THE AMNESIA PROJECT

Barbara Winkes

For D.

Chapter One

Dani

2003

It was the summer that should have been the adventure of our lives. The three of us, Alice, Joy, and I, were going to New York City for the first time, ten days to explore what seemed like a magical place to us. Sure, we had all gone out of state for college, but this was different. This was the first day of the rest of our lives, or something similarly melodramatic I would have come up with on the verge of twenty-two.

I was unsure about many things. I had an internship lined up with a bank, thanks to a friend of my dad's, and I didn't even know if I still wanted to go to business school afterwards. Then there was this other thing...I couldn't handle too many uncertainties, so I tried not to think about it too much. The girls who had been my best friends since junior high deserved the truth though. In New York, on a relaxed evening after a couple of drinks, I was going to tell them, and I knew they wouldn't judge me.

The drama started a week before our departure.

When I picked up Alice to meet with Joy in town, she all but stormed out of her parents' house, slamming the door. I didn't think much of it at that time. Alice always had a flair for theatrics.

"You won't believe this!" she said, and I realized she was so angry she was close to tears.

"What happened?" Mr. and Mrs. MacGregor were among the most laid-back people I knew, so I couldn't imagine what made her this upset.

She sat in the car, slamming that door too, making me wince. "Easy."

"Wait until you hear it," she said darkly. "I can't believe how sneaky they are. Mom and Dad want us to take Paige to New York with us. They already booked her a ticket!"

"Oh."

"That's all you have to say?"

That was all I had to say on the subject. I shouldn't say more, or my big revelation could become awkward very fast. I agreed with Alice. Taking Paige was not a good idea. I understood their parents' reasoning—with Alice's seventeen-year-old sister along for the ride, some activities were off the list. We would have to be a lot more mindful with an underage girl around. Girl. I was sure Paige would object to that word, but that's what she was.

"Dani? Really? We can't even go to a bar if we have to babysit her all the time!"

"Yeah." I wondered whose idea this was, Paige's or their parents. Either way, Alice was right. Not that we had planned to get drunk all the time, but we would have to take care of her while we were there, and it would be a lot harder to find the right moment to share my secret. "We can go to restaurants though. Sneak a few beers or a bottle of wine into the hotel."

"We could do the same here," she said impatiently. "Hell, it's what we've been doing in college. I'm not going to New York to buy a bottle of wine from a supermarket. This is so unfair. It's like they won't accept that we're adults now."

"I didn't think we were going just to drink." The words came out harsher than intended, and Alice shot me a surprised look.

"That's not what I'm saying. Of course, we were gonna do the sightseeing and all, but...You don't seem to have a problem with this. Maybe you should be the designated babysitter then."

I blushed a bright red at her suggestion, relieved that she couldn't see it in the dark.

"Come on, that's not fair. If it's a done deal, then we should make the best of it."

Alice leaned back into her seat with an exaggerated sigh.

"Easy for you to say...but yeah, I guess we have no choice. Don't get me wrong—I love my annoying little sister."

That, I knew for sure. Alice had once shared that her parents had adopted Paige as a baby. They were usually close.

"I just wanted this to be something that we did together, you, me and Joy, before we all go separate ways and never hear from each other again," she added.

All of a sudden, I understood a lot more about her somber mood.

"That's not going to happen."

"How can you say that? Brad already told me that he doesn't want a long-distance relationship. Why would we be any different?"

"Because guys are like that. We're friends. We'll always be friends."

My heart was beating uncomfortably fast. What if, once they knew, they didn't want to be my friends anymore? Where would that leave me? Was finding the truth always worth it, no matter the costs? I had no idea.

"Are you sure?" Alice asked.

"Of course I am. We chat once a week or so…It's not that hard. We won't lose touch, just because we can't hit the bars every night in New York." I laughed because the thought seemed absurd. "It's still going to be amazing."

"Promise me," Alice said, her tone so serious it startled me.

"Sure. I promise. Lighten up, Paige is not a baby."

For sure, she wasn't. In the past four years I'd only seen her sporadically. She was all grown up, and the fact that I'd noticed, only added to my confusion. That, I wouldn't share with any-one, ever.

"All right then. Make the best of it—that's what we're going to do."

"Exactly."

For a moment, I considered moving up the moment of truth, testing these two women who meant so much to me…Did I really mean as much to them? I was too scared. Somehow, I thought that the change of scene, the Big City, would help me to take that step, to be honest to myself and to them.

Hey, maybe they wouldn't even think much of it—or they already knew?

Joy was waiting for us at the local bar, and she took the news in stride.

"It could be worse," she reasoned. "We don't have to take my brothers." We all cracked up at that. Yes, Paige MacGregor should be easier to handle than Joy's fourteen-year-old twin brothers. In theory.

We had all been wrong about so many things.

⁂

As we got closer to our departure, Alice seemed to come to terms with the changed plans, while I got more nervous by the minute. Joy, Alice, and I knew everything about one another—except for some small details I was going to share. We trusted each other, and we could often communicate without words. Throwing Paige into the mix was probably not a good idea.

Once they knew, she would, too, and what if she was uncomfortable around me? *I* was uncomfortable at this point, but I couldn't deny the excitement that gripped me, too, when I finished packing. After our trip, I'd be looking for a job in addition to the internship, and an apartment. Joy was going to L.A., Alice would go to law school. She was right—it wouldn't be that easy to stay in touch, but we'd try. After all, we had something special.

Mom and Dad drove me to the airport, and we picked up Joy on the way. In the drop off zone, we met with Alice, Paige, and their parents, and said our temporary goodbyes.

"I'm glad Dani is with them," Mrs. MacGregor said with a wink. "She's always been the most responsible."

"Mom," Alice protested, while my own parents were unabashedly content with the praise.

I had mixed feelings about it. This was supposed to be the best trip ever...and once it was over, everyone would know. It was early in the morning, but the temperature had already risen to a balmy eighty degrees. I cast a quick glance at Paige who was wearing shorts, a tank top, and flat sandals. No, not a baby. She gave me a bright smile, and I quickly looked away, suppressing a sigh.

"We have to go now. We have to check our luggage, and I'm sure there's a line at security."

That's me, Dani, always the responsible one.

Alice and Paige hugged their parents, I hugged mine, while Joy waited patiently, and then we were off to the big adventure.

The line at security was long indeed, and by the time we made it to the other side, it was almost time to board, which was fine with me. Joy was browsing the paperbacks in the bookstore,

Alice leafed through a travel brochure. Paige sat next to her, listening to music on her MP3 player.

This was really happening. We were going to New York City. It would be a different atmosphere than it would have been only two years ago, but the spirit was stronger than ever, Karen, a college friend, had assured me. She said I would love it.

Karen knew. She'd also said I'd breathe easier—"at least in Central Park," she added with a laugh. "I'm serious. You'll see, you'll be a lot more relaxed about everything, and your friends will be too. Good luck."

I could use some of that, no doubt about it.

"Hey."

I jumped when Paige sat next to me. Lost in thought, I hadn't noticed her come over.

"I've been making the rounds," she said. "I wanted to thank you too, for taking me. You didn't have to."

Really? I didn't know we had options. "It's no problem."

"Oh, I know it is for Alice. She has barely spoken to me the last week."

So, Alice wasn't adjusting that easily to the change of plans after all. Sure, it made a difference, but there was no use in crying about it now.

"I'm sorry about that. I don't mind."

"It's my first flight," Paige said, her cheeks flushed with excitement. "I so hope I won't be sick. Sorry. That's gross."

"It's okay. That's unlikely anyway. It's actually fun, the take-off, and being up in the sky..." Why was I rambling? "I'm sure you'll enjoy it."

She gave me a long look, enough to make me squirm.

"If you say so, then I'm sure I will." Her words sounded innocent enough. When our flight was called, I all but jumped to my feet.

Joy had to tear herself away from the bookstore, and Alice closed her brochure. If she was still mad with Paige or their parents, she didn't let it show.

"Come on, girls, let's go. New York's waiting for us."

Since the MacGregors had booked for her late, Paige couldn't sit with us, which didn't seem to bother her or Alice. Paige shared a row with a grandmother traveling with her four-teen-year-old granddaughter. We were sort of relieved that we didn't have to check in with her every minute, and that we were far enough to order a drink without her noticing. Not such a bad start.

Alice, Joy, and I toasted to our trip with the sparkling wine—babysitting or not, we would have an amazing time before adulthood got the better of us.

It was in the afternoon when we arrived at our hotel, just a ten-minute walk away from the Empire State Building. In an instant, I had forgotten about my troubles, and I could tell from Alice's wide-eyed look that she felt the same. We had traveled a bit, seen other cities, graduated from college—big deal. This was nothing like it.

Who cared that we couldn't go to certain places with Paige around? We'd go sightseeing, shopping, visit restaurants and bookstores right at the heart of Manhattan. Ten days, kicking it off with a restaurant visit after hitting the stores in Times Square. I was looking forward to a quick shower and change of clothes, though, being the responsible and serious one, I'd have to wait in line. Trying to save money so we could still be close to the action and stay for as long as we wanted to, we had booked one room for all of us. One bathroom. That meant we would have to be quick and efficient, and someone would have to see to that.

Sitting on the windowsill, watching the bustling city below, I knew we'd have a great time, but I had second thoughts about any planned revelations. What if they completely mis-understood? I had known them for such a long time. We were comfortable around each other, undressing, dressing, it was no big deal. What if it suddenly became one? Maybe this was a conversation better done from afar, one of these days when we'd hang out online together and I had actually someone to present to them. Another big step, sometime in the future.

"Dani, your turn," Paige said as she came out of the bathroom clad in only a towel. She said something else, but I had already locked the door behind me.

We spent the evening exploring Times Square, visiting the shops and just generally enjoying the atmosphere. Even though the sky was almost dark, the many billboards made it feel like daylight. I had been tired earlier, but not anymore. We had talked about this for so long, and we were finally here!

We walked a few streets farther to find ourselves a place to eat.

Paige looked hopeful when the waiter came to take our or-ders, but Alice ordered a Coke for her, while the rest of us went with a beer. I wasn't going to argue. She was underage after all. If we didn't bring her home safely, the MacGregors wouldn't be amused.

"To us," Joy raised her glass. "May we remember these days forever."

Thinking back to that moment, it sounded like a foreboding.

❦

The next morning after breakfast, we walked up to the Met where we spent close to three hours. Joy loved museums, and she always infected us with her enthusiasm. I knew that Alice had talked to Paige in the bathroom the night before. Whatever they had said, there seemed to be some sort of cease-fire between them. I watched Paige standing in front of a painting from the 19th century collection, studying the two women. She was wearing a short dress today, her hair in a ponytail.

I tried to look past her at the painting, which wasn't easy.

It was becoming incredibly harder to look past Paige, which told me it was a bad idea to stay home for a job. I needed to go somewhere I could build a life, with someone who understood what I was going through.

We had a snack on the rooftop terrace and spent most of the afternoon in Central Park, before heading back to our hotel to get ready for the evening. When we had arrived at the door of our room, Alice held me back.

"Dani, could you do me a favor?"

"Yes, sure," I said without thinking. "What favor?"

"Look, I know we wanted to hang out downtown a little longer tonight, but it's only the second evening, so there's time for all of us..."

I didn't understand what she was saying.

"I was thinking...We take the subway, walk around some more and go eat somewhere. There's this bar I really wanted to try, but of course we can't go with Paige. What if we take turns? If Joy and I went after dinner, and you took her home for the evening, would you be okay with that? Please. I'll take another night so you and Joy can go. I think Paige wouldn't mind hanging out with you for one evening."

Now that I did understand her, I didn't know what to say.

"Please," she repeated, misunderstanding my hesitation. "I know it's not great, but it's the best we can do under the circumstances...We can't smuggle her in somewhere."

"Of course not. I don't mind. I'm actually pretty tired. We'll take the subway back up and hang out in the hotel until you guys come back."

Alice hugged me. "Thanks, Dani, you're the best!"

"Don't I know it."

All banter came to a halt when an hour later, we walked past Ground Zero. Even though the area was as busy as everywhere else, it felt different, heavier. For several minutes, none of us said anything. It was only when we got close to the waterfront, the millions of lights from the windows of skyscrapers at our backs, that we broke the silence.

"How about Italian tonight?" Joy suggested. Those little decisions seemed so trivial...and even bigger decisions looked different to me, in the grand scheme of things. I would tell them. I wanted to. The most important thing you could do with your life was to use the time wisely. Tomorrow would be the day.

After dinner at a restaurant in Little Italy, we went separate ways—Joy and Alice renewed their makeup in the restroom while Paige and I went to find the nearest subway station.

"My parents really didn't think this through, did they?" she asked, sounding miserable.

"I'm tired," I said. "Whatever they are up to now, I don't think I am."

"You don't have to be so nice. I'm ruining your vacation."

"Come on, don't be ridiculous. You're not ruining anything."

We found the station and bought our tickets, then tried to get past the turnstile. After three futile attempts, the friendly person behind me helped me with it. I admit I'd had some preconceived notions, but all New Yorkers we'd run into so far had been nothing but nice. I finally got to the other side, catching my breath. All of a sudden, having Paige with me seemed like a lot of responsibility. I didn't want her to feel bad, but there was no denying her presence complicated things for all of us.

I still wondered what bar Alice and Joy wanted to go to—they hadn't given me any details.

We made it to the hotel without any incident. After some time in the bathroom, getting into PJs, it was just the two of us, nowhere left to go. I sat down to look at pictures I had taken.

"Can I see?" Paige asked.

"Sure."

She sat next to me on the bed, a little close for comfort. I made room, handing her the camera.

"So..." I began, scrambling for something to say. "You're going to college this year?"

"Yes. I'm really excited. I can't wait to get away from high school."

I could imagine. She was smart and opinionated, which made a small-town high school not the easiest place for a girl to be. I thought of my first year in college. I remembered feeling alone and uncertain many times, but I always had Alice and Joy to turn to at least. I hoped Paige had good friends like that. There were many opportunities to stumble, and not all of them were of the academic kind.

"What are you going to study?"

"Political Sciences and Women's Studies," she said. "Equality is everything, but to change the rules of the game, you need to learn how to play it first."

"Makes sense."

"Yeah." With a sigh, she put the camera aside. "I hope I can make things right with Alice before that."

"What do you mean? She loves you. And she knows that this was your parents' idea. Not that it bothers me, or Joy, for that matter."

"I don't know, I think she's really changed this past year."

"We all have. You'll see, once you move out from your parents', it's all very different."

"I guess." She held my gaze for long enough to get me flustered.

11

"Anyway. You'll be fine. Just take it one step at a time."

"I think that's great advice. Thank you."

She leaned in to kiss me, an honest to God adult kiss. I should have stopped her right away. As it was, I had been dreaming about kissing another girl for months now, like this, and if I was honest, Paige had appeared in those dreams too...

Dreams were safe.

This reality was not, because it exposed me within seconds—my confusion, my hopes, my inappropriate thoughts with her body so close to mine. This was Alice's little sister, Paige McGregor. I all but jerked back, my face flushing with shame.

"I'm so sorry. This will never happen again, I swear."

Paige looked amused.

"What if I want it to happen again? Don't you?"

"No. No, we can't do this."

"Why not? It felt pretty amazing to me."

Which wasn't the point.

"You're seventeen, remember? I could go to jail! Oh my God. Alice would make sure I'd go to jail."

Paige shook her head.

"Come on. I'll be eighteen in a few months. I agree that we shouldn't tell anyone yet, but...You enjoyed it, didn't you? I could tell."

She probably could. It occurred to me that she might be more experienced than I was, that she might have done this with a girl—girls?—her age. It didn't matter. It didn't change the years between us, or the fact that I wasn't ready to come out to the world. Now I couldn't even tell Alice or Joy because I felt like they would know.

"You like me," Paige insisted.

"Yes, I do. Of course I do." I raked both hands through my hair. "I just didn't think...I didn't know..."

She smiled, touching my hand gently. I withdrew it.

"It always surprises me when someone doesn't know, because I think it must be so obvious, but I guess you had to figure out some things for yourself. I understand that. I've been there, and I don't have any more doubts. If I can figure out what field I want to work in for the rest of my life, what makes you think I don't know who I love? I want you, Dani," she said with all the misplaced confidence of a teenager. Paige might have kissed a girl before, but her choice of words told me she was nowhere near ready for anything else. If I was honest—neither was I, and all of it told me in no uncertain terms that I was right to put a stop to this right now, regardless of my feelings, or hers.

"We don't have to wait," she added.

"What part of going to jail did you not understand? You're an amazing person, Paige. You'll find someone your age...when the time is right."

"You don't even want to give this a try, even though you're attracted to me?"

Why did she have to keep torturing me? There was no way—at least not for the next five months, and even after that, what would it look like? I couldn't imagine Alice or her parents being any happier once Paige made it past the eighteen mark.

"I'm sorry," I said again. "You are much too young. We are in different places in life, and..." More platitudes. "Nothing can happen right now, you know that." That was a bit more honest. "In five months, you'll be away in college. But if you come home for Christmas, I'll probably be there, and we could...talk." It wasn't great, but it was the best I could come up with for now.

"Sure we could. I think I'd like to go to bed now."

"Okay. No problem."

Paige retreated to the double bed by the window that she shared with Alice, drawing the sheets up high, even though it wasn't cold in the room.

I stayed where I was, staring into the dark after we'd turned off the lights, blinking back tears. My timing sucked, big time. Instead of coming out to my friends as planned, I had found out that Paige liked girls, too, that in fact she liked me. If this had happened half a year later, I might have thrown all caution in the wind. Now, I wasn't sure if I hadn't made a mistake. It wasn't fair to make her wait and think we had a real chance—but I didn't want to hurt her. Who knew what we'd all do in six months? She would probably meet someone in college. Like I said, my timing sucked.

I wanted her too, but there was nothing I could do about it.

I was jolted out of my sleep when Joy and Alice arrived, giggling as they tried to maneuver the room in the dark. Someone stubbed their toe, curses following, then more giggling. I was irrationally resenting them for having so much fun when my evening had taken an abrupt turn to complicated. Still, I pretended to sleep, and I assumed Paige did the same, because no one could sleep through this noise.

Both Alice and Joy were slightly hung over and pale at breakfast, but they'd obviously had a good time, and their appetite wasn't corrupted too much. They didn't seem to notice that Paige avoided my gaze and had hardly touched the food on her plate.

I didn't know what to think or to say. In the light of day, last night's revelations felt unreal. However, Paige, withdrawn and sulking, made it clear she hadn't forgotten.

None of this was her fault. She hadn't ruined the trip for any of us. I hoped that I wasn't about to but being honest would be a lot more difficult.

Chapter Two

Paige

Kissing Dani was every bit as exciting as I imagined it to be, even if the following conversation wasn't. Yes, I probably should have expected her to react that way, after all, she wasn't out to anyone yet—but for a moment, she let herself go, and that's when I had hoped she might be willing to go all the way. My first time. With Dani. I wanted that so much it almost hurt, but obviously it wasn't going to happen anytime soon.

Maybe it would be her first time too, though I had a hard time imagining that. In five, six months? I had to be realistic. There was no way that a woman like Dani would stay single for this long. I had my chance, and I blew it—or maybe she'd flat out lied when she said she liked me too.

No.

That kiss told me everything I needed to know, and we would have had all the time in the world. Joy and Alice had come back to the hotel around three-thirty after doing the barhopping Mom and Dad wanted to keep them from.

Dani said no, because she didn't want me as much. It hurt. I wish I could go home, not see her every day for the next eight days. I'm sure Alice would have liked that. All of them would have liked that. At this moment, I resented our parents for sending me along, as if I could keep Alice from doing anything.

I finally gave up on breakfast and sipped my coffee instead. It was funny how Alice and Joy were partying all night, and I was the one hung over. Maybe they would be okay with me staying in the hotel today? I suppressed a sigh. Not a chance.

Joy suggested exploring the neighborhood around the hotel a bit more and doing some more shopping this morning. We hadn't made it to 5th Avenue yet.

Dani agreed, but she gave me a quick look as if wondering if I was okay with the idea, blushing before she looked away. I didn't care anymore.

I couldn't believe it. I had seen the way she looked at me, had felt how much she wanted to kiss me.

I couldn't help it. My thoughts kept revolving around that moment. I wanted to cry. Her half-hearted rejection was more painful than anything, knowing that she was trying to let me down easy by suggesting we might talk this over again once I was eighteen. How could she think I'd move on so easily, forget about her once I was in college?

She wasn't that much older. In a few years, nobody would blink an eye.

It was another hot day, and I realized soon that despite copious amounts of sunscreen, I was going to get sunburn on my shoulder. I should have worn something with sleeves. Should have, could have...

Joy and Alice were walking in the front. I lagged behind a bit, because I was afraid Dani would try to talk, reason with me some more. I heard all her points yesterday, I didn't think I could stand any more.

Who wanted to walk on this street anyway? Crowds of people were waiting for buses, some getting on, some still waiting for theirs to arrive. I should have had something to drink, I realized as I felt the headache coming on. It was hot, and loud, and I wished I'd stayed in the air-conditioned hotel room. We had to cut through lines or walk around them, people with suitcases, some with kids in strollers.

I forced myself to smile at a baby—my misery wasn't their fault—and saw Joy and Alice had gotten further ahead, not even once looking back. Maybe they were trying to lose me on purpose?

Why did I do it?

I was going to tell Dani about all the important things I wanted to do with my life, maybe even run for office someday, because there was so much work left to do for us...all of that seemed laughable now. All of a sudden, she was so close, and I caught a whiff of her shampoo. Everything after that was so natural, unavoidable.

The crowd was getting tighter, and I was a little light-headed with lovesickness and dehydration. I'd have to ask the girls to stop for a moment. A smoothie would be perfect...Someone's arm brushed against me, and I shrank away from the contact. Alice and Joy had crossed the street while Dani was still waiting at the light. Why didn't they stop and wait?

Somebody pushed me to the right, or maybe that was just a ripple effect from the group.

"Hey! There's no need to be rude." I tried to get out of the throng of people surrounding me, all taller, blocking my sight. I only had a moment to realize that the bus to my right was smaller than the others, a dark van. "No...wait...excuse me, I need to—"

A gloved hand clamping over my mouth cut off my words. My heart was racing frantically, blood rushing to my ears. I was going to pass out any moment. I struggled, to no avail. I was lifted into the van, the doors sliding shut after at least four other people climbed inside. I felt a prick to my arm, and then the world slid away. I didn't even have enough time to fear my unknown fate.

***

Dani

I turned around to look for Paige who had been dragging her feet all morning. I couldn't see her. At first, I wasn't even alarmed. There were many people blocking my sight, and I expected her to show up any moment. She didn't.

Joy and Alice were already on the other side of the street. If I tried to shout, they wouldn't hear me, so I pulled out my cell and hoped Alice would notice it was ringing. Alice hardly ever missed a call, and rest assured, I saw her flip it open.

"Hey, can you slow down for a bit? I don't see Paige."

"What do you mean?"

"Well, she can't just shove people aside. Come back here, and we wait for her?"

The silence on the other end made me realize that my voice sounded...anxious. There was no reason. We simply hadn't picked the best street for our morning walk. In a few minutes, we'd regroup, maybe get a snack somewhere and then tackle the shopping day.

By the time Alice and Joy had crossed the street back to where I was standing, there was still no sign of Paige, and I was beginning to worry. She wouldn't go back to the hotel without telling any of us, except...She probably didn't want to talk to me at all.

I turned to look up the street where we'd come down. Most of the buses had departed, and it was a lot less crowded. I couldn't see her.

I couldn't panic, because then Alice would.

"Maybe she went back to the hotel?" Joy said.

"Why would she do that?" Alice asked, unnerved. "She's not supposed to go anywhere without us."

"Maybe she was pissed that we didn't take her yesterday."

"She was okay with that," I felt the need to say. "Let's go all the way back up. Maybe she bought something to drink, or someone needed help."

Yes, Paige would jump in if such an occasion arose, but what if she was the one needing help? It was hot and humid. A person could pass out from that, especially if they forgot to drink enough. We hurried up the street to the next crosswalk—no Paige.

I felt sick. I could tell from Alice's imploring look that she hoped for a solution from me. Knowing I couldn't give her any made it all worse. The scenarios kept playing in my mind—if she had passed out, or, God forbid, been hit by a car, wouldn't we have heard the sirens? Maybe not. There were so many noises at any time, sirens, honks, people. The city was quickly losing its magic, feeling too loud, too scary and overwhelming.

"We check at the hotel," I said.

"What if she isn't there?"

I glared at Joy, but she was serious, didn't back down. Alice started to cry.

"I knew it was a bad idea to bring her with us!"

"Both of you, calm down. Let's go back to the hotel now."

Joy asked me again when she thought Alice was out of earshot.

"What if she isn't there?"

"Then we'll go to the police." I prayed that wouldn't be necessary.

Those moments passed in a blur, and yet they are etched into my memory, sharply, indelibly. Paige wasn't at the hotel, and the concierge hadn't seen her since we left this morning. Alice hadn't stopped crying. She wasn't much help. Joy tried to calm her while I called the police, hoping somebody would tell me that we were all overreacting, that Paige would show up any moment.

Paige didn't magically materialize, not when I talked to the officer on the phone, only noticing I was crying too when he spoke to me softly, asking me to repeat the information. He promised they'd send someone over.

This surprised me though. I had expected he'd ask us to come to the station.

"That's not necessary. You stay where you are. A detective will be there in twenty minutes."

"It's room #410. Please hurry."

"Detective Jacobson is on her way," he assured me.

After I'd hung up with him, I walked past Alice and Joy to the bathroom where I washed my face, taking in my shell-shocked expression. I had just reported Paige missing.

How was that possible?

Alice would have to call their parents. We couldn't put it off much longer.

Detective Jacobson arrived a few minutes later, true to her word. She was dressed casually, her long brown hair in a ponytail. She looked tired and jaded to me, the impression igniting a cold fear in me before she'd even said a word.

"You have to know we're taking this very seriously," she promised. "Can you tell me exactly what happened?"

The trouble was, we couldn't tell her much. We were walking down the street, slowed down by the crowds waiting for their respective buses. There had been a few food carts along the way, selling overpriced snacks and bottled drinks to tourists. A fenced off construction site to the left.

"I realized she'd fallen behind," I said. I sounded desperate. That's because I was. I somehow needed her to believe that this wasn't my fault, that I couldn't have done anything differently.

"A colleague of mine is checking the hospitals as we speak," Jacobson said, then she paused to regard Alice. Alice's face was still tear-streaked.

"Did Paige ever talk about running away, or give you any indication that she might have plans like that?"

"What the—" Alice jumped to her feet. "Are you crazy? Paige was—is," she corrected herself hastily. "An honor student. She's going to college in the fall, has it all figured out. There's no way she would run away. Besides, she just came out to me and our parents. Everyone was okay with it. She's happy, even said she had a crush on someone."

"Did she say who?"

"No, and why would it matter? No one knows us here."

"Okay." Jacobson's tone was calm. She was unfazed by Alice's outburst. "We will talk to your parents. Is there anything else you can remember?" The question was for all of us. Joy shook her head.

I hesitated a little too long.

"Danielle?"

"No. I told you everything. Please find her."

"We're doing everything we can," she said, which was not enough to make me feel better. On the contrary, I began to imagine what she had seen in the course of her career, and how she really felt about the chances of someone disappearing on a street of New York in broad daylight. Somebody had to have seen something, if they could find the vendors…Why didn't we think of that? I gave myself the answer—because at that moment, we'd still hoped to find her at the hotel. Did we waste time coming here first?

Jacobson's phone rang, and she excused herself while Alice picked up her own cell phone in trembling hands.

I waited, feeling like I was intruding on this private conversation. I couldn't imagine telling anyone what Alice had to tell her parents now. Jacobson spoke to them as well.

I was terrified, and yet, after the detective handed the phone back to Alice, I all but backed her into a corner.

"Could I ask you a question?"

"We haven't heard anything from the hospitals so far," she said, continuing when she realized that wasn't my question, "Sure, go ahead."

"Do you think she could be okay? I mean, how often does it happen that someone is reported missing, and you find them and they're okay?"

"It happens," she said. "Let's not jump to conclusions." Her pained expression, probably unintended, confirmed my worst suspicions.

"Everything happened so fast. One moment we were walking down the street, and then she was just...gone. What do you think it means? If she's not in any hospital, what could that mean? Did she just wander off? Did someone kidnap her..."

"Try to breathe," she instructed softly. "In, out. Slowly. That's it."

It wasn't until then I realized that I'd started hyperventilating. Jacobson studied me for a moment.

"Is there anything else you'd like to tell me, Danielle?"

"I already told you everything. I don't know...This just seems so crazy. Alice isn't rich. There is no reason to kidnap Paige unless..." I couldn't finish the sentence. It was too horrible to think about. Unless money wasn't the reason. "I'm sorry," I said through tears I couldn't hold back. "No, there's nothing."

She squeezed my shoulder gently and then turned to Alice who had finished her call as well.

"Mom and Dad are going to be here later tonight," she said, now sounding eerily calm. "Will you stay here?"

Jacobson shook her head. She handed a card to Alice. "I'll be back. This is where you can reach me meanwhile. The moment we find anything, I'll let you know."

"Thank you," Alice said. The door fell shut, and for a long moment, all of us seemed frozen in time.

What should we do?

⁂

Joy and I stayed. Sure, changing our tickets would cost us a lot more, but neither of us was thinking about that. Paige was all we could think about while we were waiting for Alice and her parents to return from long conversations with the police.

Mr. and Mrs. MacGregor had booked a room in a hotel across the street from ours. I was scared they might blame me, because I blamed myself. Why didn't I pay attention? I could have seen something, done something...I couldn't even tell anyone the reason why Paige had been so unhappy that morning. It was both a blessing and a curse that Joy and Alice hadn't noticed. I'd be alone with this until...until we found Paige. Or the rest of my life. These thoughts made me feel even guiltier. We didn't know where Paige was, if she was still alive, if she was suffering. The MacGregors stayed polite and kind, never breaking down in front of us.

When they came to tell us that Detective Jacobson had no news, after ten days were gone, and we had to return, I did.

But I still carried the secret home with me. I knew I had to make it right. Somehow.

Chapter Three

Dani

2016

When I came home that night, Lois was sitting on the couch reading a paperback. We shared a quick kiss before I was to disappear into my office like every night.

"Dani, wait," she said, putting the book aside. "I thought we could go out for dinner tonight?"

I hesitated. She had a point. There was nothing new waiting for me in that room, the same files, the same questions and regrets. I did enough overtime as it was, and even though we worked in the same building, we hardly saw each other anymore.

"Let me check something first?"

"I made reservations for seven. Hurry up."

"Sure. Thanks." I gave her a smile before I headed for my office, closing the door behind me.

I had every reason to be grateful for Lois who didn't seem to mind, or at least got used to sharing her life with someone who was obsessed. Yes, that was the best way to describe it, even though I had become pretty good at fooling those around me. I was successful at my job, in a solid relationship, and we shared a nice home together.

And every evening I spent hours in my office, going over every little detail, adding information gained over the years, from resources I shouldn't use in that way. I couldn't help myself.

There was no new information regarding Paige. That day in New York, she vanished without a trace, and no one had seen her since. I had tried to find Paige's biological parents but couldn't come up with anything I didn't already know—her biological mother had given her up when she was very young. It was a dead end. I was looking for patterns. Women who had gone missing under similar circumstances, the same year, in the same age group. Too damn many women disappeared every year, too few returned to their families safe and sound.

I remember being uncomfortable with Detective Jacobson, sensing that she wasn't optimistic, and now I knew why. She had retired without ever being able to close that case. That day, I had seen my future, and every day, I was becoming her a little bit more—jaded, hopeless, fighting a losing battle against the evil out there.

Sure, I'd be pleasant company for an evening out.

Lois knew better than to ask too many questions. Being a civilian employee of the police department, she was nevertheless aware of the stakes. She understood that I couldn't let go. One day, I would find out what happened to Paige.

Obviously, not today.

There was a hesitant knock on the door, preceding Lois into the room.

"I don't mean to rush you, but we should leave soon."

Our apartment was only a few blocks away from the main street, so we were able to walk to many restaurants and bars. I could use a drink. Today, two girls who had disappeared from a group home had been found safe. Sometimes we were lucky. Too often, we were not.

"That's okay. Let's go."

"Your mom called earlier," Lois said when we were out on the street. "They'll come for dinner on Saturday night."

"Oh. Okay."

Whenever Mom and Dad were around, I had to work a little harder at appearing normal. They'd been shocked when, after returning from the New York trip, I abandoned all my plans, and instead of the internship at the bank, joined the police academy. I had never once mentioned an interest in that line of work, and they knew I had one sole reason. I disregarded any warnings and well-meant advice, saw it through, lucky enough to have mentors along the way who believed in me.

They, of course, never knew the whole truth.

"I heard you found the girls from the group home."

"Yeah. It's a good day." Good days, bad days, it was all relative.

"You know, you can take an evening off. It won't make a difference—" Lois stopped as if only now realizing the ways in which I could interpret her words.

I wasn't looking for a fight. I was tired.

"You're right."

She couldn't suppress the smile at my admission. I couldn't blame her. She had waited long enough to hear those words from me.

I still couldn't chase the thought from my mind that a relaxing evening with my girlfriend would mean betraying Paige.

I had planned to sneak back into the office after dinner, but Lois had other plans. I couldn't bring myself to disappoint her like I had so many times in the past weeks. Late at night, I was wide awake from too much caffeine and sugar—I shouldn't have had that dessert—wondering if we had a real chance, or if I was just stringing her along. Mom and Dad liked her, all her co-workers highly respected her, and I...She helped me take a moment to breathe every once in a while. I valued her affection, her intelligence, except I didn't love her. Perhaps I still didn't know what love actually was—experience didn't always translate into knowledge. My feelings for her didn't come with the same intensity, which was sad, considering. Right now, Paige, and what could have been, was nothing more than an illusion. It wasn't for that reason I held on, or at least that was what I was trying to tell myself. I had hurt her. I had to make it right either way. For a long time, hoping to get the MacGregors closure was part of my motivation, but now, both parents had passed away, and Alice didn't talk to me anymore.

By the time I moved away to work for a department halfway between New York and the small town where we had grown up, she had stopped answering any of my messages or emails. It was Joy who had told me about the parents. Alice was now married. She had a young son. They were moving on with their lives, but I couldn't.

I had never told anyone what happened between me and Paige that night, not even Lois. I was too ashamed. The Mac-Gregors had asked us to look after her, and I was the one who had let her slip away. It was only fair that it would be up to me to find her, and deal with whatever I would uncover...If only I could be sure I'd get there at some point. I turned away from Lois, drawing the cover up high.

⁂

I kept playing along, making breakfast for the two of us before work. Usually, we both grabbed something on the way. I could tell from Lois's gaze that she had questions, but she didn't voice any of them. Some subjects were too difficult to tackle even between us, even when things looked good on the surface.

Guilt was always so prominent I could have set a third plate and cup for it. For what I did, and what I didn't do.

I had moments when I wondered what might have been, if Paige hadn't been so disappointed in me, or if I hadn't done what was right, or at least, seemed right to me. We could have been together. I could have found the courage to come out to my friends. In fact, I never did, because Alice didn't talk to me, and Joy didn't seem to care.

I didn't think about coming out or dating at all after New York, though four weeks into the academy, I was brave and desperate and wanted to get it over with. I went to one of the two lesbian bars in town and got drunk enough to hook up with the first woman who said yes. The experience had to be worse for her, because I cried most of the time for reasons that had nothing to do with her. I never saw her again.

Since then, I had dated a few times, but it wasn't until Lois that I found someone who could handle my past.

She was holding my hand on the table, smiling gently.

"I swear I'll keep my promise. I know what this means to you. I just wanted you to let go for one night—not forever."

"I know. Thank you for that."

"Will you be okay with your parents here?"

Weekends were usually reserved for more searches and filing. Lois knew I'd get antsy if we had to sit down and make small talk for too long.

"I'll be fine," I said.

❧

The woman in the armchair looked peaceful, as if she was sleeping. She wasn't. Earlier that night, while Lois had tried to keep my mind off the person always in the room with us, Dr. Brittany

Dawson had taken her own life. On the table next to her, there was an empty pill bottle, and a half-empty bottle of red wine.

The name sounded vaguely familiar to me, and when I took a look at the shelf behind her, I knew why: She had been a famous surgeon, written a few books and often appeared on TV shows, at least until a few years ago.

It seemed obvious what had happened.

There were footsteps behind me, and I turned to my partner, Detective Viola Marsh.

"The wife just arrived," she said. I winced.

"Yeah. She's devastated, obviously, but she had some interesting things to say. Come with me?"

I cast a last look at Brittany Dawson before I followed Viola along the hallway to the den where Elaina Dawson was waiting for us. They had taken the same name, I realized.

"Mrs. Dawson, I'm Detective Ryder. I'm so sorry for your loss," I said.

"Thank you." Her fingers tightened around mine in a painful grip. She looked around as if to make sure no one heard us. "Let's go to my office, please?"

I gave Viola a questioning look, and she shrugged. Elaina was probably still in shock.

When we had all sat down in the spacious office, Elaina began, "I already told this to your partner, but I want to make sure you are taking it seriously. If Brittany did this, and I'm not sure she did, it's because someone made her do it. She was, as you probably know, successful. She was happy." Her voice broke. "There is no way she'd go there, ever. We talked about everything. Whenever there was something bothering her, she would tell me eventually. The only way she wouldn't was if she thought it could put me in danger."

"Do you have reason to believe that she—or you—were in danger?" I asked. "Did you receive any threats?"

"Brit was fairly famous, so there was hate mail, fewer in the past few years."

"What changed?" Viola asked.

Elaina retrieved a paper tissue from the box on the desk, wiping her face. "I'm not sure if you noticed, but she was less in the spotlight, concentrating more on her work at the Mason clinic. I don't get this. She was the star there, too, everywhere she went! Everyone loved her."

Somehow, that hadn't been enough, and Brittany Dawson found herself in a place so dark she couldn't see a way out. I could sympathize. I hadn't ever seriously considered the option, not when I still didn't know the truth. There had been moments when I was confronted with likely scenarios of what Paige might have gone through...and the darkness beckoned.

"Was she all right with those changes?"

"Of course. We had planned them. Brittany wasn't depressed. She didn't need any medication. Someone made her do this," Elaina insisted. "Whether they actually gave her the pills or convinced her somehow...She wouldn't do this. Not now."

Tears were streaming down her face as she opened a drawer in the desk, took out a folder and laid it in front of us.

It said 'Adoption.'

Dawson and her wife had been in the process of adopting a child. I agreed that her death was highly suspicious.

"Where were you last night?" I asked.

She shook her head with a smile that didn't reach her eyes.

"I know you have to ask that. Family first, right? I'll make it easy for you. I was on a plane coming back from New Orleans. I was at a conference...the two-hundred something people on the plane, including captain and crew, can certainly vouch for me."

"I'm sorry. Did Brittany have any relatives?"

"Not that I know of. She was adopted, and her parents passed away ten and seven years ago. Look, she didn't go on those shows or write the books to be famous. In fact, Brittany was a very private person."

It was remarkable how Elaina went from being logical and pragmatic to devastated and back again. Grief left deep marks, always. So did guilt. I knew a thing or two about that, even though I'd never let myself grieve for losing Paige. If I did, it would mean I'd given up. Not yet.

"We will talk to her colleagues at the clinic. Thank you."

"Find who made her do this," Elaina said. "Find them and make them pay."

"Don't worry, that's exactly what we're going to do," I answered, ignoring Viola's quizzical look.

From the director of the clinic, a center specializing in brain surgery, to the other surgeons, to every employee we talked to, no one could imagine what could have made Brittany commit suicide. Some of them knew that she and Elaina had planned to adopt—I couldn't detect any envy or homophobic undertones.

Brittany was a hero and a saint. She had saved many lives in the operating room.

Viola and I headed back to the station when she got a call from the lab, something out of the ordinary on her computer.

"Maybe she was undiagnosed," I mused. "Or she knew and was afraid they might fire her?"

Viola shrugged. "Even undiagnosed, someone had to notice something. What if she made a mistake and tried to cover it up? That could drive a person over the edge."

Sure, it could. I was pretty decent at my job, and still, I couldn't close that one case. It was wearing on me, had done so steadily for the past thirteen years.

"I'm curious to see what the lab has for us," I said. "They seem financially sound, but there could be surprises as well. Adopting a child is not easy or cheap."

"Yeah, but Elaina is right. You don't make a decision like that lightly."

I wouldn't know. Most of my life came down to one single motivation. What would I do if that was gone? I didn't care for the answers. I had to do my job, find answers for someone else.

⁂

Down in the lab, neither Viola nor I were sure what exactly we were looking at on the screen. It looked like a jumble of letters and numbers.

"That's right," Hawkins, head of the lab, said. "Aside from a few family photos with her parents and her wife, we don't know what's on her computer. There are a bunch of folders and files, some on the surface, some hidden deeper."

"And you can't tell us what's in those files? Financial records, letters from a secret lover?"

She gave me a wry grin.

"You think I'd show you this if I knew what's inside? They're encrypted."

"Don't you have programs for that?" Viola asked.

"Smartass. Sure, there are things I can try, and believe me, I tried every single one of them, to no avail. I've never seen this kind of encryption outside of top secret government material."

That sounded almost science-fiction to me. Brittany Dawson had been a renowned brain surgeon, the star of a world-famous clinic. She had helped people who came to her under the most desperate circumstances. What had she been hiding?

"Are we sure those are her files?"

"You think the wife put them there?" Hawkins asked. "With the setup of the computer, I'm not sure anyone except her could access those."

"Well, if you can't access them, who can?"

"I know I need some sort of help. I hate to admit it, but…" She pointed to the nonsensical mix of numbers and letters. "This is all I have. I'll contact the FBI and see what they can do."

I thought of Elaina whose emotions were all over the place. Grief…guilt…was she really just a good actress? Both of the women had money. What if she wanted Brittany out of the way, and those secrets in the encrypted files were hers?

I couldn't help feeling like we'd stepped into a hornet's nest. Never mind the pressure of solving what was at the very least the suspicious death of a celebrity.

We definitely needed to bring in the big guns on this.

I called Elaina and asked her if she knew anything about hidden files on Brittany's computer.

"I have no idea, but if I had to guess, they might be patient files," she said. "Brit worked with some famous people, and I'm sure many of them wouldn't want to have their brain surgery made public."

"Do you know who did the encryption?"

"Again, I have to guess, but wouldn't that be her employers? Look, she never gave me that many details, especially lately, and I was fine with that. She needed to be in her zone, you know?" Her voice wavered once more. "God, that sounds so terrible. I should have asked those questions, right? I should have made more of an effort."

"This is not your fault," I said. "But it's important that we find out what's in those files. If you can think of anything…"

"I'm sorry. I wish I could help you."

I spent the rest of the early afternoon poring over financial records, beginning to think I might have chosen the wrong line of work. Then again, I was alive. It was hard to argue with that.

The Mason clinic had to make obscene amounts of money to pay her this much. Then again, if they had celebrity patients, as Elaina had suggested, it was an explanation. Still. Money obviously hadn't been a problem, unless there were other, darker secrets we didn't know about yet. Debts? A gambling problem?

"Danielle. It's good to see you. How are you?"

"Chief. I'm good, thank you." I rose to shake his hand.

"I hear you caught the Dawson case. Any major development yet?"

"Unfortunately, we're on hold for the moment," I told him.

"You're doubting it was a suicide?"

"No, not yet, but there is something odd to it."

"You think you have time for a coffee while on hold?" he asked with a wink. Chief Larkin brought out the old school charm with every woman he encountered, regardless if said woman was in a committed relationship with another woman, or a man. He had taught me a lot, from the moment I made detective, my years with Missing Persons, to my recent transfer to Major Crimes.

I could make time for a coffee.

"Of course."

I was obsessed, there was no doubt about it, but my situation would be a whole lot more desperate if it wasn't for his guidance throughout my career. He had guessed that my motivation to become a cop wasn't random, and he encouraged me to build a safety net around it, focus on doing my job so I could do what I needed to.

"There might be a chance we'll never find her," he'd said, "but there'll be others like that, cases you can close, closure you can give to families. I'm not saying you should give up, but that, you can do in her honor."

I was still living by those words. In Paige's honor. I wondered what it might take to break the encryption of those files.

"About your case?" he said when we had both gotten a coffee from the break room. "I was under the impression that it was pretty cut and dried. Of course, it's getting a lot of press as well, so it might be best for the family, the wife in this case, to wrap it up quickly."

Yet it was Elaina who thought someone might have driven Brittany to suicide.

"I get that, but there were some red flags regarding files on her computer. In any case, the autopsy will be later today."

"I know. I'll be there."

I didn't say anything, but the surprise must have shown on my face.

"Brittany Dawson's parents were good friends of mine," he said. "I owe it to them."

I understood about debt, not the financial kind.

"I guess then I'll see you later. I have to get back to work."

"Any news on...?"

I shook my head.

"All right, Detective Ryder. I'll see you later."

I tried to concentrate on my folders, but my mind kept going back to the Dawson case. We would have to wait for the final results, but it was unlikely that the medical examiner would rule it anything but a suicide, and the mysterious files weren't enough to keep going.

There was no viable suspect, no motive—and Brittany had certainly known the amount of pills she needed to take in her wife's absence. How horrible for the both of them.

What was in those files?

I knew Hawkins had made some calls, but I'd know if she had heard anything yet. I would likely have to let it go. I was bad at that.

I opened one of my files, with the picture on top of it that always made my heart skip a beat. The first night, Times Square. Before I screwed everything up.

I had a vague idea of what she might look like today, a computer printout from a program I shouldn't have used for personal purposes in the first place. It was hard to determine a pattern—so many young women vanished under mysterious circumstances and were never seen again, alive that is. My job gave me options, but it also cruelly opened my mind to all the possibilities. Human trafficking. Random offenders operating alone. Statistically, the person most likely to harm a woman is someone close to her, but that was impossible. We'd been in a city where we knew nobody.

I had bothered Detective Jacobson a few times with questions and theories, only to learn that she had followed all those avenues. They'd had a few girls missing in the week following a big sports event, some game that none of us had known or cared about—this was why they had sent a detective right away. As it was, it didn't make a difference. A small percentage of those girls had been found, and there was no connection whatsoever to Paige.

I looked at another file. Caitlyn Hoyt, reported missing by her husband. She'd only been a few years older than Paige, back in 2003. She and the husband were on an anniversary trip to New York. At a restaurant, she went to the restroom and never came back. Since the circumstances were so similar, I had followed up on the case when I learned about it.

"Why are you coming here if you can't tell me anything new?" the husband had snapped at me. There was another woman living with him now, looking tired and scared. I couldn't help thinking that Caitlyn might have been better off, wherever she was now, and it gave me pause. No. Paige wouldn't run away, ever.

Just like Brittany Dawson wouldn't commit suicide, ever?

Did we really know those closest to us?

I had thought Joy, Alice and I would be friends forever, now we barely send a couple of greeting cards a year between us.

There was a soft knock on the door, startling me nonetheless. This room was like a time machine at times, transporting me to several moments along the way that were all laden with uncertainty.

Would we ever learn Brittany's secrets?

Would I ever be able to sleep at night without wondering what Paige was doing now, or if she'd been dead for a long time?

"Come in," I said.

To my surprise, it wasn't Lois who opened the door, but Elaina Dawson.

"I just found this with a note. Brit said to be very careful whom I'd give it to, but I guess you qualify." She held up a USB key.

"It might have the same encryption as the files on her computer."

"That's the thing," she said. "It's only a simple password. I could open them."

2003

She sounded calm and collected as she walked the attending surgeons through the procedure, one that she had done a few times now. Business as usual, for the greater good, no reason to falter.

Brittany Dawson hoped that her hands wouldn't shake. She couldn't afford to make things worse because the situation was already bad. She forced a smile for her attentive audience.

"There's no doubt that we are breaking ground. From here, the possibilities are endless, but we also have to remember this progress comes with huge responsibilities. Precision is key. A kind of precision you never knew you needed, with tools you never knew you would use someday. Forget about everything you've seen before."

The expressions of the people listening to her ranged from amazed to concerned. Some believed it couldn't be done. Some believed it shouldn't be done. Some couldn't wait to get started.

It didn't matter what they thought. Every one of them had made a deal with the devil, and the devil had come to collect.

Was it better to ask forgiveness than permission?

She didn't know anymore.

I'm sorry, she thought as she raised the scalpel.

Chapter Four

Paige

2003

I woke up scared, feeling a vague pressure, like the beginning of a headache, my vision blurry but slowly clearing up. My heartbeat didn't slow down even though the room that came into view wasn't threatening at all. It looked like an average private hospital room. The window to my right didn't give me much information as to my location—it was grey and cloudy outside. The lamp on the ceiling cast a soft glow. Fluid from an IV bag was dripping into my veins.

The sudden assault of disjointed and violent imagery hit me without warning. Something terrible must have happened! I tried to get up, but my body wasn't cooperating, fear sending my heartbeat into overdrive.

Behind me, a door opened, and someone came rushing in, a woman in a nurse's uniform.

"Ms. MacGregor, what's wrong? Please, try to relax."

"Where am I?" I managed.

"You're safe now. You were in an accident, but you're going to be okay."

"I...I don't feel any pain."

"That's because of the medication."

"Where are my parents...and Dani?" Funny that Dani came to mind first. For some reason, I couldn't even remember much about her, or the last time we talked, the thought filling me with anxiousness. I really wanted to talk to Mom and Dad. They would help me figure out what happened.

The nurse looked uncomfortable.

"It's best I get the doctor. He can explain everything to you. The most important thing for you is to recover."

"Have my parents been notified?" I asked, frustrated with the non-answer. "In that case, I should call them."

There was no phone on the nightstand. Why?

"I'll get the doctor for you in a minute. Please, don't move." She arranged the IV bag, and to my dismay, the fluid seemed to flow faster.

"No, wait!"

"You really need your rest. We'll clear this up in no time, I promise."

I wanted to protest, but I couldn't fight the effect of whatever was in that bag, my body growing heavier each second, my lids closing. My last thought was that this couldn't be right because my parents, Dani, Joy, and Alice would never abandon me. I knew I was in trouble. Why would the nurse lie to me about an accident? Why was there no phone?

The drug-induced sleep was deep and heavy, leading to a series of disturbing dreams. Every once in a while, I felt that someone was in the room, but maybe I was dreaming that too.

My lids continued to feel too heavy, and not being able to move or open my eyes sent me into a panic occasionally, which was followed by the door opening and a soft voice speaking to me. I didn't know how much time had passed, hours, days, but I never saw my family or friends. At some point, I became convinced that, for whatever reason, they wouldn't come, and I was all alone.

Eventually, a doctor came to explain my situation to me. I was still in the same hospital room, the same bed, feeling heavy and uncomfortable. No one had asked for me.

"I'm sorry to say that doesn't surprise me after what you'd told us about them," he said.

"What?" I couldn't even remember talking to anyone.

"You said you left the house the moment you turned eighteen. Your parents were cold and indifferent, and your sister's friends mocked you at every occasion. They wanted you gone."

That's not true! I held back the instinctive reaction as my mind searched for an explanation. I couldn't find any. There was a vague recollection of heated words that I'd exchanged with someone...Alice? Mom?

"I'm really sorry. Now that you're more aware, I'll send in the psychiatrist to help you sort this out. Let's talk about your physical condition first."

"I was...in an accident?"

My tongue felt heavy. It seemed like they kept me under for quite some time, which meant I must have had serious injuries.

"Yes, you were. We had to repair some internal injuries which we did successfully. Your leg was broken. Our biggest concern was the trauma you experienced on impact. We had to operate on your brain."

I was stunned and terrified at the same time. I only now realized that my left leg was still in a cast. "Is this why I can't remember?"

"Partly." He reached out and touched my arm gently, the gesture startling me. "Look, we will continue to do what we can to help you through this. I know it's a lot to take in. Our psychiatrist will talk to you in more detail, but I can tell you it's perfectly normal if you feel confused or can't remember the accident or other incidents. Chances are that your memory will return for the most part."

"What if it doesn't?" This was a nightmare. I felt like I had something important to do, people to talk to, but as it was, I couldn't even leave this bed.

"As I said, we'll do our best to help you with the healing process. Today, we need something from you, too. I'd like you to try and stand up for me. Slowly."

Nothing easier than that, right?

The moment he assisted me into a sitting position, I began to hyperventilate. What had happened to me? I had been living in this netherworld for so long now I was afraid to move. Afraid that I might not be able to.

"Take your time," he said. "It will all come back to you, I promise."

My mind flashed back to something the doctor had said earlier. "Why did I leave home? I'm not eighteen yet. Why would I say that?"

As we talked, he carefully guided me out of the bed and to my feet.

"As I said, there are some things the psychiatrist is better equipped for. However, you had identification with you when you were found that stated you are eighteen indeed. This is going well, Ms. MacGregor. In the next few days, you'll be able to make it to the bathroom by yourself."

I blushed hotly when all the details of my situation registered with me. How was it possible I never even noticed...? I wanted back into that bed. I wanted answers, but even with the doctor's help, staying upright required all my attention.

Eighteen? What happened between New York and now? Wait...I planned to go with Alice and her friends, but did that ever happen? I had some muddled memories, but I couldn't tell if they came from something I'd seen in a movie, or reality.

"What car was I driving?" My heart beat hard against my chest. "Was anyone else hurt in the accident?"

"No, you were alone."

I breathed a sigh of relief, my eyes welling up. He finally let me sit on the edge of the bed.

"It's hard to concentrate," I admitted, "but I need to know. Please tell me what you know...and about that operation."

"Of course. You deserve to know," he said, "but first, let's get you back into that bed."

I was feeling sick, a drop of cold sweat snaking down my spine. I had the feeling it wouldn't get better.

Chapter Five

Lois didn't follow us into my office. I tried not to get ahead of myself, but if Elaina came by at this time of the day, it had to be important, right? It had to be something.

"Okay, let's take a look," I said, and gestured for her to sit down.

"You can't tell anyone about this," Elaina insisted.

"If there's any information relating to Brittany's death, there has to be an investigation. Don't you want to know the truth?"

The truth—it was a gift most people underestimated.

"Of course I do," she snapped. "I also want to live."

I couldn't help thinking that grief was driving her interpretation of the situation. Yes, there was the matter of the encrypted files, but only a few hours earlier, Elaina thought they might be patients' files—which made sense.

The USB drive contained several folders, within them documents that didn't tell me anything, lists, numbers, and abbreviated words that I assumed were famous brain surgeon jargon.

I clicked on another folder, pictures this time. They were all women, ages teens to early thirties.

"Who are they?" I asked. "The patients from the encrypted files? I don't recognize anyone famous."

Elaina shrugged.

"I don't know. I didn't recognize anyone either, but that doesn't have to mean anything. The Mason Clinic has various ongoing studies, so maybe those were participants. Whatever this is, Brittany thought this information could get me in trouble. I need you to find out why, please!"

"I'll do what I can," I said, still clicking through the photos, then back, pausing.

"What is it?" Elaina asked.

I debated with myself whether I should tell her, and what she would do with that information, if anything.

The picture was the same I had in one of my own folders. Caitlyn Hoyt. How was she connected to Brittany? Who were the other women?

"Nothing," I said. "Can I keep this? I promise you, I won't tell anyone yet, not until I find out more. If this is the key to why Brittany killed herself, we'll find out."

I was no step closer to determining Paige's fate, but this was an exciting turn of events. At the very least, I might find out if Caitlyn had left her husband of her own free will and take her off my list. Progress.

"Yes, please keep it. I feel better if you have it instead of me."

I couldn't blame her.

"Thank you for trusting me with this. I'll get back to you as soon as I know more."

I couldn't do all of this from home, so I came in to work early, determined to run as many of those pictures as I could before anyone could think of raising questions. It was still dark outside. I was motivated. After comparing the pictures against my files last night, I found another match: Annette Montgomery, twenty-two at the time, disappeared without a trace from a hiking trip she took in 2006 with a female friend. I had called the friend on the phone, and it didn't take me long to determine they'd been more than that. In 2006, they couldn't get married in their state, and both of them would have been fired from their workplace if their employer knew. No one had seen or heard from Annette until now.

Annette. Caitlyn. Both from my files. Was this the beginning of the pattern I'd been looking for? And did it mean anything for Paige? Her photo hadn't been in the folder, but that brought me back to the encrypted files. What if there were more pictures? Had Brittany known what happened to these women, or had they suffered brain damage at some point that kept them from contacting their families? So many of them?

Checking my watch, I didn't think Hawkins would be there yet, neither could I reach the director of the Mason Clinic. I wanted to make sure I hadn't overlooked anything when it came to Brittany's employer.

One by one I ran the pictures through the missing persons database. Of about three dozen, I got close to twenty hits. I stared at the screen, alarmed at the picture unfolding. I had focused on aspects resembling Paige's case, but these were all missing women, the details, year, circumstances, all over the place, though they all fit within a certain age range. If this was a sex trafficking ring, most of the victims would likely be even younger. Whatever their connection was, to Brittany Dawson and to one another, there was something sinister going on. Another mystery to solve.

I printed out my results and put them into a drawer I locked, then I headed for the lab. Hawkins was there, frowning over some test results.

"Hey," I said, startling her.

"Do you make it a habit of sneaking up on people?" she grumbled.

"No, just for you. Bad news?"

"No." She swiveled her chair around to face me. "I'm pretty busy this morning."

"I won't be long. Did you hear anything about those encryptions on Dawson's computer?"

I noticed a minute hesitation when she answered.

"No, but I don't see what we'd do with those now anyway. The case is closed, isn't it? The ME ruled it a suicide. A celebrity with a high-profile, high-pressure job—it happens."

"Check with them anyway. If anyone can tell us what's in those files, I want to know."

"You're bored?"

"Just let me know, okay?"

She gave a terse nod.

Twenty-five minutes later, Eric Johnson, the director of the Mason clinic, was more forthcoming than my colleague, agreeing to see me without an appointment.

"It's been a shock for all of us," he said. "Brittany was family. Can I ask what this is about though? You do have her financial information, don't you?"

"We do. I'd just like you to take another look at the numbers."

"Sure, no problem. What am I looking for?" He studied the papers I gave him, month after month of Brittany Dawson's earnings. Johnson answered the question himself. "This is odd. Let me make a quick call."

I waited while he punched in the numbers. The person on the other end of the line was obviously in the payroll office. He asked a few questions regarding payments made to Brittany in the past year, and then hung up.

"That's what I thought. Look, don't get me wrong. We certainly valued Brittany's contribution, and compensated her accordingly, but this is not the salary we paid her. Even if she had worked here full-time..."

"You're saying she didn't?"

The mystery was just getting bigger. Brittany had had an unknown source of income from a job she either hadn't told Elaina about, or Elaina lied to me.

"She did twenty, twenty-five hours. She didn't talk about her other project though. I assumed it was for a new book, but I can't say for sure."

"Do you have any idea who might know?"

He shrugged. "Brittany was well-liked, but she didn't really socialize. She came in, did her job—brilliantly, I might say—but I never saw her go out with her colleagues. If I should guess, they were mostly in awe, or intimidated by her talent. She worked wonders."

"And you didn't try to make her work for you full-time?"

He laughed. "I wish I could have! She said no, so there must have been something else close to her heart."

My phone rang, and I excused myself. Viola.

"Are you planning on coming in at any time today? You know we have half a dozen witnesses on the Webster case to interview."

"Don't worry, I'll be there soon," I said and ended the call. "Thank you so much for your help, Dr. Johnson."

"You'll be in touch if you find out anything new? I mean, it's still so hard to imagine. Brittany had her quirks like all highly gifted individuals, but I can't believe she was suicidal...I guess sometimes even those closest don't know."

"Unfortunately, that's possible. I'll let you know."

I left his office with more questions than answers, but somehow, that had me excited. All of a sudden having a real chance at finding out what happened to these women was exhilarating. Even if Paige's photo hadn't been in that folder—she could still be mentioned somewhere else, in one of the encrypted files.

I called Lois and left her a message. I'd be home late tonight.

After a shift that didn't seem to end, I drove straight to Elaina's house. I needed something from her, and for that, I had to make some revelations.

"I'm not sure if I'm in the mood for that. As you know, I'm preparing a funeral." Her tone kept changing quickly enough to give me whiplash. This was the same woman who had asked me just yesterday to leave no stone unturned in the search for answers.

"I understand that, but it would help a lot if I could do this. The women you saw in that folder...most of them have been missing for eight to ten years, and more. There must be a reason why Brittany compiled those photos, and why she kept the other files encrypted. I think she was protecting those women."

"From what?" Elaina asked, doubtful.

"That's what I want to find out, and I believe once we know, it would give you closure, too."

She sank into a chair, wiping her face in a quick, angry gesture.

"Frankly, I don't know. What if we find out that Brittany was just really unhappy with her life? I don't know if I could live with that kind of closure."

I sat down across from her.

"It's true, there's no guarantee as to what we'll find out. But these women's families have been waiting for a long time. I will have to pass on those files, but first I'd like to see if there's anything that will help. Everything that might tell us about her secret project."

"What project?" she asked, puzzled. "She worked sixty and more hours at Mason."

"Director Johnson told me something else."

Elaina contemplated this new information for a moment, then she nodded.

"Okay. Let's get to work."

We spent the next hours poring over paperwork, every single square inch of Brittany's office. At some point, Elaina ordered dinner from a local Thai restaurant. She offered me a glass of wine which I declined. I needed a clear head, now, tomorrow when I presented my case to the higher ups. I wondered if Chief Larkin was still in town. If he could back me up with the lieutenant, we might be able to set up a bigger task force...find those women.

Find Paige.

As it was, we still didn't have anything to crack the code we'd found on the USB drive. Abbreviations of names, and what else? License plates, social security numbers, coordinates? Nothing panned out so far.

At the back of the bottom drawer, I found a page torn out of a newspaper. Here we were struggling with encryptions and codes, but the real clue came to me in a very old-fashioned way. There was a sticky note, the letters "C H" and a phone number written on it.

53

I scanned both sides of the newspaper page and eventually stumbled across a small paragraph about a shooting involving a man named Christopher Hoyt. Earlier this year, Caitlyn Hoyt's husband had died in a shootout with someone he got into a fight with. Alcohol was involved. Apparently the two men knew each other.

I stared at the note as the seconds ticked by. If this was the one thread to start with, the whole story could unravel.

I typed the numbers into my phone, disregarding the late hour.

After four rings, a man answered.

"Hello? Who is this?"

"Can I talk to Caitlyn, please?"

"You have a wrong number. There's no Caitlyn here."

"Please, wait—"

He had already hung up. I thought back to the theories that had been floating around in her case, that she might have tried to escape from an abusive relationship. If that was true, she probably used a different name. I'd try to trace this number first thing in the morning.

"I really appreciate you bearing with me," Elaina said ruefully. "Half of the time I think it's bad to stir up things, but then again, I need to know. If I could have done anything...I need to know. That sounds crazy, doesn't it?"

She didn't know who she was talking to.

"I completely understand. I'm afraid I have to go now. There's something I need to work on, so those cases can go forward."

"If you want, you can work on it from here. You can always sleep in the guestroom."

I considered my options. It would indeed help if I could continue here, get a few hours of sleep and then drop by home in the morning to change clothes and pick up some files.

"Are you sure that's all right with you?"

"Actually, I'd feel safer. I don't know if I'm paranoid, losing my mind, or if there's actually something to fear."

"I think it's better to be safe than sorry. If Brittany was afraid of someone, we will find out."

Lois wouldn't see me tonight after all.

⁂

The number belonged to a Jason Geller, a contractor who lived about two hours from here, married, three children aged one to seven. Was Mrs. Geller Caitlyn Hoyt? If that was the case, did she know that her ex-husband was dead? Even so, there might be some legal consequences in her future, as the police had assumed a crime and opened an investigation. If she'd married Jason while still legally Christopher's wife, no one could do anything about it now. She had reasons to stay hidden.

I needed to talk to her, if only to exclude her from my list, and find out how she'd ended up on Brittany's.

When I knocked on the lieutenant's door, he called me in right away. To my surprise, we were not alone. Hawkins and Viola were present. Unfortunately, I couldn't reach Larkin earlier.

"Detective Ryder," he said. "It has come to my attention that you've made some new inquiries into the Dawson case."

"That's what I wanted to talk to you about. Dr. Dawson kept a file of photos and other information that lead back to several cases of missing women. I think I found Caitlyn Hoyt, and once we know the content of the encrypted files—"

"What difference do you think it's going to make? Look, the medical examiner's findings were clear. Dr. Dawson killed herself. Your case is closed. You can pass on any information regarding Ms. Hoyt to your colleagues in Missing Persons, but I believe you have other open cases to address."

"Yes, but—this could lead us to solve many other cases. There must be additional information in those files."

"Maybe, and maybe there isn't. I advised Hawkins to withdraw her request for an analysis."

"What?" I couldn't believe it. "That doesn't make sense!"

"Excuse me, Detective? I'm not sure if you are aware, but the resources of this department are not infinite. We have to work with solid evidence. Until you can tell me for sure that there's more on this than celebrity patient names, it ends here. Now go back to work."

"Sir," I said tersely before jumping to my feet and heading out. Viola followed me.

"Look, I'm sorry."

"Yeah, you should be. You could have backed me up in there."

"Really? You make me wait, make the witnesses wait and ask Hawkins for jobs on the side? I'm really sorry, but that's not how it works. Everyone here knows you have an agenda, and that missing women are a trigger for you—but you're not in Missing Persons anymore, and you can't expect everyone to fall in line."

"Some of them were teenagers! You don't want to know what happened to them? You don't care?"

"Low blow, Danielle. I do care about every one of them, but I also need to still have a life. Think about that for a moment."

Angry and frustrated with the outcome of the argument, I went back to my desk to do some paperwork, wondering if I could have another conversation with Chief Larkin. He, too, had suggested that wrapping up the case as soon as possible might be for the best, but there was new evidence. Maybe I could get him to help me.

Brittany's computer would be returned to Elaina. I wasn't sure what I could do with those files, but I needed to have them. I also needed a couple of days off.

Not much later, I was back in Lieutenant Thorne's office, groveling just enough for him to accept my apology.

"I am sorry. I never meant to call your authority into question. I have to ask you a favor, though."

"Suicide cases are always tough," he acknowledged. "The loved ones want explanations, any explanation other than the obvious, and sometimes we can get drawn into that."

"It's possible that's what happened with me. I was wondering if I could take a couple of days." Thursday and Friday—that would mean that I didn't have to return until Monday. It would give me enough time to take a little road trip and visit Mr. Geller. If he and his wife had any information that would help me solve the mystery, I'd have to think long and hard about turning them in. They hadn't actually pretended a crime happened, just didn't correct the assumption. Caitlyn didn't have any family, and now the husband who had been looking for her, was dead too. What good would it do to mess with her life once more?

I was going to tread carefully. There was a chance Jason Geller didn't know whom he had married.

"I think that's a good idea. Get your head straight. I'll have Pierce work with Marsh in the meantime."

"Thank you so much." I wasn't exaggerating.

I didn't talk to Viola, or anyone else for that matter, on my way out. At home, I searched the internet for a motel or B&B in the vicinity of Geller's address. There was a pub in town that offered rooms on the upper floor. No booking online. I called the number, got myself a room, and then went to pack.

"We're going somewhere?"

I turned around to find Lois standing in the doorway, looking resigned. She already knew that this trip didn't include her.

"I'm sorry, but there's a lead I have to follow. I expect to be back on Sunday at the latest."

"What about your parents?"

I suppressed a curse. I had completely forgotten about the Saturday night dinner. I really wanted to see them, but...this couldn't wait.

"You think you could entertain them for an evening? I might even make it back in time, but for sure I'll pay for breakfast on Sunday."

"I guess I have no choice. They'll be disappointed."

I straightened to embrace her, wishing I could give her a good reason as to why I had to let her down for a vague promise—again.

"You think it might be about her?"

"I don't know yet. I might solve a Missing Persons case."

"Then you have to go, right?" She sighed. "At least you're not cheating...even though sometimes, it feels like it."

"I'm not."

"I know. Have a safe trip. I'll have to get ready too. I'm meeting some friends for dinner."

"Sure. Have fun."

Cheating? This was crazy. My only hope was to deliver this piece of the puzzle, so Alice, Joy and I could deal with the consequences, whatever they were.

If I ever found Paige alive, there was no reason why she'd still be attracted to me. I just didn't want her to hurt, because the last time I'd seen her, she was, and it had been my fault.

Chapter Six

Paige

2003

I was healing, though that was a relative term when it came to my state of mind. I felt like I didn't know who I was anymore. Those feelings were probably not surprising given the accident and the subsequent surgery.

The psychiatrist, doctors and nurses helped me get back on my feet, literally and then when I came closer to the moment of leaving the hospital. I was terrified. I wanted to call somebody, reach out, but according to what I had told the staff, there was no one to reach out to. My family had rejected me, and I decided to run away, leave them, school, a job, I wasn't even sure. What had I run away from?

"You're a remarkable young woman," the psychiatrist assured me. "I've reviewed your case together with your physicians, and I have to say that the surgery isn't enough to explain this massive loss of memory. Chances are that some of the traumatic events happened before the accident, and your reaction to them is not purely physical."

When it rains it pours, right?

"I don't know what to do," I said, crying again. I'd been crying a lot in the past weeks, when the fog in my mind started to lift and I realized the gravity of my situation.

"Be assured that we won't kick you out. I can make an appointment for you with our social worker, and she can help you settle in, wherever you choose to stay. You should remain in the vicinity for a while longer though, because with such an extensive surgery, you need regular check-ups. You've been through a lot, Peggy. We can help you."

Paige. My name is Paige. I had given up on correcting people, and I had no leg to stand on anyway—all my papers identified me as Peggy MacGregor. Why would I carry the purse with all the identification of someone who looked like me, was the same age and height and born in the same place? Peggy. Paige. It didn't matter so much anymore—I had other problems to deal with, like finding housing and employment.

"I would really appreciate that. Frankly, I'm scared of the final bill." The thought made me physically sick. I should have left a long time ago, but then again, it wasn't that long since I could walk around by myself without attacks of vertigo and headaches. The doctors here had a reason for wanting to monitor me.

"You don't have to be. Most of it is covered by your insurance, and the rest...our community comes together in cases like yours. Don't worry about it."

I wasn't sure what that meant, but there was too much on my mind anyway.

"Thank you."

"It's all right. We give back when we can."

True to his word, I had an appointment for two days later. My bloodwork was next to perfect, and the psychiatrist didn't think I'd present a danger to myself or my environment.

Now, there was the matter of Tom, my boyfriend, whom I had only vague memories of, but who came to visit me every day since the staff thought it was okay. He, sadly, could confirm frequent fights with my parents and sister until they decided I should no longer stay with them. It was frightening to hear the same story again and again, a story that I had told, too, apparently. How else could they know?

I should have been grateful. Gloria, one of the nurses, often stopped by during her breaks to chat. She had become a friend.

I already felt crowded. Then again, the social worker would hopefully help me stand on my own feet. I needed it.

I needed to start all over again from the life I had imagined was mine. Reality turned out to be so bad I needed to imagine it in the first place, and maybe it had tainted me. There were helpful and kind people all around me—a shadow of doubt always remained.

Gloria came with me to my appointment with the social worker, and she offered me a room in her apartment until I could get a job—or until "Things with Tom get really serious," she said with a wink.

"I was going to start college," I said. "I really need to look into places." I'd always thought that by my eighteenth birthday, I would already be enrolled, but here I was, basically an orphan by my family's choice, with no money. I would have no place to go if it wasn't for the kindness of strangers.

I saw the look Gloria and the social worker exchanged. Sympathy—pity? Did they think I couldn't do it? It was true, I had trouble concentrating, and it was probably all related to the accident, or the subsequent surgery. I had always been good in school—at least I thought that's what I remembered.

"This is important to me," I insisted. After having little privacy for what seemed like a long time, I needed to make my own decisions.

"Maybe you should put off those major decisions for a while," the social worker said. "Take the time you need to figure out what you really want."

"That's right," Gloria chimed in. "You and Tom want a family, right? It's best to start young."

Wait, what? We had talked about that?

All of a sudden, I had the urge to run, though I wasn't sure I could make it far.

I wasn't sure where to run to. My new friends—and some old ones I had trouble remembering—only wanted the best for me, didn't they?

❧

Dani

2005

I went back to New York City on my own, two years after Paige disappeared. Phone calls and emails between me, Alice and Joy already were sporadic. When I asked them if they wanted to come, both of them quickly found an excuse not to. Alice was spending the summer with her boyfriend's family. Joy had to help out her parents during a renovation.

Maybe I was paranoid, and they did have a good reason not to join me. I wasn't sure what I was hoping to find…but something drew me there. I knew I had to go.

It seemed impossible that time just went on, as if nothing happened. I had raged, grieved, been stunned to realize that the world kept turning, regardless. Days, weeks and then months had passed, and the two-year anniversary of that day was coming around.

I took my car this time, drove all the way, only stopped a couple of times for meals.

I was exhausted when I arrived, but I still took a shower and went out to a restaurant we had visited that summer. As I was sipping my beer, I remembered the arguments Alice and Paige had had, the night Alice and Joy went clubbing.

When Paige kissed me.

I still hadn't told anyone. There had never been a right moment. It felt selfish, to draw anyone's attention from the fact that Paige was gone, somewhere out there, unhappy or worse.

Every once in a while, I questioned the wisdom of going to the academy instead of business school. I wasn't queasy, but the things I saw on a daily basis were reminders and nightmares of what might have happened to her.

I missed her. The truth was, I had a crush on her since the last time I had come back home from college, when I could no longer pretend to myself I was looking for a boyfriend...When I started to realize I wasn't just interested in anyone. Somehow, being attracted to her had made everything worse. I was paying for my sins.

I was wallowing in self-pity, all by myself in New York City.

Later, I hailed a cab to bring me back to my hotel, the same hotel we'd stayed in two years before, where I cried myself to sleep.

In the morning, I went to a coffee shop to have breakfast. A coffee and muffin in front of me, I sat at my table, watching busy people hurry past the window.

I had a mission too, but I was stalling. I wasn't sure if I could do it, and whether I should be relieved or upset that Joy and

Alice weren't here. Finally, I left and walked all the way to the place where it happened, the street where we'd lost Paige.

Like the last time, travelers were waiting for buses and shuttles. Of course, no one had the slightest idea about who I was, or why I was here. No one remembered but me.

Walking down the street, stopping at a light that had turned red...Joy and Alice had already made it past...

I turned around, startled when I saw the woman with her back turned to me, same build, same height and hair color...I started walking towards her when she turned to kiss the man behind her.

She wasn't Paige. My imagination and grief were playing tricks on me.

I went back to the Met, standing for minutes in front of a painting that she had admired. I thought of all the plans we'd had—in the short run, for that trip, and the more distant ones.

She was in love with me. If I had respected that, we might not have lost her.

I knew I had to go home empty-handed—but I would be back.

❧

Dani

2016

Present

I was on the road early in the morning, leaving the city behind. It felt like a weight was off my shoulders, even though there would undoubtedly be consequences for my actions.

Maybe I was lucky, and the Gellers would quietly accept my visit and not notify any colleagues of mine...or my lieutenant. If I was really lucky, no one would ever know. I could keep their secrets, and they could keep mine.

My reprieve wouldn't last long. I was afraid that if I didn't turn up for Sunday breakfast as I'd promised, Lois would soon have enough of me. It gave me pause to realize I wasn't that afraid of the possibility. Yes, I liked her, I liked the companionship, and frankly, the sex. At the end of the day, it was one more responsibility taking me away from the mystery I needed to solve. Again, I had lied to her, because I didn't think she'd take it well if she found out this was all my idea. I had passed on the information to Missing Persons as ordered, but I couldn't leave it alone.

I could feel it in my bones that Caitlyn, if I found her in the Gellers' house, had answers for me. I just knew it. I stopped halfway for breakfast at a rest stop, enjoying a coffee and a piece of cheesecake, then I drove the rest of the way straight. I only stopped briefly at the hotel to check in and freshen up, then I made my way to the Gellers. The community they lived in was a bit further out than I imagined. The suburban feel of the area and its cookie cutter houses depressed me. It looked like the coming of age of a bunch of jocks and their high school sweethearts.

The house Jason shared with his family was on the first in a large, almost symmetrical half circle, another half circle of houses behind. Who or what were they trying to summon?

I parked on the curb and walked up to the house. I had a prickling feeling at the back of my neck, and turning, I could see movement behind the next-door neighbor's window. Nothing surprising so far. When your neighbor was practically on top of you, curiosity was a given. It made me cringe that there were people who chose to live like this. Then again, it was none of my business, right? A few days out here would remind me why I loved living in a city.

I rang the doorbell once, waited, then another time.

The door opened, and I came face to face with Caitlin Hoyt aka Mrs. Geller.

"Ms. Caitlyn Hoyt?" There was alarm on her face, and I had only a split second before she decided to slam the door in my face. I caught it in time. "Caitlyn, please, I need to talk to you for a moment. It's important."

Someone's life could depend on it. I'm not sure it would have been fair to use that, given that I had no idea if Paige was alive. But she had to be. She had to be.

The other woman let go of the door, her shoulders slumping.

"My name is Katie Geller," she said. I heard children's laughter from inside the house.

"I need to make lunch," Caitlyn/Katie added. "My husband is coming home in a few minutes, and he won't like seeing you here. He doesn't like people bothering us."

I detected more between the lines than I wanted to.

"I don't want any trouble for you or your family. I know you escaped your former husband." It was worth a shot. "You might want to know that he's dead."

Something in her expression changed, a hint of emotion visible.

"Who are you?"

"My name is Danielle Ryder. I'm a cop, but I'm not here on an official assignment. I am interested in the circumstances of your disappearance."

"Why?" she asked, her tone cool and sarcastic now. "You want to charge me for pretending a crime happened? That's rich, especially since the police never do a thing when you need them."

I assumed she was talking about the times she tried to escape from Christopher. Maybe she had even tried to press charges.

"I'm so sorry this happened, but you could really help me. Caitlyn."

"I told you, my name is Katie."

"Okay. Katie. Can you tell me what happened the day you disappeared? Was that your choice? Did someone take you?"

Her eyes started welling up.

"Please leave. I can't help you. My husband will be mad when he finds out I stood here chatting with you instead of starting lunch."

The pieces fell into place to reveal a horrible picture. Maybe she had run away during that vacation with Christopher Hoyt, but Caitlyn hadn't found a better life, on the contrary.

"I'll make sure you're safe," I said.

She didn't look impressed. "Other cops have said that before. Look, I don't have time. I don't even know what you're talking about. I need you to go now."

"I'll be back."

"Please don't. You'll only make things worse."

Make no mistake, I planned to make things a lot worse—for Jason Geller.

Speak of the devil. He arrived as I was still contemplating how far I could go with this without exposing either of us too much.

"Go," she hissed as his car pulled into the driveway.

I didn't want to leave now and risk her getting beaten up because lunch wasn't on the table.

"And who do we have here?" Geller said with a charming smile, kissing his wife. I didn't miss Caitlyn cringe. I had seen abusers who could put up a pleasant front before. In fact, most of them were pretty good at it.

"Hi, Mr. Geller." I let my voice go a notch higher, into a chirp that fit my lie better and would hopefully not tip him off. After all, he'd heard my voice before. "I'm here for market research, and I'm visiting families in the area. I was hoping your wife could take a few minutes' time to answer my questions."

"And she said yes, right, darling?" This time, the smile didn't reach his eyes. "That's my lovely wife, she just can't say no. Go ahead, talk to the lady, I'll say hi to the kids in the meantime." Another flinch as he patted her back and then disappeared into the house. She wiped a hand across her forehead, her sleeve riding up to reveal the bruise around her wrist.

"You have to let me help you."

"I don't have to do anything. I need to take care of my children. If you must know, yes, I ran away from Christopher, and it was a good decision. Don't come back here. I have a different life now."

This time, she closed the door in my face. I stood for a moment, then turned to my car, one step, two, then I heard the scream. Something breaking. Children crying.

I called 911 and identified myself after giving them the address.

I ran back to the front door, hand on my gun as I entered the house. There was a dining area and living room to the left. On the right, in the kitchen area, Jason Geller was choking his wife.

"Let her go!" I yelled at him. Two of the children watched from the gallery, crying.

"Get the hell out of my house!" Geller's gaze darted around wildly, falling on the knife block.

"Don't even think about it. I'm a police officer. Backup is on the way. Let her go."

"I don't have to listen to you bitch!"

He was loosening his grip slightly, though, and Caitlyn frantically gasped for air, coughing.

"Suit yourself. You're under arrest for assaulting your wife and..."

There were sirens, at first distance, then loud enough to alert me that the local police had arrived. "Get away from him, Caitlyn," I said. "We'll figure this out. Go get your kids."

"What the fuck are you doing?" he yelled.

Behind me, other cops entered the house, and I holstered my gun, turning around with my hands raised.

"I called 911 to report this man assaulting his wife. I'm Detective Danielle Ryder. My badge is in the inner pocket of my coat."

"Lies," he muttered while Caitlyn ran to her kids, pulling them into a group embrace. A female officer came to check my badge, and I let my hands fall to my side. "Thanks for coming right away. I take it this was not the first call to his house."

The officer looked at her partner, both of them seeming uncomfortable. "We don't have that many calls in this area. Can you tell us what happened?"

"Mr. Geller here was choking his wife in front of his children."

"She's lying. Got herself access to our house with lies, disturbing our family. I bet she's not even a real cop."

"Mr. Geller, we need you to come with us," the male officer said. I told him that Geller hadn't been read his rights yet, and he continued while his partner stood by. I went up the stairs to look after Caitlyn. I hoped they could hold him for the weekend at least, so that could help her to formulate a plan.

Over the heads of her children, Caitlyn addressed me "Get out." It sounded like speaking was causing her pain, but her message was urgent, unmistakable as she gripped my jacket. "I don't want to see you here ever again." She was still afraid, which was no surprise.

"He won't be back right away. My statement will…"

"Do nothing," she said bitterly. "You'll see. I have nothing more to tell you. Don't ever come back. Jason has a gun too."

"Okay. Whatever you do, you should call someone, make sure it's safe for you to stay here. I can talk to the police about a restraining order, and all you have to do is—"

"Detective Ryder," the female officer called me. "Could you please follow us? We have a few more questions."

"Yes, sure."

I had done the best I could to explain the situation to local law enforcement officers—and of course they had to check my credentials. By late afternoon, I had various furious messages from the lieutenant, and one, calmer, from Chief Larkin. One from Viola who asked me if I had freaking lost my mind.

I called each of them back, explaining on three different voicemails that I had saved a woman from getting choked to death by her husband, and that I wasn't sorry about that. Also, I could take Caitlyn off my list, but that, I kept to myself.

The day's work done, I went down to the pub, all eyes going to me as if they had never seen a single woman walk into a bar. Perhaps it was really inconceivable to them, because the women here were all with men, and there were only a few single guys.

I didn't care.

All I wanted was a decent beer or two, and something to eat. A couple at a table shared a plate of nachos that didn't look all that bad. I sat on a barstool and ordered said plate with a Corona.

After ten minutes, the first guy asked me if I was alone here and interested in company. I said no. That didn't stop the second one. I would have shown him my gun, but I wanted to get blitzed, and that doesn't mix well with firearms.

The police officer I had talked to earlier walked in, and after that, the advances stopped. He nodded to me but had fortunately as little interest in small talk as I had. After the third Corona, still convinced I'd done the right thing even though coming home would not be easy, I decided I needed to get some sleep. When I got up, my coat slipped from the chair I'd parked it on to make sure everyone got the message, and something fell out.

For a moment, I just stared at the photo, dumbfounded. Where had it come from and why—? I recognized Caitlyn first, of course, I had seen her only a few hours ago. The photograph showed a group of women, at a street party or a barbecue maybe. They all smiled into the camera. At least four of them were from my list, Brittany Dawson's list and...*oh my God.*

The folded picture fell from my hand, sailing to the floor.

Second row, third on the left.

"Paige," I whispered.

～

2003

"I don't feel good about this," Dr. Brittany Dawson admitted. "We're not there yet. She's not ready."

The assistant project manager moderating the meeting, frowned.

"How so? We've invested quite a bit. You and your colleagues have done extensive work, and now you're telling me we have to delay?"

She looked around the small groups, doctors, psychiatrists, administrative staff, all eager to optimize the path to their shared goal. What was that, she wondered? She had done—and was still doing—superior work to help trauma victims defeat their memories. Her technique was unique in the world. She didn't make them forget what happened but enabled them to sort it out in a way the brain wouldn't overwhelm them with flashbacks and nightmares. In order to keep the money flowing for these projects, her job was now to create disintegration.

"It would be better," she said. "Give Dr. Knight more time."

The psychiatrist shrugged. "We're on our way, but I suppose there's a limit to what we can achieve with our means."

"I need you to get back in there," the assistant project manager said. "Our sponsors won't wait forever."

"Our sponsors don't have the skills and knowledge to understand what it is we're doing here!" Brittany saw the shocked faces all around. No one ever raised their voice in this room.

"You all know what to do. This meeting is over. Dr. Dawson, can I have a word?"

She saw Knight's sympathetic expression.

"Yes, sure."

Her colleagues filed out of the room, and then it was just her and the APM. He wasn't the only one—each oversaw one group, and frankly, Brittany didn't think they had the knowledge or skills to truly understand what they were doing here. She, of course, had, and it frightened her, but the money could help so many people. She wouldn't always be around. She had to train others. There wasn't enough time in the day—she barely saw Elaina as it was.

But it was for the cause, not the one the APMs and their bosses were talking about, but her own.

"Is there a problem?" he asked.

"No, no problem," she hurried to say. "Everything is going according to plan—just slower than we expected."

"Then make it go faster."

"There's no saying what damage we could do—"

"I don't care!" He regained his composure quickly, his face turning into an unreadable mask again, but he couldn't fool Brittany. Everyone here had an Achilles heel, something to lose.

"I'll see what I can do," she said, and then, gave in to the foolish impulse she knew would get her into trouble. "How did her leg get broken?"

"You know that. It was a car accident."

"Okay. I'll get ready."

"You better," he warned. "I don't want to have to report a liability on our team."

"That won't be necessary," Brittany said. "I'll prepare everything for tonight."

Chapter Seven

Paige

2014

When we returned from couple's therapy, I felt tired and antsy at the same time. In theory, there was a number of issues as to why a couple was required to attend these sessions—in reality, everyone knew, in the clinic, and everyone we met out on the sidewalk. Social pressure was part of the process, and today, I was sick of it.

I doubted myself for it, knowing that I was the reason why we had to go, and why our neighbors were already talking behind our backs. I didn't have much time to indulge in self-reproach, though. I had to cook dinner. After a stern look and maybe a speech from Tom's mother, I had to take care of my children.

My children.

After all these years, the words still had an odd ring to it, or did that just happen a few weeks ago? It was hard to tell. I was happy, and fortunate, wasn't I?

For some time now, I had been living in a fog I didn't know how to get out of.

What was wrong with me? I was fulfilling my destiny, as a woman, as a wife and mother, and yet I couldn't be happy about it. Yes, there had to be something wrong with me.

I was staying up late, always something to do or to prepare for the next day, so I could crawl into bed when Tom was already asleep. I wished I could sleep in the guestroom, be left in peace for eight hours at a time, or infinitely.

"It's against our fate," he said, desperate. "It's not natural."

Maybe he was right, but I couldn't help the way I felt.

I had the fantasy that his mother would have put Mia and Colin to bed, leave us alone early so that we could have a quiet evening, talk about the things we said in the therapist's office, the advice he gave us. The moment I walked through the front door, I knew it wasn't going to come true.

"Peggy, Tom, you're home. I take it everything went well? I made dinner. Look who helped."

The table was set indeed. I wanted to cry at the state of the kitchen. They weren't of any substantial help when cooking. The only difference they made was to create a bigger mess I'd have to clean up later. On the bright side, that would discourage Tom from trying to work on our marital problems.

I could sense his mother's curiosity directed at me like a laser. Everyone knew that when a therapist was involved, it meant that a couple had sexual problems. I'd had two children within a short time, now almost six years had passed without another pregnancy. It was a miracle that I'd gotten away with it for so long. I had to be grateful for Tom being so clueless, and kind even. He didn't put on much pressure until his family and friends got together for an intervention, and he still didn't get it. I almost blurted it out right there at the therapist's office: *I don't want another baby.*

I was already overwhelmed with taking care of the two we had, with everything around the house that wasn't a man's task. I wasn't supposed to take a job outside, though lately I'd been dreaming about it—do something other than pick up after them, speak to people other than Tom, his parents, and the neighbors. The guilt was crushing those thoughts every time. Mia and Colin were healthy, smart, and happy children. What more could a mother ask for?

"That's great. Thank you so much," I said with as much enthusiasm as I could muster, which wasn't all that much these days. I hugged Mia and Colin, and we sat down to eat.

I didn't look up, wanting to avoid the concerned glances I knew my husband and mother-in-law were giving me. They were good people. They worried about me.

I didn't want anyone to worry about me. I was fine. I just needed a break, that was all.

I felt a flash of nausea, out of the blue. What if a break wasn't enough? What if therapy wasn't enough?

In the decade of living in our little community, I hardly ever heard of couples separating. Divorce wasn't an option, and in the case of unbridgeable disagreements, the children often ended up with the husband—because they had the money to support them.

But that wasn't going to happen, was it? We weren't going to split up. I finally dared to look up at my children who enthusiastically wolfed down the spaghetti Millicent made, as if I rarely ever fed them. I couldn't imagine being without them...but I was so tired. Maybe I could convince Tom to stop the sessions. Several of his friends were doctors, if we could get just one of them to lie for us...I'd gladly take the blame and say it was because of me. Yes, there would be blame, together with some sympathy and pity, but that was better than being kicked out of your home with nowhere to go.

My family abandoned me a long time ago. The community was all I had, and I was truly happy here. I needed to get it together.

The rest of the evening passed in a predictable manner. Millicent stayed for dessert, then a coffee, then a little nightcap while I did the dishes, gave my kids a bath, had them brush their teeth and got them to bed.

When I came down the stairs, Millicent was fortunately ready to go. I eyed the bottle of red wine on the table. Women of childbearing age were cautioned to watch their alcohol intake. Just one glass. I wanted it badly.

"I'll come by when you go to your next session," she said with a smile. "It's really no problem. They're great children. They take after their daddy." She pinched Tom's cheek, unaware of the insult she had just made. Or perhaps she was, aware.

"Thank you, Mom."

"That's very generous of you," I echoed. A babysitter would be so much less complicated. We had the money, but both Tom and Millicent would be indignant if I ever brought up the subject. After all, I was already causing so much trouble by not fulfilling a part of my wifely duties.

When she was gone, I cleaned up the last glasses from the table and carried the wine into the kitchen where I poured myself a glass, taking a hasty sip as if someone was going to take it away from me in a second. And another sip. It felt good, my body starting to relax.

Tom walked into the kitchen and embraced me from behind.

"That wasn't so bad, right? I think he had some good pointers for us."

I didn't like where this was going. Yes, I wanted to talk, but that didn't seem to be what was on his mind.

"I'm tired."

"I know," he said, "but you heard what he said. We should try anyway. We have to, at some point."

I understood that this wasn't about individual desires, or the lack thereof. There was a time when I didn't hate intimacy, found it mildly pleasant at times, even. Today was not one of those days, and I couldn't pretend otherwise.

"Can I just finish that glass?" My tone was harsher than I intended.

"Yes, of course," he said, taking a step back. Maybe he was hoping that the alcohol would mellow my crankiness enough for us to be normal again, husband and wife. I wasn't all that certain, but if we had to follow the therapist's advice, this was one way to go.

There was something else Tom didn't know. I might not enjoy myself, but what was more important, I wasn't going to be pregnant.

***

Paige

2016

Present

I wiped my hands on my apron, realizing they were shaking. I had seen the flashing light of the police car in the distance, heard the siren. Close. Too close. The Gellers weren't our next-door neighbors, but Doreen came over earlier this morning and told me that Jason had been arrested, and something about a woman with a gun.

I couldn't understand what was happening—our neighborhood was usually quiet, and everyone knew one another.

It deeply disturbed me that the outside world could intrude abruptly like this. The police didn't come to our house yet. I hoped they wouldn't. Something about that possibility terrified me, and I already had enough problems of my own.

I lifted the lid off the pot, a gust of steam hitting me.

Why couldn't Tom just leave it alone? Lately, he'd been bringing up fertility treatments. Almost everyone in the community had more children than we had. People were whispering about the Gellers, too, even though Katie had a toddler at home, and her last pregnancy had been difficult. The Gellers had three children. Four or five were more like the average, and couples would tell you proudly how they were trying for more.

I couldn't help getting irritated at those conservations, but then again, they were simply living the life they wanted, right? Wasn't I?

There were always compromises. I regretted bitterly that I hadn't been a better friend to Katie, wrapped up in my own misery that seemed trivial in comparison. I wasn't such good friends with Doreen either, but she had supplied me with birth control pills for years now, and it didn't cost me an arm and a leg.

However, if Tom insisted on treatments, the doctors would soon become suspicious, as there was no reason why I shouldn't become pregnant.

I didn't have it so bad—Tom wasn't violent like Jason Geller, and I didn't have to run after six or seven kids turning the house upside down.

Why couldn't I be happy?

What would it take?

Lately, I had entertained the crazy idea that I might try to find my parents and sister, confront them.

Clearly, I had too much time on my hands.

For now, I needed to find out what happened to Katie. I had to make sure my husband didn't figure out that not only was I avoiding him, but I had been buying contraception on the black market.

First, I had to get lunch on the table.

A day like any other day...

❦

Dani

2016

Present

I had picked up the photo, my coat and got upstairs to my room where I once again called the Geller's residence, not surprised that no one picked up.

I spread out the files I brought on the floor, made a new list as I cross checked the photo against my previous information on the missing women.

Paige MacGregor
Caitlyn Hoyt/Katie Geller
Annette Montgomery
Tammy Grey
Margaret Allen
Ashley Benning

They were all in the picture, smiling as if they weren't connected by that dark spot in their history, family members and friends who had desperately searched for them. The letters blurred before my eyes. What happened to them? Why did none of them ever call or let their loved ones know that they were okay?

Did they know each other's stories?

This couldn't wait until tomorrow. If Caitlyn had slipped me the photo, she had to be aware of a bigger picture. I needed to talk to her, right now. I was hoping that with Jason out of the picture, even for a short time, she'd be more eager to talk. I couldn't leave her alone.

Not anymore.

I went down to the reception and had to ring twice before an employee arrived and grudgingly called me a cab. Then I was off to the Gellers once more.

The house was dark when we arrived. I felt truly sorry, but this might be the moment I had been waiting for, for over thirteen years. I couldn't stand to wait another minute. The cab driver didn't ask if I needed a ride back—he took off after I gave him the money. I had a bad feeling. Like the first time, no one opened after the first ring of the doorbell. The second and third went unheard as well.

I walked around the house, noticing that there was no light behind any of the windows. There was a small gap between the hedge and fence where I could squeeze myself through, and a moment later, I stood in a medium-sized backyard with a swing and a sandbox. As I stared at the darkened house, my blood ran cold at the thought that they might have let Jason out earlier. What if he had come back here and killed Caitlyn? Maybe I was exaggerating, but I'd learned that you could never turn your back on an abuser. I was out of my jurisdiction, and I was about to trespass. I also had found the first sign of life from Paige in many years. She was alive. The profound, staggering relief was only beginning to catch up with me. I had to call Alice and Joy. I had to notify my colleagues about the other missing women. But first, I had to make sure Caitlyn was okay.

The sliding door between patio and living area opened almost silently, and I stepped into the house. I found a room that must have been shared by the two older kids—empty. Next, a nursery. Had Jason taken the children, or was he still locked away?

There was no one in this house. Probably Caitlyn had scooped up the kids and brought them somewhere she felt safer. I hated it when the victim had to be on the run, couldn't stay in their home because they never knew when the abuser would be back.

This required more than just one person. I needed help. I wanted to knock on all of these doors and look for Paige, but there was something I had to do first.

I called the lieutenant.

❦

"Ryder, have you lost your mind? Don't believe for a second that your half-assed apology will be enough to get yourself out of the mess you created, and you know I'm not talking about helping a woman in a domestic violence situation—I'm talking about harassing her for the wild goose chase you've been on for a decade. This is a friendly warning from someone who doesn't want your career to go down the drain, and don't get me started about calling at this time of night—"

"Lieutenant," I finally interrupted his angry rant. "I have good news."

That silenced him for a moment.

"I believe I found Paige MacGregor." My voice trembled a bit when I said her name out loud. "Her and five other missing women, including Caitlyn Hoyt. Caitlyn slipped me a picture of a group of women, and they were all there."

"Okay," he said, calmer now. "I sense a 'but.' Where are you?"

"I'm at Caitlyn Hoyt's house. Inside actually. There's no one here, and please, hear me out. I made a judgment call. I didn't know how long they were going to hold him, and I was worried for her life."

"Do you know if he's out already?"

"No," I admitted, "but we need to find her. We also need to interview everyone in this community to find the other women. Could you send me Viola? I'll coordinate with the local department."

"It's been many years for most of these cases. What makes you think it can't wait until tomorrow?"

"I can't wait until tomorrow. Please. We have the chance to solve six cases at once."

"Will you be okay handling this?" he asked.

"By the letter of the book, I promise."

I left the Gellers' house and called myself another cab. I got a black coffee and a pack of gum from the Seven Eleven across from the hotel, and then I made the call.

We met at the top of the cul-de-sac where the Geller's house was located.

They sent the same pair I had met earlier today, and a male detective named Jarrod. I presented them with what I had.

"I came because I had reason to assume Caitlyn Hoyt was living here. Obviously, the situation got out of control quickly."

"Why didn't you tell us earlier that you suspected her to have run away from home?"

I frowned at the detective's wording, but I had something to save me. Tonight, I wouldn't back down.

"I was hoping Caitlyn would trust me enough to talk to me—"

"Which didn't work out."

"But I'm surprised you don't know. When I found the Gellers' phone number, detectives from our Missing Persons department followed up first."

It was his turn to look surprised.

"We never heard from your people," he insisted. "Besides, if you thought they were here first, why did you come on your own?"

"Because the missing women seem to be related to a case I'm investigating."

"Murder?"

"Suicide," I said, growing impatient with him questioning me. "Do you recognize any of those women?"

"Katie Geller, obviously," the policewoman said. "And this is Annie. She's in my yoga class," she added, her tone apologetic as if that was something to be embarrassed about.

I pointed to Paige.

"Have you ever seen her?"

None of the local cops could confirm.

"All right. My partner will be here in a little while, but we don't have to wait for her. Let's go."

"If you allow," the male detective said. "I'll take the lead on this. This is a well-respected community, and if we must disturb them in the middle of the night, we damn well better be careful about it."

"Why, what are they going to do?"

He didn't give me an answer.

⁂

The first three houses we visited had similarities I found every-thing from mildly irritating to chilling. It was as if people in this community had found each other and agreed on a certain lifestyle, which included living in houses that were almost

85

carbon copies of one another. At the first door, we found the Andersons, Terri and Jim. I didn't need a second look to realize that Terri was Tammy, who had gone missing during a vacation with her husband and child. I knew the husband had eventually sold their house and moved the family to South America hoping for closure.

"I know I look a lot like that woman, but I can assure you it's not me. Jim is my husband. We have four beautiful children together, and you're waking at least one of them right now."

"My wife is pregnant," Jim Anderson said. "Is that all...?"

"We'll be gone in a few minutes," I promised. For tonight, at least. To my relief, this couple didn't seem to have the abusive dynamics that had been so obvious in the Geller house. "Mr. and Mrs. Anderson, could you tell me if you have seen any of those women before?"

"Sure. Katie and Annie are my closest neighbors," she said. "Annie's next door, but you might want to be careful, her kids sleep very lightly. Katie...I don't now, I think she might have left."

"She's married," Jim reminded her. "She can't just leave."

Had I missed something? Terri/Tammy didn't seem to feel threatened though. She shrugged.

"That is true. She will certainly come back."

Caitlyn/Katie, Terri/Tammy—I had been right to expect Annette Montgomery behind the next door.

"My husband isn't here right now," she said anxiously.

"Can we come in for a moment?"

I could tell that she'd rather decline. I showed her my badge which she studied for a long time.

"This is Detective Jarrod and two officers from the local police department. Annette Montgomery?"

Her eyes widened. "No one has called me that in a long time. Come on in."

Unlike Terri/Tammy, she didn't deny who she was. We all sat down in a living room that looked a lot like Caitlyn's and Tammy's. The décor differed slightly, but the layout and overall look of those houses was the same. Annette picked up a toy car before she sat in an armchair.

"Why are the police looking for me now?"

"The police have been looking for you since 2006," I said in disbelief. There was only so much denial I could handle, and I was coming to the end of the line. What was wrong with them?

"I don't understand," Annette/Annie said, looking confused.

"You remember the hiking trip you went on with your girlfriend?"

"Oh yes, what an unpleasant experience." She actually blushed. I knew the statements of their loved ones by heart, devastated, pleading with the police to bring them back.

"Unpleasant how?"

"Well, I didn't want to go in the first place. I don't enjoy camping." Annette shuddered. "I assumed I owed it to her, because I was going to break up with her, tell the truth. I take it she didn't deal with it very well."

"What is the truth?" Detective Jarrod asked. "My understanding is that you vanished from that hiking trip and your partner reported you missing."

"Partner?" Annette shook her head with a wry laugh. "That's what she thought. That was my old life. I made a mistake. I was hoping I had made that clear to her, but obviously she didn't understand. Listen, I didn't vanish. I met someone, fell in love, and I am married now. I have a family."

"You have children?" I prompted. She didn't need any more of an invitation.

"Three, number four on the way," Annette shared proudly. "I'm really sorry about all of this, but I didn't know, okay? I was just trying to live my life in peace."

A peaceful better life, something that Caitlyn had sought, and Annette as well. For some reason, all of the women in this neighborhood seemed extraordinarily fertile.

There was something that didn't fit her story though.

"You were both activists at the time. I just find it unusual—"

"Detective," she interrupted me wryly, "did you listen to what I just said? It was a mistake. I was in my early twenties. I didn't know better."

"And now you do?" Was this some kind of cult?

"When I met my husband, my purpose became so much clearer. I left all the false promises behind and did what I was destined to do—start a family."

"You also left college behind?"

Her eyes narrowed. "You're going to judge me for that? Do you have children?"

I didn't see any point in answering her question, but I had noticed the shadow crossing the female officer's face.

"No one's judging anyone, Annette."

"Annie, please."

"Okay, Annie. Our problem here is that we have several open cases, women who have gone missing, and they are turning up here in this community. Did you hear about anyone else?"

She shrugged.

"I saw you went to Terri's house. And Katie's husband was arrested. It's a trying time for all of us."

"What did you hear about them?"

"Nothing. Like I said, this feels very intrusive. If any of them has a story like mine, let me tell you we don't dwell on the past. We live busy lives."

I still couldn't fathom how Caitlyn had gone from one abusive relationship to another, or why Annette, a passionate lesbian activist, had become a poster child for a lifestyle out of the fifties. I couldn't keep up with all the questions multiplying in my mind. It was as if someone had invented completely new lives for these women, leaving who they'd been before their disappearance, only a faint memory.

"Too busy to notice when one of you is being abused?"

"Detective Ryder!"

Jarrod was right, this was uncalled for, but something about her self-righteous tone got to me. I had met Rose Kerry, the girlfriend, who had spiraled into a deep depression after Annette vanished. Did the people here ever watch TV or go on the internet? Read the newspaper? It didn't occur to me until now that I hadn't seen a TV in any of the homes yet. For sure, I'd be up all night taking notes.

"I'm sorry," I said. I showed her the same picture, and she identified the same women as Tammy had, plus Ashley Benning who was now Sheila.

All this time, changing names, partners and cities, those women had never talked to each other about their past? I found that hard to believe.

"Can you tell me when this picture was taken?"

"I'm not sure, but it was probably the community gathering last summer."

That sounded ominous to me.

"And you don't know all the women?"

"I told you before," she said, a hint of anger to her tone. "Why don't you believe me? They might have been someone's guest, or new to the community. Like I said—we're busy."

"We'll be in touch," I said. "Thank you for your time."

Outside, we met with Viola who had arrived in the meantime, and I caught her up on what we had found so far.

"This is crazy," she remarked. "None of them was aware the police were looking for them?"

"Apparently not."

"They are friendly, keep to themselves," Jarrod added. "There was no need to harass them."

"Harass them?" I echoed. "I can't believe that no one ever became suspicious, and no one recognized them."

He shrugged. "Those are all cold cases. You know as well as I do that there's no shortage of girls and women who go missing every year."

Unfortunately, I couldn't argue with that.

"Look, it's late," he said. "Why don't we come back tomorrow, start with a fresh perspective?"

"No. You saw those women, the stories they told, as if they were rehearsed. We need to keep going, identify the others before someone has time to get ahead of us."

"Someone, who?" he asked. "What if they are telling the truth?"

What kind of detective was he anyway? Tammy, Ashley, Caitlyn, and Annette—that made four of them ending up in the same neighborhood. So far. It couldn't be a coincidence.

I had successfully pushed the thought from my mind that we could find Paige exactly like this, living in an alternate reality where she apparently had no access to modern means of communication, and had turned into a proud 1950's housewife.

No. Not her. Paige was seventeen when she disappeared.

Then again, Ashley Bennett had been sixteen on the day she went to see a football game with friends from her high school, and never returned.

"Let's see Ashley Bennett," I said.

Chapter Eight

Paige

2016

Present

From the kitchen window, I could see the headlights of a police car in the distance, as I sipped my tea slowly. Sneaking out of the bed in the middle of the night, with the kids fast asleep and my wifely duties fulfilled, the silence was my only escape.

I found it hard to say no to Tom who was trying so hard, so desperate to make us work, because there was really no alternative for either of us. I didn't doubt that he loved me. Lately, I had come to the shocking conclusion that perhaps I didn't love him, that I was incapable of love.

The signs were all there, weren't they? I was struggling to connect with my children. Terri and Annie were overjoyed to announce their pregnancies. When Sheila had told us, Katie and I had exchanged a look. *Thank God for Doreen and her never-ending supply of birth control pills.* We both suspected that the money we gave her mostly went for liquor, but we were all adults, right? Able to make decisions about our own lives.

The police seemed to be going from house to house. Would they blame us for not interfering with Katie's marriage? What could we have done? I had heard stories of women calling the police, and nothing ever happened. Besides, none of us knew anything for sure...then why did I feel so guilty?

They were at Sheila's now.

Did this have anything to do with Katie at all, or were they looking for an escaped felon?

Truth be told, I would have liked the focus of everyone's attention to be on someone other than me and my marital troubles. Perhaps over time, Tom would find someone else...Not that we could get a divorce, but we could both mostly go our separate ways, leave each other alone. It was definitely not normal to feel that way. I looked at the car outside of Sheila and Graham's house again, filled with an inexplicable longing...and terror. I turned away from the window and went up the stairs into the bedroom, back to my sleeping husband.

Another day that I wasn't pregnant. It was a good day.

⁂

Dani

Ashley Benning a.k.a. Sheila West and her husband Graham couldn't imagine why anyone would have reported her missing. She didn't remember the football game or what happened at all. She had visited a local college for a while, where she met Graham, fell in love and got married.

Ashley was blinking back tears as she told us that they had adopted twins as she couldn't have children of her own.

"The photo, of course. That was at our last community gathering. Annie and Terri are friends with Caitlyn, but I'm not surprised they don't remember us. They hardly spoke to me and Peggy. Sometimes, the husbands can be peculiar about these things," she said and affectionately smiled at hers.

I held my breath.

Peggy.

"She lives here?"

"Yes, just down the street."

"Thank you. Thank you so much." I got up from my seat and, to the surprise of the local officers, turned to leave. Viola caught up with me in the hallway.

"Danielle, wait."

"This is it. That's her."

"Likely, but please, take a moment and breathe, okay?"

"I am breathing. I need to see her now, and then I need to call her sister and tell her that she's still alive. In fact, we'll have to notify relatives of those other women. Wow—whatever happened, the paperwork will be endless. Let's go. The locals can wrap up here."

"I agree that there's something strange about this," Viola said hesitantly. "Maybe you should wait until tomorrow."

"No. All the other stories I know only second hand. We'll have to look into that, wrap up all the loose ends, but it's different with Paige. I know that whatever she'll say, she had no reason to disappear. I know what she wanted to do with her life." My voice became slightly breathless as I hastened my steps, jogging the last few. Viola hurried after me.

"Dani. Wait!"

"She didn't leave. Someone took her."

I was ready to keel over, but I couldn't stop now. My hand was shaking badly as I knocked on the door. This could all be over within minutes, everything I had worked for so hard in the past thirteen years. Alice, Joy, Paige and I...we could have a life now.

The door was opened by a man in his late thirties, wearing a bathrobe over pajamas.

"Yes? What's the hurry?"

"I'm Detective Ryder, this is Detective Marsh."

"We don't know where Katie Geller is, if you came to ask us that. We have an early start tomorrow."

Talk about forthcoming. My mind refused to put the pieces together, even when Viola said, "Thank you, but we need to talk to your wife for a moment."

Wife.

Peggy.

"I don't understand why, but..." He stepped aside to let us in, and I stepped into another carbon copy of the houses we'd seen before. There was a significance in that, for sure.

My heart skipped a beat when she came down the stairs, like the man clad in a robe over nightwear. A grown woman. Paige.

Alive.

"Paige," I said. "Oh my God, Paige."

She looked startled, pausing on the last step.

"The police are here about Katie?" she addressed the man. *Her husband.*

Something was horribly wrong.

I stepped forward.

"Don't you recognize me?"

Viola gave me a strange glance as if she was trying to determine whether I was going to make it through this moment without passing out. She had reason to be anxious. I could hardly breathe. No matter what strange bubble these people lived in, this was Paige, and she knew me, and I knew her. She had to remember that.

"Dani," she finally said. "I didn't know you were with the police now."

"I've been trying to find you all those years, I..." I was choking up. "Everything will be okay, I promise. I came to take you home."

I knew I'd crossed a line even before I felt the sharp jab of Viola's elbow in my side, and the man Paige was apparently married to, angrily asked, "Can anybody explain to me what the hell is going on?"

We all heard a door open upstairs, and the footsteps of small feet on the upper floor. Like the other women in the community, Paige had children.

I had waited for this moment for over a decade.

I felt more at a loss than ever before.

What had they done to her?

2015

Brittany Dawson blinked against the blinding sunlight.

"Isn't it a beautiful picture?" the assistant project manager asked. He seemed to truly enjoy the sight. This wasn't the first community gathering she'd been invited to. Every time she hoped to find a good excuse, but never succeeded. It was her reward and punishment all in one, a constant reminder of the endless possibilities. They had thought of themselves as Gods and acted accordingly.

She shuddered.

"You helped create this," he said. "You wanted to make the world a better place, and you did. This is what you will always be remembered for."

She wanted to throw up. Brittany accepted the plastic cup filled with beer from one of the women, hoping she wouldn't talk to her. She didn't want to talk to anyone. She wanted to go home to Elaina and tell her everything. Brittany knew that wasn't an option. She couldn't put her in danger as well, her and their shared dream. Maybe it was still possible.

It was like a carnival around here, so many people, many of them young children.

It was true, she had created this. The future. The nightmare. She would have to face the consequences.

Dani

2016

Present

"I don't know what you imagined," Paige said softly. "This is my home."

The husband, Tom, had grudgingly conceded to the fact that both parties had a lot of questions, and so we sat in another living room. This was different. I felt wide awake, more than I had in years.

"You might not remember. We are trying to find the answers, for you and the other women. Do you remember anything about your abduction?"

"What?" Tom's eyebrows shot to his hairline. "Are you accusing me of anything?"

"Of course not." Viola shot me a warning look, but her tone was placating. "It has come to our attention that at least six women who went missing between 2003 and 2006 are living in this community under different names. Your wife, Paige Mac-Gregor, is one of them. We are trying to figure out how it was possible that nobody knew they were reported missing."

Paige frowned, shaking her head.

I couldn't get over the fact that she was here, alive. Confused like the others, yes, but alive. All else we could work around.

She was beautiful.

Inappropriate to think that now. Something might have traumatized them so badly that they chose not to remember.

"You got this all wrong," Tom insisted. "Peggy wasn't abducted."

"Her name is Paige."

"Tell them, darling," he said.

Paige looked upset, but she obliged.

"I do remember you, sure, and I don't even understand what we're talking about here. My parents...I'm not sure you know I didn't have a very good relationship with them. They kicked me out when I was—"

"No," I interrupted her sharply. "That isn't true. I was there. We went on a trip together, and you disappeared. That is what happened. Let's call Alice, she can confirm everything."

"Now?" Tom and Detective Jarrod echoed.

"I don't know that I want to talk to Alice," Paige said, her tone cool. "Back then, no one was there for me, no one cared. I don't owe her or my parents anything. Ask them."

It would have been better for all of us to continue this tomorrow, but we had gone too far already.

"I can't, Paige. Your parents passed away."

I saw the disbelief in her face, her eyes welling up. "Is that another lie?"

"It's true. Alice is your family, and she's been waiting for this news forever. Let's not make her wait any longer."

"Tomorrow, then. Let me talk to her tomorrow."

"I'd say that's a good idea," Viola said. "We'll be notifying the families over the course of the next day, shed more light on these stories."

"Katie's husband used to hit her," Tom said with unveiled anger. "Are you sure it's a good idea to stir all of this up? Are you going to notify him too?"

"Her husband isn't going to bother her. If you're talking about Christopher Hoyt, that is. I understand that Jason Geller is still in custody for the same reason."

Paige looked at her feet.

"Paige, please, look at me. What do you remember?"

"I was in a car accident," she said defensively. "I was eighteen at the time—no one could stop me."

"You were seventeen the summer we went to New York."

"Are you going to argue all night, or will we be able to get a little bit of sleep?" Tom intervened. "I understand you have to tell the sister, even though the family never gave a damn about her. They even changed their phone number on her! We'll be here tomorrow, just give us a little bit of peace."

"That's fair enough," Viola concluded. "We have lots of work to do right now."

✿

Back at the hotel, I promised Viola I would sleep for a bit as well, after making some calls. The hardest...first. Alice picked up after six rings, snapping at me.

"Dear Lord, what do you want from me?"

The last time we had spoken was over two years ago. The last time she'd picked up the phone.

"Alice," I said, my voice breaking again. "Alice." For some reason, I couldn't get out the words. This was too big, altering everything.

"Are you drunk?"

Funny coming from her...Joy kept telling me that while Alice had a good life on the surface, with a husband and her son, Paige's disappearance had changed her. She was drinking. She'd been blaming me, I knew, even though she'd never learned the whole story...But I didn't spend thirteen years of my life on this one single purpose because of that. I'd done it for Paige, and for me.

"No, I'm...We found Paige."

"Stop it. That's not funny. I'm hanging up now."

"Please, don't. It's true. I swear."

"Like all the other times?" she asked sarcastically. I couldn't blame her. In the first years, I had been so eager and enthusiastic. I'd been jumping on every clue, getting all of our hopes up, only to have them plummet again.

"I saw her," I said. There was a long silence on the other end, and for a moment, I feared she had hung up.

"Where?"

I told her how the clues in another case had led me to one of the missing women, and from there to this town with its strange community.

"I'm leaving right now."

"Alice...wait a second. There's something you should know."

"I knew she was unhappy because she had that crush on you," she said dismissively.

"That's not it. It's...hard to explain. She thinks that she left on her own and got into a car accident. Or maybe she actually did have an accident, we still have to figure out the timeline. She thinks that your parents kicked her out of your home."

"What? What the hell happened to her, did she suffer brain damage or what?" Behind the sarcastic tone, I could sense her fear. I felt the same. I didn't know, and it was driving me crazy. Tomorrow, I'd see her again. Tomorrow, in the light of day, everything would be better.

"There are a lot of questions we need to answer right now, in her story, and those of the other women. It would be best if you could bring some sort of ID for Paige. Could you let Joy know?" I gave her the address of the hotel. "If I'm not there, call me. I'll see you tomorrow, then."

Another long pause, then she said, "Thank you, Dani."

"There's no need...I'm just glad."

I called Rose Kerry last, and we both cried. I had wanted to take some notes, but I fell asleep in the middle of the bed, still fully clothed.

For some reason, this had been some of the best sleep I had gotten in years. I woke up hopeful and intensely motivated, eager to see Paige again, solve the mystery, but mostly convince myself last night hadn't been a dream.

I met Viola in the breakfast room, and we started gathering notes. In the course of the day, we'd be joined by other cops who could now close cases, and relatives of the missing women. Alice, Rose Kerry, and Ashley's/Sheila's parents were on their way. No one had reached Tammy Grey's husband yet.

Caitlyn Hoyt was still at large, while her current husband faced assault charges.

Everything was in motion.

"She looked good, healthy, right?"

"Yeah. She looked as good as someone possibly can after you spring that kind of news on her," Viola remarked dryly.

"Thank you for being here," I said. "I don't even know where to start. This is...massive."

"No kidding, but you're welcome. You've been waiting a long time, and we both know those stories don't always have a happy ending."

I flinched, reminded of when I had lost Paige, all the unexplored emotions and unanswered questions that had been left behind. I still couldn't get over the life she seemed to have chosen for herself, so different from the one I knew she'd wanted.

She'd wanted *me*.

"All right, we still have to find Margaret Allen. I suspect that when we do, the story will be similar—a name change, memories that clash with what loved ones told the police. How do they all wind up in the same community, living a life that's contrary to what they intended?"

"Some of them were very young, Viola reminded me. "Goals can change."

"Annette was an activist. Paige was out and proud. I don't think they would change their mind. Something must have happened, a concerted effort to push them off track."

"Whoa, this is getting bizarre." Viola put a generous amount of sugar into her coffee. "So far, we have no proof that any kidnapping happened. I have to say, they all look like *Stepford Wives* to me, but then again, that's their choice. Aside from Hoyt, none of them seems to be in an abusive situation. She obviously found a way out the first time, hopefully now, if they get to him."

"I don't see why they shouldn't. I gave my statement. I can testify that he was choking her. Damn," I said. "Whatever the story turns out to be for the others, she was trying to get away from a bad situation, and here she is, stuck with another idiot, and three kids."

The waitress came by to fill our coffee cups, and I picked up a piece of fruit from my plate when it came to me—I wouldn't make it to Sunday breakfast or even dinner. Since two of the women had disappeared in my jurisdiction, Annette and Ashley, I had reasons to stay a bit longer. I wanted to coordinate with the other cops, see if between us, we could put the pieces together.

Lois would be disappointed.

At the moment, I couldn't bring myself to care. I'd have to warn her.

Paige

I didn't want to get out of bed. I could hear Mia and Colin playing in their rooms, and Tom had already gotten up as well. I had to go down and make them breakfast, but I couldn't bring myself to move.

I was so scared, that Dani might come back, that she might never come back, and then what? I'd be left with these bits and pieces of lies and the truth, and I didn't know which was which.

It was hard to remember anything before I woke up in that clinic where everyone was so friendly, focused on my recovery and building a life better than the one I had before.

My parents had kicked me out. My sister and her friends, that included Dani, had never been anything but nasty to me, so I saw no alternative to getting into my car and leaving. At least that's what I had told them, in lucid moments, before the surgery.

Not true. According to Dani, my parents were dead. I couldn't touch that grief at this moment even though I felt like

I was on the verge of crying. But I had been feeling like that for a long time.

What now?

Dani had seemed friendly, emotional even about this visit. She was a cop now. Something about her made me uncomfortable though. I didn't have to prod much—I remembered that at some point, I had feelings for her that weren't natural, that could have endangered my future. Why did I even have those feelings when she, too, had been mean to me?

I remembered feeling hurt, scared and alone, but at least her reaction sent me on a better path.

Or did it?

What if the problems I had in my marriage stemmed from something darker, something I had tried to suppress all these years, but was coming back to haunt me? No. I was just tired.

The trip to New York Dani had been talking about...had she told the truth? If they had treated me so badly, why had I gone with them in the first place, and when did that accident happen?

I wanted to turn back time to before she knocked on our door.

I wanted answers, but at the same time, I wasn't sure I could handle them.

And there were other women who had been reported missing, who had found a home in this community.

Was it Dani's intention to destroy it all, tear families apart?

I might be naïve, but even after everything I knew happened between us, I couldn't imagine she could be this cruel. Of Alice's friends, I had always liked her best.

Dani

Lois, to my surprise, took the news well.

"It's fine. This is great news. I can call your parents. They'll want to know about this."

"Thank you. How are you doing?"

She laughed, sounding nervous. "You're asking me that, after you just solved the big mystery? This is amazing. You must be so happy."

"I am. Thank you for understanding."

"I'll let you go," she said. "I'm sure you have a lot of work to do right now."

"That's true. I'll call you again."

That was much too easy—or maybe she fully understood the magnitude of these developments?

Viola and I spent the morning at the local police department, advising Jarrod, another detective and a few uniformed officers on strategy. We sent information to departments across the state and country—some of the cops who had worked on these cases were already retired, others were grateful to be able to close their cases. The FBI would send a couple of agents, the lieutenant told me, to help clear the fog surrounding these bizarre stories.

I wanted to see Paige again, but I had to be patient. I wanted to see what was going to happen when Rose met Annette—and I had to speak to someone at the local hospital, find out more about that car accident. The police report Jarrod had given me was more than sketchy, and the date was unreadable. All we knew was that the accident had to have happened after Paige's disappearance in New York City.

She said she'd been eighteen. What happened in those months? Who was responsible?

Chapter Nine

Paige

2003

After my release from the hospital, I took Gloria up on her offer and moved in with her. I didn't feel so good most of the time. Stress headaches, I was sure. It felt like my life was slipping out of control, my past and my future.

Tom had proposed, and I didn't know what to do. How could we know if we were compatible if we didn't even have sex yet? I liked him, liked spending time with him, but the thought worried me. I still hadn't looked into going to college. With each passing day, that goal seemed to be further out of reach, though Gloria didn't think that was a bad thing. I was lucky to be able to talk to her, to have her as a friend. She always seemed to know what I should do.

"Come on, don't be so silly," she advised one evening. "Tom's a good guy. He'll take good care of you...and I wouldn't kick him out of my bed, but forget I said that. He loves you. What are you waiting for?"

"I'm not sure," I admitted. "Tom wants children."

"You do too, right? You have to be sensible about this. Those chances don't come often in life."

"I don't think I can do it."

I could see the alarm in her face, and, for a split-second, I wondered why this was so important to her. Perhaps, unlike my family and so-called "friends" from home, she truly cared about me?

"You'll be just fine," she assured me, and refilled my glass. I was still on medication, but Gloria had said that a sip of wine with dinner wouldn't hurt.

There was a long dark gap after that conversation, and once again I woke up in a hospital bed, panicked out of my wits.

A somber-looking doctor explained my situation to me: I had collapsed in Gloria's living room, and she called 911. They discovered that there had been some bleeding in my brain, and they had to operate right away.

Tom was my rock in those days after. I was well aware of how much I owed him, and frankly, he made me feel safe, being the only constant left in my life.

The next time he asked me, I said yes.

❧

Dani

2016

Present

Rose Kerry was heartbroken after the confrontation.

"We wanted to get married. We wanted to have children together." She was crying.

"I know this is hard, but we wanted to give all loved ones a chance to talk to the women, see if it would help with their memory."

Like I had helped with Paige's? Annette, "Annie," had made it very clear that she wasn't interested in picking up where she'd left off with Rose. She considered it a "sinful lifestyle" that she had escaped.

"It's like she was brainwashed," Rose said.

It made me wonder how extensive Paige's injuries had been in that accident, thirteen years ago. One story by itself could be explained...but that still didn't bring us closer to understanding how all these women had wound up in the same community. It was a long shot, but I wanted to go back to the firm who had built these houses, and the realtors who had brought couples and families into these strangely similar homes.

It was like entering a time machine.

"I know, but I promise you, we will find out what's behind this."

If she looked a little doubtful at that, I couldn't blame her.

Rose didn't know where Annette's parents were. The old phone numbers didn't work any longer. It seemed like grief had driven them off the grid.

I put more hope into Alice, assuming that she had kept Paige's personal things. Paige's birth certificate had to be among her parents' things. There had to be something.

Hospital records.

I wanted to know the truth about all these stories, but most of all, I needed to know Paige's—what else was new?

I had never seen any case like this.

Caitlyn Hoyt was still hiding from the world with her children.

I was running mostly on caffeine and excitement that I found Paige, and that she was alive, no matter how bizarre the circumstances. It was time to go see her again.

Viola and I were minutes away from her front door when Alice called.

"I'm at your hotel," she said.

"We were going to see Paige. Let's meet you there."

"Oh my God. I'm not sure if I can make it there in one piece. I'm already shaking."

"Should I send someone...?"

"No, I'll be careful. I don't want to wait any longer."

Viola and I parked on the sidewalk where we waited, until Alice pulled up behind us in her white Subaru. We got out of our respective cars. I was aware of Viola studying us with curiosity as we walked towards each other, hugging awkwardly. Ever since Paige's disappearance, seeing Alice, the few times I had, was never anything but awkward. She gave me a small smile.

"I'm nervous," she admitted.

"That's okay." I was too, still, more than she could ever imagine. "Let's go see her. Did you bring the papers?"

Her face fell, and I braced myself. This wasn't going to be as easy as I had hoped.

"It's really strange. I kept a box of all of Paige's papers. I couldn't find it. I'm sorry about that. I will look again when I'm back home—I hope it didn't get lost in the last move."

"We'll worry about that later." I turned around to look where Paige stood in the front door, her composure signaling apprehension.

Alice walked towards her, then stopped about a few feet away as if she didn't know how to react. I was about to follow when a tug on my sleeve and a firm look from Viola held me back.

"Give them a second, okay?"

I supposed she was right. She just didn't know how hard every second that the mystery and the smokescreens persisted, was.

Eventually, we followed Paige and Alice inside, not exactly invited, but they couldn't keep us out either. They had yet to hug. I wanted to hug her, but maybe the same thing that held me back, made it hard for Alice as well.

It was like an invisible wall. Peggy Bond. Married with children. This wasn't a strange coincidence. Paige knew that the MacGregors had been her parents, that Alice was her sister—just like the other women, she had created a completely different reality using the same characters, why?

Alice, forewarned, was happy to greet Mia and Colin, her niece and nephew.

"I can't understand why everyone is so concerned all of a sudden," Paige said beside me. "Nobody was before. I spent a long time in the hospital after the accident, and the only people who came to visit me were from the community."

"That's because we didn't know where you were, Paige. We couldn't find you."

She gave me an odd sideways look.

"You were looking for me? I'm sorry if I've been wasting your time. I have a different life now."

I didn't ask her if she was happy. Maybe I was too afraid of the answer. I needed to get her and the other women in front of a psychiatrist, so they could sort out the memory loss, manipulation, and lies. I didn't think Paige was lying. She truly believed what she was saying. Someone had lied to her, repeatedly, successfully.

"I can see that. We are trying to establish a timeline, what happened to you—all of you—between the day you disappeared and now. Do you have your birth certificate?"

She shook her head.

"I must have left my parent's house very quickly. Did Alice keep it? I am sure that it says Peggy. I know my passport and driver's license do."

"But you had them before your wedding?"

"Of course, but my first name was the same. They were all renewed after I got married. I can show you."

"Yes, I would appreciate that."

I couldn't help it. I felt terrible admitting it even only to myself, but those old feelings were still there, regardless of what our lives had become. They weren't the only reason why I had spent the last thirteen years trying to find her, but for sure, they were part of it. I still didn't know how much she remembered about that day in New York City, and with Alice around, it wasn't a good moment to find out.

She opened a drawer in the living room, took out her passport and handed it to me. "Peggy Bond. That is who I am."

My jaw dropped a little when I saw the date of birth. I have to admit there was even triumph.

"This isn't right," I said. "The year of birth isn't right. You were born a year later than that."

Paige shook her head again, denial, protest, I wasn't sure.

"Do you remember who gave you this? Who told you about your family?"

"I didn't need to be told! I remembered!"

I didn't quite buy that.

She took a deep breath.

"Okay, I see how you could think there's a story here, but I've been telling you the truth. I wrecked the car I rented. I woke up in a hospital, I had to have surgery, and Tom and Gloria were there for me."

"You were supposed to go to college."

"Was I? How would I have paid for that? I don't think you understand. That accident, it changed everything for me, not all for the worse. I found people I could rely on..."

That stung.

"...but at the same time, I needed to think of my future. I made decisions—I'm sorry if you don't agree with them."

"That's not a simple matter of disagreement, and you know it. When did you get married?"

"A few months after the accident," she said. "What? I was almost nineteen. So I had my children young. Are you going to arrest me for that?"

"Hey, why don't we give her a little more time," Alice who had joined us, suggested. "I don't care if she wants to call herself Paige or Peggy. She's alive. That's all that matters."

Paige cast her a grateful smile. Across the room, Viola signaled for me to come over.

"Alice told me that Joy will be coming too," Paige said, her tone resigned. "I thought I could have them over for dinner tomorrow...You can come too, Dani, if you want. It seems like everyone is sorry, so I should give them a second chance, right?"

"I'll be there," I said. Chances were, I'd be in her house before that.

Outside the house, I told Viola, "Where the hell are the locals, what are they doing? We need more people on this. I want to bring in all of the husbands. Something is off here."

"What do you think this is going to achieve?" Viola asked calmly. Sometimes, her laid back ways could get on my nerves, and this was one of those moments.

"The false identification, those strange cookie cutter houses, there is a pattern."

"Yeah, but none of the women except Caitlyn were harmed, and her husband is behind bars. It's not like the authorities are completely blind around here."

"They were to the fact that a minor got married without the permission of her parents. Paige's passport says she was born in 1985. That is not true. She would have turned eighteen at the end of the year she disappeared, but according to the papers she has, she already was eighteen."

"That is strange," Viola admitted. "Let's check in with the others if they found anything similar."

A few quick phone calls revealed that we had one similar case: Ashley Bennett, now Sheila. With all the others, birth dates matched their real ones. Jarrod told me that they had found Margaret Allen, now Mandy. She was married with five children and one on the way. The detective who had worked her case, a Marilyn DeShawn, was now retired, but she had agreed to join the friend who had reported Margaret missing in 2002. So many names, so many stories.

"I want to talk to all the husbands but focus on Graham West and Thomas Bond. I want to know if they were aware that they married minors," I said grimly.

Viola's expression was somber, but for once, she didn't disagree.

I was wondering if Paige would still want me at the dinner table after I brought in her husband.

This was ridiculous. She had just come out. She wanted to go to college, and if anything, she'd been much too young to decide on having children. If she'd been a minor when she got married, a judge must have been involved—her parents didn't know any of this, so they couldn't have consented. Questions over questions, and very few answers. I couldn't lose focus now, let my emotions get in the way. Too much depended on the outcome.

Later that night, Alice, Joy, and I reunited in the pub below the hotel. What a crazy ride in only hours since I had found the picture Caitlyn gave me. I was exhausted, exhilarated, and afraid.

I hugged both of them, and all of a sudden, we were all in tears, grappling with the impact of the past thirteen years. The shock when we had to realize Paige was gone, somehow inexplicably ripped from our lives. The profound relief and happiness—and the confusion.

Viola stood in another corner, talking to retired Detective DeShawn.

We were trying to bring some sense of order into this, together. Once that was achieved, I could allow myself to think of what the next chapter of my life could be.

❧

"You saw her passport. Peggy was confused after the accident. She only vaguely remembered the people in her life, but she knew who hurt her, and whom she could trust."

I didn't like Bond's attitude. Truth be told, I didn't like him at all.

"So, she was confused, and hurting, and you thought it was the best moment to take advantage and marry her, a seventeen-year-old?"

"I didn't know!" He had raised his voice as well. "Hindsight is 20/20, sure, but I had no reason at the time to be suspicious. We hadn't been together that long, but I knew she was the love of my life, and I made sure she was eighteen before anything happened."

"Eighteen on false ID."

"I told you, I didn't know!"

"Then tell me something you do know. I'm very interested in your side of the story, because the timeline doesn't add up at all. After the accident, you asked her to marry you. You claim you knew her before, but the truth is, that accident must have happened shortly after Paige, her sister, another friend, and I went to New York City. Paige disappeared. She was seventeen!"

"I never heard any of that. All I knew was that she was trying to get away from a family and so-called friends that treated her badly. You guys went to New York, maybe, but she was already with me. And when that accident happened, Gloria and I were the only ones that took care of her. If you want to accuse me of anything, do it already."

He seemed genuine. I couldn't yet decide if that was better or worse. What would happen to Paige once this illusion shattered into a million pieces? What would happen to the children?

There was a knock on the door, and Viola stepped inside, Jarrod behind her.

"Dani, could you join us for a second?"

On the other side of the door, Marilyn DeShawn was waiting for us. She looked uncomfortable.

"Jarrod and I were just comparing notes," Viola said. "I spoke to the lieutenant as well."

"Okay."

"The cases of the missing women are all closed. They will have to get identification in their real names again, and the local police will work with the FBI on how those false IDs got into their hands."

"What about West and Bond? They married girls who were underage!"

"Those two are a little more curious," Jarrod admitted. DeShawn said nothing. "That's why we're going to speak to the families and offer the women housing until this is all legally sorted out."

That was better than nothing. "All right. What about the others?"

Admittedly, I liked the solution of Paige being away from Tom for a while.

"We are following every angle," Jarrod said. "It will be easier once we've set up the task force with the FBI. You can be sure we want to get to the bottom of this."

That sounded too much like a dismissal to me.

"We'll be around for a bit longer, I assume."

"The lieutenant told me to come back and contact him if you wanted to use up vacation days," Viola informed me.

DeShawn still hadn't spoken.

"What about you?" I addressed her. "Don't you want to know the whole truth?"

"It's out of my hands now," she said uneasily. "I accompanied Margaret's former partner, because she asked me to." Margaret Allen, now Mandy.

"Partner in what?"

"They had just started a business together."

"That's all?"

She looked around the small group. "All else you would have to ask her."

⚬

Viola and I had lunch together before she left town. I still thought the lieutenant was making a mistake, but of course I wasn't calling the skills of the other cops into question. They would update us so we could properly close all of the cases.

"It's not so bad," I tried to convince myself rather than her. "If she has some time to herself, Paige will remember, I'm sure. Then I can finally bring her home."

Viola stared at me in disbelief. I didn't think I deserved that kind of reaction. Paige would want to go home at some point.

"Home to what?" my partner asked softly.

"Excuse me? I don't think she's even started to work through what happened to her—whatever we might still find out, notwithstanding. Her parents are gone. Alice..." I wasn't sure how to say more without betraying my friend.

"They'll look into the husband some more, but for all we know, they are a family. She has given no indication that she wants to separate from him. Neither have any of the others, for that matter, except Caitlyn."

"This is not right, and you know it. DeShawn called them partners."

"Business partners."

"You saw her expression, like she was holding something back. I bet they were a couple. So were Annette and Rose. Paige came out shortly before she went missing."

"They might be bi—or they did change their minds. They were all pretty young. What are you saying?"

I couldn't say it. I didn't know how.

But Viola had known me long enough to put the pieces together.

"Oh my God, Dani. You were in love with her. You still are."

"No, that's not true, and if it was, it wouldn't matter. Rose felt like Annette was brainwashed. Think about it! Three women disappear at a young age, all of them out and outspoken lesbians, and they end up in Cookiecutterville with a dozen kids between them. Something crazy is going on here."

"I'm not saying it's all in your mind."

"Gee, I'm so relieved."

"There is something strange going on," Viola continued, ignoring my sarcasm. "I'll give you that. But if the lieutenant thinks it's all right to leave it in the hands of the task force, I think it's right. You found her. That's close to a miracle. Now you have to let go a little. You're too close to all of this."

I couldn't deny that I was. Still, the idea of leaving Paige behind made me nauseated. I couldn't do it another time, too afraid something bad was going to happen, that she'd slip away again.

"I'll talk to Thorne, beg him to let me stay. If I have to use up my vacation time to make sure she's okay, then so be it."

"What's Lois saying about all of this?" Viola asked.

"What do you think? She understands that I'm doing my job."

"Only this isn't your job, it never was, because you decided to follow up a lead on your own. Does she know how you feel about Paige?"

I got to my feet.

"I was twenty-one that year. We were just walking down the street, damn it. There were so many people, we were separated for a minute or two, and she was gone. Does Lois know I felt guilty every day of my life because I didn't pay attention? I think she can imagine. This is not the moment to be jealous."

"Rose Kerry is going home. So will Ashley's parents, and Alice, eventually. I believe you imagined many different endings of this case, but you didn't think she could have a life..."

"A life built on lies, and there's a lot of work yet to be done to prove that. Drive safely, Viola. I need to get back."

I couldn't be in her presence anymore. She had put her finger on too many open wounds, and the pain was more than I could bear.

Chapter Ten

Paige

2016

Present

The last time I felt this alone was when I woke up in the hospital, after my accident.

Tom had to go to the police station. It had been hours, and he hadn't come back. He didn't say much, but I knew he was mad about having to take a day off work, since no one could tell him how long it would take.

I still had to cook dinner for my sister and her friends who were very kind to me so far, but I feared that this could change at any moment. And Dani.

Part of me wanted to be alone with her, and another was terrified of the idea. It was all chaos in my head. I remembered that she came over to my parents' house at times, usually to see Alice, when they were home from college. I remembered finding excuses to go into the room, or to talk to her. I remembered being so excited when my parents told me I could go to

New York with them...wait. When was that? And when did the accident happen? Before...after...how could I disappear and not know that people were looking for me?

Paige. I tried it out on my tongue, feeling something reverberate in my mind. Paige. I said it out loud, my own name. If someone was watching me now, I had to look like a crazy person to them.

Peggy. My name was Peggy Bond.

What if they arrested Tom and he wasn't going to come back? I had no job, no income. Would Mia, Colin and I be homeless? At least they were still in school. I hoped no one was harassing them about the latest events. I had no idea what to do, or what the hell to cook for dinner, but my thoughts were wandering back to Dani.

There was no way I could think about her like this any longer. I was a grown woman, a wife, a mother, everything a woman could possibly be, right? It was much too late to cry about college, and what would I do with a degree anyway?

She would leave eventually, like the other cops, like the woman who claimed that she and Annie were together in what, another life?

It didn't matter. Time had run out on us a long time ago.

Still, I found myself standing in front of my closet, wondering what to wear for the evening, while my husband was being interrogated by the police.

Truth be told, for all my fears, this was the most excitement I had seen in many years.

❧

Dani

In the afternoon, before dinner at Paige's, I went to the hospital and asked about her case. We didn't have a warrant for her medical records yet. I couldn't imagine what the hold up was, since the urgency was so obvious to me, but I found one of the doctors who had treated her thirteen years ago.

"Oh, I remember that case well. She was lucky we have one of the most renowned trauma centers here. At first, it didn't look too bad. She was a little banged up, a clean break to her leg. We ordered a head CT and discovered extra-axial hemorrhage. That's when there's bleeding inside the skull, but not the brain tissue," he supplied helpfully. Even so, it sounded terrifying.

"So you had to operate?"

"Oh, yes. Mrs. Bond was lucky. We caught it early, the surgery was successful. Of course, she was young and healthy, which went in her favor."

"Still, she has problems with her memory to this day."

He frowned as if hearing this for the first time. "Not that severe, in her case. The follow-up looked good. We could eventually release her, and I hear she has a family now."

"Do you remember who came to visit her?"

"Sad story. The parents and sister didn't want anything to do with her, and she couldn't even reach them on the phone when she was well enough to try. Gloria, a nurse who worked here, befriended her, and there was of course her boyfriend."

"Who paid for her medical bills? If she was here under a false name, she couldn't have had insurance?"

"I believe the boyfriend did."

Intensive care after brain surgery? Bond had to have money.

I had asked half a dozen people about Gloria. Everyone remembered that she and Paige got along well, but no one knew where she had gone.

"Yeah. Thank you for your time, Doctor. We might contact you for some follow-up questions."

"Of course. Anything I can do to help."

As I drove back to the town's police station, I couldn't help feeling that Thomas Bond knew a whole lot more than he had told us, and maybe the same went for Ashley Bennett's husband Graham West. If we concentrated on those two, maybe there was a chance we could unravel this tangled web of lies. The moment we could connect either of them with the people who had provided the women with false ID, these men would have a lot to answer for.

I wanted to have a shot at Jason Geller, but before I reached the station, I received a panicked call from Paige.

"You said you'd help me," she said sounding frantic. "I need help. The police are in my house again."

Depression, anxiety, paranoid tendencies, all of those would come to no surprise, the doctor had told me. The brain was so complex that it was hard to predict the effects of surgery in the long run—but in Paige's case, the bleeding had been caught early, and she had been successfully treated. They let her go, assured that her prognosis was good. We would need to look at the medical history of all the women, find out if there were any more eerie similarities.

"Calm down, Paige. What happened?"

"Please, I need you to talk to them. They say Tom can't live with me until a judge determines if our marriage was legal. We didn't do anything wrong! I had all the papers, and I was eighteen at the time."

"You weren't...but Tom says he doesn't know, and I believe him. It will be okay." I said the latter sentence through gritted teeth. Of course, this was hard for her now, but she'd be better off if she could learn to live with the truth over time.

"I'll be right over," I promised.

Bond was still under investigation, as were all the husbands. So far, we couldn't come up with any intentional wrongdoing, except in Geller's case.

When I arrived, I found Paige in the middle of a desperate negotiation. The kids were nowhere to be seen, in their own rooms, I assumed. Bond stood next to her, looking exasperated.

"It's Tom's house," she told the policemen. "I can't kick him out. I'll go."

The officer looked uncomfortable but nodded. "I guess that can be arranged. I will check—"

It hurt me that she thought it was okay for her, not him, to leave their shared home. After all, he had taken advantage of her confusion. Then again, the further apart they were, the better.

"I'll help you," I said. If I talked to her in a neutral place, maybe the four of us could get together tonight for dinner, and something would jog her memory. "You can take your time, pack for you and the kids."

"What the hell are you talking about?" Tom asked angrily. "These are my children. They aren't going anywhere. They need to go to school tomorrow. You have disrupted their lives enough."

"Sir..." The policeman cleared his throat.

"Shaw, you know that I know your father, right? I'm not sure what he'd make of your conduct right now."

I couldn't believe what I was hearing.

"Mr. Bond, this isn't helping your case. We don't intend to disrupt anyone's life, but we must determine if Paige was able to consent to this marriage legally. We're not singling anyone out. She and one of the other women were underage the date of the wedding, and they had already been reported missing by then."

"Dear Lord, how many times do I have to tell you I don't know anything about this? My wife's name is Peggy. She was legal when we married," he repeated stubbornly. "Peggy, you do what you want, but Mia and Colin stay here."

"Tom, please. I'm sure we'll be back soon."

"I need them here. I need you here."

"I know. But we have to go along with what the police say. So this can be over soon."

Did she really mean that? In trying to determine what was true, and what not, I was starting to feel almost as confused as Paige.

However, she was willing to trust me. That's all I needed to know.

"Do I have a choice?" I wasn't sure if Bond's question was directed at me, or Paige, or the policeman he had threatened a moment ago. Either way, the answer was the same.

I followed her upstairs to the bedroom where she took a suitcase out of the back of the wardrobe and started to put neatly folded clothes inside. She halted abruptly, turning around, her expression desperate and longing.

I finally pulled her into a close embrace. She was crying, but my vision blurred.

"I don't know if I can do this—I don't even know what this is. Everything is falling apart."

No, I thought, holding her close. Everything is finally coming together.

❧

Paige was silent, apprehensive, as we drove. Mia and Colin were quietly playing in the backseat, though in the rearview mirror, I could see the boy studying me with curiosity—or suspicion, I wasn't sure. They were too young to understand that their mother was likely forced into the only life they knew, and that disrupting it wasn't a bad thing.

I understood that she was scared, but I actually felt more optimistic. I had booked a hotel room for her that was a bit out of town and nicer than the B&B I still stayed in. Maybe I would change, and I assumed that Alice would want to as well.

We'd take it one step at a time. There was a restaurant across the street, and I had asked Joy and Alice to come there later. In the small pub below the B&B, where everyone in town went, I felt like under a microscope. I was confident that we could make a little more progress away from it all.

While I waited for Paige and the kids to settle in, I called Jarrod and learned that Geller made bail.

"What the—?" I stopped myself short of cursing within earshot of Mia and Colin. "What happened there? Now we'll never find Caitlyn. She's scared. She won't come back. Chances are, he'll find her first, and then what?"

"What happened was the law," he said sarcastically. "We couldn't keep him forever. He's not rich or stupid—he'll hang around and wait for his trial."

"Let's hope that's true." I was about to end the call, but then I remembered something. "We need to set up appointments with a psychiatrist for the women, to determine their mental health status for starters, and get a complete medical history as well. Could you take care of that or..."

"Yeah, sure, I'll get on it," he said. "You're not going home?"

"No." He didn't need to know about those vacation days. "Thanks. Let me know when we can start."

I saw Paige standing in the doorway, looking pensive.

"Is everything okay?"

That should have been my question. I decided not to worry her about Geller. If anyone was in danger from him, it was Caitlyn.

"It's all right. All we need to do is concentrate on figuring this out now."

She quietly closed the door behind herself.

"What's going to happen next? When can we go home?"

"I would have preferred for you and the kids to stay home. You did nothing wrong."

She laughed wryly.

"Really? I don't remember half of it, maybe I did something horribly wrong, and that's why my memory shut down. All I know is that Tom took care of me when I had no one. He doesn't deserve this...suspicion. People are going to talk, even when they have no idea what it is they are talking about."

I couldn't deny that.

"You will go in front of a judge, tell your story. If Tom only ever saw the documentation you have with you now, technically, he didn't commit a crime. There's a lot I don't understand though. He's nine years older than you."

Paige nodded. "That's not a crime either."

She was right. Legally, we probably couldn't touch him, but a twenty-seven-year-old dating an eighteen-year-old was still taking advantage, no matter how you put it. Regardless, something had happened in between, that made Paige go from an out and proud lesbian to a 1950's housewife. I couldn't believe that people changed like that.

"We will ask you and the other women to speak to a psychiatrist."

"Why?" she asked, alarmed. "The policeman who came earlier said it would be okay if we just updated our papers. I swear I didn't mean to deceive anyone! When people told me that it was my name, and I had given them the papers to prove it, why would I have doubted it?"

"That's okay, don't worry about it. They'll ask a few questions, and hopefully have an idea about what caused your memory loss."

"Well, you know what it was in my case." She sounded sad. "They had to operate on my brain. It can mess with just about everything. They told me that in the hospital, so I'm not surprised."

I thought about what she said. It seemed that the memory loss came in different degrees—Caitlyn, for example, was aware of her past, the abusive husband. She didn't seem to fit in, yet was connected to the big picture in some way. We needed to interview her again, in a context where she knew she'd be safe. Annette Montgomery remembered her former lover, just in a completely distorted way.

"I have a few more questions for you," I said. "This is more like brainstorming, so we can figure out the complete picture. I swear, none of them is a trick question."

She perched on the edge of an armchair.

"Based on what I think I remember, I shouldn't trust you or my sister, but I guess my fate is in your hands now. If this helps bring my family back together, I'll do it."

"I am not deciding your fate. You are free to go whenever, or wherever you like—and frankly, you don't have to answer any questions if you don't want to."

"I know. Let's do this."

"Okay. I'll need a few names. If you were married in church, who did marry you? You had your children in the same hospital where you were treated after the accident?"

Her eyes widened.

"I didn't go to a hospital." Paige blanched as if I might judge her for that. I was simply baffled. Of course, there were women who chose not to have their children in a hospital, but I doubted she, or the other women, were making those choices here. More and more, this "community" seemed more like a religious cult, but what exactly was their deal except the obvious, make sure the women were barefoot and pregnant at most times while the men did their world domination, we-are-better-than-you thing? Groups like this had a doctrine, a leader. They didn't emerge out of nowhere. In my opinion, none of the husbands qualified to be the clever manipulator at the top. Abusers like Geller just took advantage of a system already tailor-made for them. Others were comfortable in it. Tom? Graham West?

The FBI should know if a new group was operating in the area—but what was the end game, kidnapping women and marrying them off, to what point?

Did they have plans with the children? This was getting scarier by the minute.

"That's fine," I finally assured her. "Your kids, are you home-schooling them?"

"No. There aren't too many options around here, but we found a good school for them."

"The other women's children, do they go to the same one?"

"Yes." Paige looked surprised. "You don't think...Come on, if something happened all those years ago, what would that have to do with the school?"

"I'm not sure."

She was probably right. This could turn out to be another dead end, but I wanted to check it off the list anyway. I was beginning to think that in focusing on the women, we might have overlooked something: The connection between the husbands. Or the children. This microcosm was like patriarchy on speed—women didn't benefit from such surroundings. Time to take a good hard look at the men, and not only the ones who claimed they had no idea when they were marrying teenagers. Part of me hadn't even fully acknowledged what it all meant, what Paige might have gone through. I couldn't, as long as we were in the middle of this.

But I was happy she was starting to question, what happened to her, what she'd been told.

Maybe my vacation time would not be enough to understand all of it, but I'd cross that bridge if I came to it. I made notes to talk to Jarrod once more about the psychiatrist, to the FBI about possible cults in the area, the school and the church. We'd have to compare the women's statements, and the men's, about the timeline, the disappearance, their relationships.

Someone, at some point, would have to slip up.

I closed my notebook with a resounding sound that made Paige flinch.

"Why don't we forget about all of this for tonight? Let's just have dinner with Alice and Joy and go from there."

Paige nodded, relieved that the interrogation was over.

❦

Paige

Colin and Mia had shown their disapproval quietly all day, but they were a little more excited about the prospect of going out to dinner. On the rare occasion Tom and I went, Millicent usually came over to watch them.

I wondered what Dani would do with all of that information, if she'd get what she wanted out of it, and what it was that she wanted in the first place. At least she didn't press on the whole home birth subject, which was an experience I remembered all too well, though I didn't care to. When I first became pregnant, everyone around me was out of their minds with joy, except for...me. I was scared. I felt all alone, overwhelmed, and I couldn't confide in anyone. Sharing how it really looked like inside of me felt like I was letting them down, Tom, Millicent, the midwife. But this was what I wanted, right? It was the natural way of things, meant to be.

The fear stayed with me all through the pregnancy. The second time, it was worse, because I knew what I was in for. I believe that if I had suggested terminating, the folks in the community would have found a way to lock me up, in prison or the psych ward. That's where women with crazy ideas went after all. The appointment with the psychiatrist still troubled me, but I couldn't tell Dani the whole story. She already had all the wrong perceptions about how we lived here—if those were choices, why was I so damn unhappy? Doreen had quickly understood why I couldn't stop crying, even though I had given birth to a healthy baby for the second time, which bode well for all the other times. There couldn't be another time. I didn't want it to be. I had kept the pills taped to the top drawer of my dresser, and I had them with me even now.

Forget about it all for one night. It was easier said than done, but I wanted to pretend, if only for one night, that I could have some time with my sister and her friends without thinking that they were out to get me. Spend time with Dani and remember the kiss that should have never been, but I kept like a cherished treasure through all these years—even through the moments when I wasn't even sure if it ever happened. I was confused. I was doomed. There were still moments when I thought about kissing her.

❦

I realized quickly that Alice was drinking too much, Dani was still occupied with all the shards of the broken picture, trying to fit them together, and Joy somehow in between. It felt oddly familiar. Could I really acknowledge, believe they all had been heartbroken about my disappearance while I was putting together a new life without them—with my husband and children in it? If I did, I'd also have to acknowledge that my parents never wanted me gone, that I misinterpreted something, or had been lied to.

I couldn't ask them or make things right. They were dead. I blinked back the stubborn tears. Dani, who cast me a quick worried sideways glance, had noticed anyway. I wasn't going to break down in public in front of my children—I was going to make it to the hotel room.

"I am just surprised," Alice said, her cheeks reddened. "Before you disappeared, you came out to the whole family. I remember that like it was yesterday. You said it was not a phase, and that you didn't need to meet the right guy. Not that anyone was having doubts, hell, you had everything figured out at that age. I remember...Sometimes I was jealous. Everything always came so easily to you. I'm sorry," she added when she realized how her words might have sounded.

Or maybe it was that I had stayed silent, secretly relieved that Mia and Colin were too tired to hear and question her words, almost falling asleep in their plates.

"Maybe now's not a good moment..." Joy ventured.

"I was wondering that myself," Dani said, "but we didn't want to talk about this tonight."

"Well, everything we talk about will lead us back to 'this,'" I was careful not to raise my voice. "I don't know all the answers. I was all by myself in the hospital, and I didn't know what to believe. I didn't remember. Tom has been a good husband—which is why I couldn't kick him out of our home."

"I understand that," Alice said. "All those years, we went through every worst-case scenario a million times. I'm just so glad you're okay. I really don't care if you're gay or not. Well, one of us already is. Dani has a girlfriend, did she tell you that?"

I couldn't help it, my jaw dropped, and various irrational emotions came at me all at once—betrayal, disappointment, anger—what had I expected? What did I want from her? I looked to Dani who avoided my gaze, meticulously folding her napkin.

"It's late," she said. "We should call it a night. The kids are tired."

"Oh, come on," Alice said. "Who knows when we'll all be together the next time? I'm sure Mia and Colin would like dessert." Predictably, they perked up at that. "And I would love another glass of wine." I might have been cynical, but I thought that was predictable too. "Speaking of the next time, I need to go home tomorrow as you know, but you must come visit me once this is all over."

I gave her a weak smile. The rest of dinner passed in an uncomfortably awkward atmosphere, but Alice didn't notice.

Maybe that was oddly familiar too. I couldn't tell the difference any longer.

Chapter Eleven

Dani

I was the designated driver that night, though I really wished I could have a drink. I'd drive Alice and Joy first and then pack my things and come back to my new hotel room. If I was honest, I needed to have a long overdue conversation with Lois as well, but I wasn't sure I could do it all tonight. Tomorrow would be another long day.

"Why did you change your hotel room?" Alice asked me, out of the blue, when we were in the car. "Are you staying much longer? I don't think I can. Don't get me wrong. I'm happy. I want to see Paige again as soon as possible, but there are people waiting for me at home."

"There are still a lot of questions," I said vaguely. Why did she have to tell Paige about Lois? I couldn't even say why this upset me so much. I wasn't planning anything, was I? Something like asking Paige if she remembered the last real conversation we had, that I said I would wait for her, and I did, in every way that counted. It would be crazy to do that, and worse, it would make me no better than Tom who had preyed on a young woman who was recovering from brain surgery. A girl, really. There were so many feelings I couldn't face, and they all had to do with my attraction to her, my resentment for him. I had chosen the higher road, and I had lost her.

What now?

Alice had been silent for a long time. Lost in thought, I had missed the storm brewing.

"Why does it have to be you? It's not like they're suspecting Paige of anything. She's not in danger. She doesn't need a bodyguard, does she? Fuck. Fuck!"

Both Joy and I flinched at the expletive.

"Alice," Joy scolded.

"Since there aren't any kids around, we can just as well be honest, right?" Alice said in a scathing voice. "I feel like an idiot for never putting it together before. You...and Paige. That's the reason you hate the husband, this is why you could never let go, because you felt guilty."

"You're wrong," I tried, but she interrupted me.

"Oh no, I see it all pretty clearly now. Is that why she was in such a strange mood that morning? Did you touch her?"

"Jesus, Alice," Joy mumbled.

"I didn't touch her! You have no idea." No idea how close to the truth she'd been, how her words had stung. I couldn't deal with their implications at twenty-one, I couldn't deal with them now. I had done the right thing. And then everything went wrong. "There are six women living in this community, all previously reported missing by loved ones who knew them, who knew better. You know it too, this is not the life Paige had planned for herself. She wanted to go to college, run for office. She had come out! Don't tell me people change, they don't, not like that."

"Is that your opinion, or wishful thinking?" Alice asked.

"I'm a cop. I know this isn't right. Something happened to these women, and I won't leave until I find out what it is."

"Suit yourself and try to keep your hands off my sister."

"Stop. It's not what you think..."

"Don't bother," Alice said, pushing the door open when I had barely stopped the car. She was gone a moment later, leaving me and Joy in awkward silence.

"Nothing happened," I felt the need to say. "I would have never..."

"I know," Joy said softly. "I also know that she had the biggest crush on you back then. We just didn't know that you were—"

"It's late. Let's call it a night, okay?"

Alone in my room, I packed, checked out and then drove back to the other hotel where I knocked on Paige's door, making sure she was okay.

She hesitated for a moment, before she said, "I'm glad you're here."

That was all I needed.

I retreated to my new room, got a scotch out of the minibar and called Lois. She sounded sleepy. Of course. Sleep was a thing that normal people did, outside of crazytown.

"I'm sorry," I said, "but we need to talk."

"I figured. You're not coming back."

"Yes...no...I don't know. I have no idea how long this will take."

"Yeah." She sighed. "That's not really anything new, so why did you call?"

"I am so sorry," I blurted out. I was exhausted. I wanted a hot bath and a good cry, but it was too early for that. This wasn't the end of the story...though it was for me and Lois. I couldn't pretend any longer. "I could understand it if you didn't want to be associated with all of this any longer. I think we should just look at the facts and..." *Coward.*

"Are you breaking up with me?" she asked matter-of-factly.

"I'm sorry," I said for the third time. "This isn't working. I know, it's all me. It's always been me."

"You think that's enough?" she said incredulously. "You call me in the middle of the night, say you're sorry, and that's it?"

I didn't think it was necessary to point out that it wasn't that late. I had to be careful. I needed to be clear, and fair—to her, and to myself.

"I don't know what else you want me to say."

"How about, what happened between the last time you called and now? Or, why didn't you ever tell me the truth about you and this woman?"

"There was nothing to tell. She was seventeen when she went missing." The resulting silence told me everything I needed to know. My tone had given me away. "Nothing happened." I kept repeating myself, and I kept lying. Between the kiss and the moment Paige disappeared, I had imagined many times what could have been. Technically, that counted. It made me guilty, because I was older, supposedly the adult one. Maybe Lois was right, and I owed her the whole truth.

"We kissed once. I told her we couldn't be together, because she was a minor."

I could sense she had many questions, none of which I wanted to answer, for none of which she would like to hear the answer.

"You're breaking up with me because of a girl you once had the hots for, who is now married with kids, is that correct so far?"

"It's not because of her." Another lie. Everything that had happened from the moment she vanished, was because of her. "It's because I can't be in a relationship right now. This is like nothing I've ever seen. These women, they were brainwashed somehow. I need to find the truth."

"That's...noble, I guess." I could hear the tears in her voice. "I'll start looking for an apartment, then."

"You don't have to—"

"Oh yes, I have to," she interrupted me. "Good luck, Dani. I hope you finally find whatever it is you're looking for."

The fact that she let me off the hook so easily was telling. Deep down, she knew as well as I did that we didn't stand a chance any longer. Perhaps we never had—the mystery had always been there, consuming me.

❦

Paige

I had strange and confusing dreams that night—although, given my current situation, that was rather ironic. My reality was strange and confusing, not much different from what my subconscious could conjure. I dreamed that Tom was in bed with me, here in the hotel room.

"No," I said, with an anger in my voice that surprised both of us. "The kids are right there, for Christ's sake."

"The therapist said we should try," he insisted. His pleading tone and gaze unnerved me. I wanted to get away, from him, this room, but there were the kids, always there, needing me, holding me back. I didn't have anywhere to go, because my parents had kicked me out. No, that was a long time ago. Dani had said I could do whatever I wanted to...and all of a sudden it was her, touching me, whispering to me in a way I couldn't resist. I didn't want to resist, to hell with all the warnings from our minister and therapist. I was nearly crying with joy. This was where I belonged, with her, in the warmth of her embrace. This was what I'd always wanted, from the moment I had first

137

imagined it. *I love you.* I could taste those words on my lips. I could taste her. If I was going to hell for it, I didn't care.

A sound in the hallway, another guest returning to their room, jolted me out of my troubled fantasies. In the other bed, Colin and Mia were still fast asleep. Remembering the images from my dream, I felt breathless. Was this really unnatural, going against what humans were designed for? Many, if not most, people in the community believed so. I had believed so, and maybe, to some extent, I still did.

What was true?

Was there something wrong with me?

Had my parents hated me because of this—or had I fallen for lies and missed the chance of saying goodbye to them? I wished Alice wouldn't have to go back so soon. I wished I could be back in New York City, seventeen, with no fear of the future, but that was forever ago. If it was ever real. I shivered, troubled by my reality and my dreams alike.

I was someone else now: Peggy Bond, who couldn't fulfill her wifely duties to save her life. I needed a psychiatrist more than I was willing to admit.

I met Dani in the breakfast room. She sat with us, and I had a hard time looking her in the eye. She didn't seem to notice. If anything, she was probably as exhausted as I was.

I let that sink in—she had never given up looking for me. In fact, she had changed careers so she could continue the search. I remembered her telling Alice that her parents had arranged an internship for her, and that she'd go to business school after.

Mia was dragging her feet, more interested in the drawing she wanted to finish than her breakfast, and Colin was drowning his pancakes in syrup. I mustered just enough energy to chide them a little, resulting in Mia starting to eat—with a pout, but still—and Colin casting a suspicious look at Dani. I wondered what Tom had told him about her.

"Detective Jarrod will set up appointments with a psychiatrist today," Dani said softly, holding my gaze. "Will you be okay?"

I blushed hotly as I nodded, all of a sudden unable to look away. It was wrong. I had chosen a different life, different responsibilities...but I couldn't stop those thoughts.

"Good. I will let you know when. I can drop the kids off at school and drive you back here. I'll have to talk to a few people this morning, but if you need anything, don't hesitate to call me, okay?"

I found it hard to speak. I cleared my throat, finally formed words. "I will...if I think of anything. I'm really sorry I'm not of much help. I'm just starting to figure out..." I didn't want to say too much with Mia and Colin around. "My parents, Alice...you. It all seems so different from what I remember, but everyone is saying the same things, so it must be true, right?"

She took my hand, and I held my breath. What if anyone saw us? The other people in the breakfast room, a couple and a family of four, didn't seem to care. Who was I kidding? If Dani was paying attention, she'd know. There was no point in any of this. I couldn't leave my family, my husband who was forced to live by himself in our house.

My head hurt from all those impossible thoughts co-existing in my head, all those contradictions. My heart did, too. I had no idea what to do about any of this, yet I was sitting here holding hands with the woman who was responsible for it all.

❧

Dani

Mia was adapting to the fact that I was around, while Colin clearly didn't like me. It was easy to tell from his openly disapproving stares. I had to remind myself that he, like his sister, had no guilt in this, and that there was no use in resenting an eleven-year-old boy. When Paige had given birth to him, she'd been younger still than I had been when she disappeared. I couldn't wrap my mind around it. I wanted someone to pay for her plans that had been crossed out, for the time lost, from her life and mine. If there was no clever mastermind behind this distortion, then Tom would be as good a candidate as any.

At least, Lois wouldn't have to live with my obsession, or me, anymore. I couldn't bring myself to regret my decision. Perhaps that would come later, when every dark corner of this story was illuminated, and Paige would go back home, and I...What would I do? Of course, I had never thought this far, and we might still uncover things that would make Paige stay far away from him. Did it make me a bad person if I was sort of hoping for that outcome?

It didn't matter. I still had a job to do.

⁂

When I got to the police station, I realized there was a meeting going on in the conference room. Jarrod was there, the cops who had been at the Geller's house the first day, DeShawn and the two FBI agents. I walked inside without knocking. I had every right to be there, even if my own lieutenant had technically not signed up on this. There were two of my cases in that pile, and in my opinion, they weren't closed until we knew the whole truth.

Apparently, they were just wrapping up the meeting.

"Detective Ryder," Jarrod said. "I don't have much time, but we have set up appointments with two psychiatrists. We've asked the women to come in. Paige MacGregor is up this afternoon," he added after a small pause.

"Her kids will be home from school."

"We have to do this as quickly as possible. We can't accommodate for everyone. There will be someone taking care of them here, but if you want, you can go get hers later. She has already consented to coming in."

"Okay. What was this all about?" I said to the female FBI agent, gesturing towards the now empty conference room. "Anything new?"

She shrugged. "Still gathering parts of the story, but we're making progress, I guess. Nothing on the false IDs though."

Then how was that progress? I didn't care to press, but caught up with one of the agents yet, eager to sell my theory.

"I don't have much time," she cut me off.

"Just a minute, please, this might be important. Can I buy you a coffee?"

She looked around as if I'd just made her an indecent proposal.

"There's something I'd like to run by you," I explained. "If you think it's a theory worth pursuing, and I think you will, we're going to need your resources on this."

"I guess I have a moment," she said uneasily, as we walked towards the break room. I would have preferred to leave the precinct, but if this was all I could get, I'd take it.

"Look, we all agree there's something strange going on, with these women missing, and then resurfacing in this community, all mothers and housewives in a context that's strangely antiquated."

She nodded. "Walking into their houses was like being in a 1950s movie. Then again…they all had something critical happening to them, and they built a new life from that."

"All together, right here? I was thinking…There must be a concerted effort behind this. You keep an eye on these things, right? There'd be information if there was a religious cult operating around here?"

"Six couples hardly make a cult."

"Maybe there are more. Maybe not all of them were forced into it originally. They could have been bribed or convinced somehow…"

Then it came to me. Caitlyn didn't seem to have suffered from memory loss. She hadn't just run away from Christopher, she had run towards something, someone offering her a better life. Was it bad luck or that person's intention that she had ended up with Geller?

The agent looked doubtful.

"That all sounds very science-fiction, and yes, we would know if there was any activity around here. There is no connection."

"Is there a connection between the men? Some sort of club, any context where they could have met?"

"To do what? Detective Ryder, I understand you helped a great deal in breaking this case, but I also hear that your lieutenant has called you home. Yet, you're still here. It's been personal for you, and maybe you're losing focus."

"All their kids go to the same school. Most of them have big families, and they can't explain how they went from their earlier life plans to this version. As you said, something happened to them that explains the changed names, the false IDs. Have you looked at their church?"

Why did it feel like I was talking to a wall, and not for the first time?

Did anyone really care about Paige and the others?

"Yes, we have. They're pretty standard 'love the sinner, hate the sin' type people. Traditional. I can't see them forging documents as part of a big conspiracy."

I had seen stranger things.

"What about the school?"

"What about it? It's closest for all of them, as you know they don't live very far apart."

"All right." I relented, realizing I wasn't getting much more out of her. "All I'm asking is that you keep it in mind. The husbands had something to gain from this arrangement."

"If you think that's something worth pursuing, I can't stop you as long as the department is still having you. We have other issues that need to be addressed. There'll be a hearing in the cases of MacGregor and Bennett soon."

"You have a date?" This was going too fast. We didn't have enough evidence yet.

"In two days," she said. "I really need to get back to work. Sorry."

I went searching for Jarrod, but he wasn't at his desk. I couldn't help notice the Katie Geller file. Making sure no one saw me, I quickly leafed through it, finding nothing of interest, except...a handwritten note, an address. Janet Tyler, sister. Why hadn't Jarrod told me? Whose sister? Caitlyn didn't have any family left. She wouldn't hide with Jason Geller's? The address, curiously enough, was of the hospital where I had interviewed Paige's former doctor. I had to go to the hospital again.

But first, I had to go pick up two kids from school who didn't like me all that much. I wanted to have a word with Paige before she went in with the psychiatrist, reassure her a little bit more.

"Where's Mommy?" Mia asked when I parked on the curb and got out to get them.

"She's at the police station to meet with someone. I'll bring you there, and then I get you all back to the hotel after." I tried to keep my tone light and optimistic, for all the good it did.

"Did she do something wrong?" the girl asked with frightened wide eyes, and her brother added, for good measure, "We're not supposed to go with strangers."

"Which is wise, but I'm not a stranger, right?"

He shrugged as if he hadn't quite made up his mind on the subject yet. To my relief, they both climbed into the backseat after all, and fastened their seatbelts. They were whispering to each other during the drive, which was all right with me. All I needed to do was get them safely to the station and hand them over to the cops in charge of watching the kids. I wanted to see Paige, assure her that everything would be all right.

Paige

I had been assured that Mia and Colin would be taken care of while I was talking to the psychiatrist in one of the offices that had been set up for this purpose at the police station. I was still nervous when I had to leave the hotel, take a cab, all the things I was not used to doing. I barely drove, and I almost never took a taxi. At least, seeing them with the two policewomen, and the kids of my neighbors, I felt a little relieved. They knew each other. They would be fine for an hour or so.

"They'll be okay." I turned around to find Dani standing in front of me, and all of a sudden, my resolve crumbled. She had to have read my mind, because she embraced me before I could stammer "I...I'm scared."

"You'll be okay, too," she whispered, and for a moment I wished fervently that the two of us could just leave, somewhere far from all of this...but where would we go? How did I get this idea that I should be running? Perhaps because one of the first things she'd said to me was that she'd take me home. Home to where? I had shared a house with my husband and children for years. All else was nothing but a fantasy...or was it?

I heard somebody call my name, and then I gently disengaged myself and walked through the open door into the office. Nothing major, just more questions, and they would try to determine if there was any way to find out what happened—why I had apparently walked away from my friends and then later ended up in that accident.

If Tom and I had been together before, I wondered, why didn't anyone know him? In the waiting area, I had briefly laid eyes on the woman who claimed she'd been Annie's girlfriend. No, wait, Annette's. I guessed I had to start getting used to using their real names.

Paige.

"Hello Peggy," the man behind the desk said, extending his hand, smiling. He looked quite comfortable given that this wasn't his usual workplace. "Or should I say Paige?"

I stood, frozen, feeling the urge to walk right out, but before I could make my body cooperate, he got up and closed the door behind me.

"Sit, Peggy," said the man who had been trying to teach me and Tom the basics of being a couple again, and why it was so important to the community in particular, and the world in general.

"My name is Paige," I said, sounding more pleading than defiant. "I don't know if you heard. I'm separated from Tom at the moment."

"Nonsense," he said, still smiling. I'd always thought he was patronizing, though I couldn't put my finger on it until I was alone in a room with him. I wasn't comfortable at all. "We have an hour. Let's see how we can work to fix the damage they've done."

Who were they? The cops? Dani?

"This will be over soon, and you'll be back with your husband where you belong," he promised. "Did you try some of the exercises I suggested to you?"

Truth be told, I had found it humiliating to talk about my sex life to a stranger, when we all lived in a context where sex was rarely talked about at all. From Doreen and Sheila—Ashley—I had learned early on that the counselors usually tried to find fault with the woman. Well, Ashley had been lucky—she couldn't have children, so once that was clear, there were no more visits to the shrink.

"Aren't we supposed to talk about the accident, and what happened before?"

"Do you remember what happened before?" He leaned closer, studying me with interest.

I shrank back.

"No need to be nervous. In your case, the diagnosis is pretty clear. Your memory was affected during surgery. So—do you remember now?"

"No." I shook my head. "They tell me that I disappeared on that trip to New York City I took with my friends. I was Paige back then. I woke up in the hospital with people telling me I had talked about how they, and my parents, had been treating me badly, and that I had run away. The papers I had with me were Peggy's."

"Such fascinating stories. Which do you believe?"

"They can't both be true, can they? When I met them again, and they told me how scared they were for me, it sounded true—but why would I make up things about my parents I can't even remember telling, and why would the nurses and doctors lie to me? It doesn't make sense."

"Maybe you shouldn't try to find any sense in this," he said. "I believe you have other things to worry about now. How can you become pregnant when you don't even share a house, let alone a bed, with Tom? That's what you want, right? To be with your husband, bring more life into this world?"

"Yes, of course." My voice was steady, and I held his gaze. I didn't know why, but it mattered greatly to me at this moment that he believed me.

"Then you have nothing to worry about. You must concentrate on the future now. Your family. There will be a hearing. It is important that this is what you tell the judge as well."

And if I didn't, what could he do to me?

I shivered hard. I wasn't sure, but the last time I had tried to do something different, something I wanted, the punishment had followed swiftly. Could Dani really get me out of this mess, or was I trapped forever? I realized I was shaking, not with fear, but with anger. Who did he think he was, trying to influence what I'd say in front of the judge? What if Tom knew that there had been some manipulation, that I hadn't been eighteen after all when we got married? What the hell did he know?

"Sure, whatever. Can I go now? My kids are waiting outside."

"No problem. I'll tell the police that you were cooperative, but can't remember anything, poor thing. Say hello to Tom for me, and I hope to see you at our next appointment as planned."

Before, I didn't see any choice, any way out of this, but now, there was a flicker of hope, sparked by this anger I couldn't seem to let go of. Someone had played with my life, made me believe that my parents didn't love me when for all I knew, the heartbreak of not knowing whether I was dead or alive, had killed them. They made me believe that my sister wanted me gone, when she had become an alcoholic after I went missing.

And Dani...Dani. I needed to see her right this moment. I walked out of the office where she was waiting for me.

"You're ready?

"I need to go to the bathroom first," I said, hoping I didn't need any more words to convince her to follow me. I was lucky. She did.

In the women's restroom, I lost my last reservations, pushed her against the door and kissed her. The sensations were so much more vivid than in my dream, the feel of her body against mine, the softness of her lips, the heat between us. She didn't even try to ask what was going on, just went with it, opened up to me, and finally, kissed me back. When I stepped back, I was shaking. Wrong, unnatural, to hell with all of that. If the couples' therapist had pushed me to do this, I was grateful for it.

Dani put her fingers to her lips as if she couldn't believe what just happened.

"Paige," she said. Surprised? Shocked? Happy? Maybe all of it.

A policewoman walked in and locked herself into a stall, breaking the spell. In the following moments, I had enough time to remember my children just a few rooms away, and Dani's girlfriend back home. What was I thinking? She wouldn't leave her for a mom and housewife who couldn't remember half of her life. Finding me had been her job, a case. Cased closed.

"Could you drive us home, please?" I asked, then became aware of my choice of words. The hotel, of course, where we would hide out until the judge declared the house I had lived in the past decade, safe.

Dani took a deep breath.

"Of course. Come on, let's go." Maybe she was thinking of the woman back home, too, the woman I was already irrationally jealous of. Because the two of them probably shared more than kisses. What was happening to me, and could I ever be back to the person I once was? Who would that be? Time was running out, and it wouldn't be long before I was back to being Mrs. Thomas Bond, left with those "unnatural" fantasies that would never come true.

"Okay, how about we order pizza for dinner?" Dani suggested, as if it was completely natural that we'd have dinner together.

I knew that Colin was slow warming up to her, but his eyes lit up at the word pizza. Of course. We were supposed to feed our children home-cooked meals, not the junk food that kids outside of the community ate. Our doctors drilled that into us from the moment of conception—or even before that. Don't do anything that could mess with your fertility, don't drink, don't smoke, go easy on prescription drugs. That was ironic, because Ashley knew somebody who provided a friend of hers with the latter.

After the meal, I let them watch TV in the bedroom—why not, I was already epically failing as a mother—while Dani poured us another glass of wine.

It was exactly what I needed for the courage to ask. Besides, I wasn't going to be pregnant anytime soon. I could have a glass of wine or more if I pleased.

"Are we going to talk about it?"

"Yeah, how did it go with the psychiatrist? You were done pretty early."

"That's because he knows me already." I drank deeply from my glass. "Tom and I had to go through marriage counseling before all of this started."

"Oh."

"Yeah, it wasn't fun. The people around here value big families. Lately, I've been...tired. That's not helping."

"Well, isn't it between you and your husband how many children you want?"

There was a petty little part of me that wanted to slap her for bringing him up, but then I remembered I was the one who had done that.

"Nothing here ever stays between you and your husband," I blurted out. "I am so damn tired running after the two of them every day, but every neighbor is on your case." She listened attentively. Wondering, judging? "Why do you care? You don't want any of this. You'll be going home to your girlfriend soon."

Dani looked straight at me when she said, "I'll stay as long as you need me, and I don't have a girlfriend. Not anymore. We broke up."

It would have been the polite thing to say something like "I'm sorry." The truth was, I wasn't sorry. I was afraid to believe what she'd just said, what it could mean, what I wanted it to mean.

How could she not know what was on my mind? Or maybe she did? Which was worse?

"You did?" The words came out as a croak.

"I'm not telling you this to put pressure on you—I know you already have lots of it. I just want to be honest with you. We didn't work out. That's all."

"Because you're still here?"

"That's a part of it, yes." She sighed.

"I'm sorry for what happened at the station," I said eventually, though I didn't mean that either. "I need to look after Colin and Mia. It's time for bed."

Dani didn't argue, and so I spent the next half hour making sure they were ready and wouldn't turn the TV back on. There were only so many transgressions I could tolerate.

"When are you coming?" Mia asked. I kissed her forehead.

"It won't be long, sweetie. Have nice dreams, both of you."

Back in the living room where Dani still sat on the couch, absent-mindedly turning the wine glass in her hands, I said, "I should get ready too."

"Probably." She made no move to get up. I leaned back against the door, crossing my arms over my chest, studying her. Remembering her, then and now. I realized that at some point in my life, I might have wanted children, have them on my own terms, give birth in surroundings that I chose.

Whenever I had dreamed my life, she had always been in it. There was no husband, no community, no shrink telling me to try to lean back and enjoy it. In the fantasy, pleasure came without effort.

Dani put the glass aside and got to her feet. I took a step, and then another, drawn by an invisible force. Magnetic. I went into her arms eagerly.

"I've been waiting for you all these years. It's been so long." Her tone, longing, need, and lust, met a pulsing echo somewhere deep inside of me. I put my hands on her back and pulled her closer to me, eager to feel and to explore. As we kissed, her hands traveled down my sides, over my hips and beneath the waistband of my skirt. My heart skipped a beat, my body ablaze with the gentle brush of her fingertips. I wanted to protest, to urge her on, but the only sound I could manage was a pitiful whimper. Yes...no...It was impossible. Maybe I'd had a chance at some point in my life, but it had come and gone. I had more than myself to think about. For the second time today, I couldn't finish what I had started.

"Please, go."

"We should talk," she said, a desperate edge to her voice. Because I was kicking her out, or because I was kicking her out like that, I didn't know.

"I can't, not right now. Please understand. This can't happen. We both need to take a step back."

"Okay, if that's what you want. I'll see you in the morning?"

I gave a wry laugh.

"Where would I go?" She didn't answer, just closed the door behind her softly.

In the middle of the room, I sank to the floor, crying. I held my hand in front of my mouth so my sobs wouldn't wake my kids who were already suspicious of Dani. My body was aching for her touch.

This was the life I could have had...but not any longer.

Whatever I said, the judge was likely to rule in Tom's favor. Men in the community always watched out for one another.

I didn't want to go back.

I was Snow White who had slept in a glass coffin all those years, awakened for a blissful but cruel moment. There would be no happy ending.

Chapter Twelve

Dani

I needed a cold shower desperately. I needed a reality check. Whatever Paige decided, it didn't mean we could just rewind to the moments before her disappearance—abduction?—and pick up where we'd left off.

Alice already thought I had crossed lines back then.

Those moments had made it painfully clear to me. I wanted her. I always had, and apparently some things had stayed intact in her memory. That didn't mean I could ignore the fragile state she was in, with everything she'd believed for the past decade crumbling. I wanted to give her time, as much as she needed...but I wished I'd taken that bottle of wine with me, just to take off the edge a little bit, sexual frustration, and a tad of anxiety—what if it was all me? What if what she really needed was a friend? But she had kissed me, many years ago, and today in the police station's restroom.

It had to mean something.

At the same time, I needed to concentrate on the other stories as well, follow other leads. The hospital. Janet Tyler. I wanted to keep an eye on Paige and her kids, make sure they were safe. I was beginning to feel like I didn't have much help.

When I came down to the breakfast room the next morning, the woman taking care of the buffet told me that Paige, Mia, and Colin had already been there, and that she was going to take them to school by bus.

I'd catch up with them later—first, I wanted to check out Janet Tyler, the woman whose name I'd found in Jarrod's file. She turned out to be another doctor, an orthopedic surgeon. She claimed not to be related to Caitlyn in any way.

"I remember Katie, sorry, Caitlyn, coming in one time. She had slipped on the floor in her home and broke her arm."

Given what I knew about Jason Geller, I seriously doubted that she'd slipped.

"You treated Paige MacGregor as well?"

Everything always led back to her. I had to make sure that whatever Bond knew, he wasn't the same kind of asshole as Geller. I wouldn't be above crossing lines.

"One time, after her accident." Like the other doctor I had spoken to, she had her answers ready. "Her leg was broken—clean break, no complications. Dr. Dawson was mostly responsible for her as the head trauma was the most concerning factor."

It took a second for that to sink in, and when it did, I nearly jumped to my feet.

"Dr. Brittany Dawson, the neurosurgeon? She worked here?"

She looked alarmed. "Not for long, and she was mostly consulting on cases. I believe her main employment was elsewhere, and of course she's writing those books."

"Did you know that Dr. Dawson died?"

Her eyes widened. So, the answer was no. How could she have missed this? Brittany's death had been all over the media. She had to have known about the women living here under false

154

names, Caitlyn at the very least. Why didn't she go to the police? Elaina might be right assuming that someone had threatened her, and she had tried to leave clues without harming Elaina in the process.

I wondered what had happened in those ORs. Did it have anything to do with why the women suffering different degrees of memory loss? Did the task force finally gain access to those medical records?

I hadn't found anything about why Jarrod had marked "sister," next to Tyler's name, but I sure had found something.

"Just one more thing. When Caitlyn came in, did you ever think of any of her injuries as suspicious?"

"I'm afraid I can't tell you anymore unless you have a warrant for those files."

"Just your impression. Please?"

"Why are you asking if you already know the answer?" she asked. "I'm sorry, Detective, but I have work to do."

❧

I brought my findings to Detective Jarrod who wasn't too impressed, with my snooping, or the conclusions I'd drawn.

"Sorry I confused you. The word sister had nothing to do with Janet Tyler, but you figured that out, didn't you? As for Dr. Dawson, she led you to Caitlyn, right? There's your connection, that's nothing new. It doesn't mean Dawson knew the whole story."

"What about the encrypted files we found on her computer, the pictures of some of the women? I still haven't managed to match all of them. Now there's Tyler telling me that Brittany worked here? That's not a coincidence."

"Maybe not, but you shouldn't go harass people while you're technically on vacation. We keep you up to date, so you can add any information we might have for your cases, to your files. It doesn't mean that you're running this investigation."

Yeah, like he needed to remind me.

"What about the medical records?"

"Nothing that jumps out. If anything, people around here are quite healthy. They don't smoke or drink much."

"Anything about the memory loss?"

He looked annoyed. "Nothing more than you already know. In MacGregor's case, the brain surgery did that. It happens. Nothing sinister there. By the way, tomorrow will be the hearings for MacGregor's and Bennett's cases. You might want to be there."

"Yes, of course. Is there anything else I should know?"

"There's dead silence on the street regarding those false IDs. This could take a long time, so be prepared to wrap up your stay here anytime soon. The women are alive and well. Maybe that's all you can do."

"We don't know about Caitlyn."

"You found her. Now it's up to this department. You should consider taking a vacation for real."

"Hm. Maybe I will do that. Thanks for the pep talk."

I had planned to catch up with Paige later when she picked up Colin and Mia from school, but I did have time for a few phone calls before.

The first went to Viola who confirmed that there was no news on Brittany's encrypted files. I had expected that. My next call was to Chief Larkin, the last ace up my sleeve.

"Danielle. How are you?" he asked. The concern in his voice didn't sit right with me.

"I'm fine, thank you."

"You're going back home soon, I assume? The lieutenant told me you are reconnecting with your old friend. It's amazing that you found her alive after all those years."

So, they had talked. I thought so.

"Yeah, but there are quite a few loose ends left. This is why I'm calling. I feel like the task force here isn't very...accommodating. I could live with that, but I'm starting to feel there's also some negligence to follow leads. I was hoping you might know someone who could look into that."

He was silent for a moment.

"Those are serious accusations. Are you talking about someone in particular?"

"The detective here keeps stalling me. Even the FBI agents don't come across as very eager, and believe me, there's a lot of work to do."

"Maybe they are just understaffed—it's a small town after all. But I will see what I can do. And speaking of understaffed, don't let too much time go by. You're needed back home as well, and you will need your vacation days eventually."

He had a point. I wasn't ready.

"I want to see this through until the end. I know there's a relation to Dr. Dawson's case. We still don't know what was in the encrypted files, and I have no idea what's taking so long."

"See, this is what I meant," he said calmly. "I hate to say it, but you're losing perspective. Dr. Dawson led you to the missing women, which is amazing. But she still killed herself, no outside influence, and you found the women. These past years have been traumatic for you, and it's no surprise. Hell, in our job we learn to expect the worst in cases like this. Fortunately, that didn't happen, and you now have clarity. You need a little time to adjust, I know, but after that it's best if you come home and do your job. These women don't need you any longer."

He could have just as well slapped me in the face. Perhaps it was true that Paige didn't need me in the long run. Didn't anyone see that we were only looking at the tip of the iceberg? It was getting tiring, trying to convince everyone. I wasn't crazy.

That's what Paige might have felt when she woke up in a hospital bed to an altered reality—but altered by whom?

"Maybe they don't need me personally, but one of them is on the run from her abusive husband, and two of them were married with those false papers when they were still underage. Tomorrow, a judge will decide whether they should go back to their husbands. I need to know that this task force is doing its job."

"I'll have someone look into that. Meanwhile, think about what I said."

"I will. Thank you."

At least that had been vaguely successful. Next, I went to find Paige and the kids, but I kept wondering about Janet Tyler and her connection to Caitlyn.

❧

I managed to talk Paige into having a coffee downstairs in the hotel restaurant while Mia and Colin were doing their homework in the room. In the light of day, with all the strange facts swirling in my mind, it was hard to think of last night, and what almost happened. My body remembered though. I could tell from her soft blush that she was thinking about it too.

"I'm sorry," I said. "I didn't mean to push you. I should have used...words first. It's a complicated situation for you, and I didn't mean to take advantage."

"I think I'm not completely innocent here." She gave me a small smile. "With the way I came at you in the restroom, how could you not interpret it like this?"

"I am listening now. I promise."

"It's hard. I don't know what to tell you. For the past years, I've only ever heard that this is wrong, against nature. For sure, it goes against the vows I've made, and I wonder what they are worth now anyway—or who I am, for that matter."

"Who told you?" I had to ask. It was driving me crazy. This had all the markings of a women- and LGBT-hating cult, but there was no obvious leader.

"Doctors, the midwife, Tom's mother, the reverend...It's common knowledge around here. I...kind of overlooked it because it didn't apply to me, or that was what I had thought. Now...I don't know what to feel. I'm so angry all the time, and I'm not sure if it's at someone who took all of this away from me, or you, because you made me aware."

"Do you still think there's something wrong with this...us?"

"I've been thinking about it a lot lately. Maybe I was always that way. Does that mean I've been living a lie? Everyone thinks I should have more children, but I don't want to. Don't get me wrong, I love Colin and Mia. I don't want to be without them, but in the beginning, it was hard. I don't think I ever felt like a new mother is supposed to feel like. I was scared and angry, and I couldn't tell anyone."

I realized she was as frustrated as I was. She needed the same answers I was after.

"Maybe the other women felt the same?"

"Sheila, I mean, Ashley, really wanted kids, but she couldn't have them. Ironic, isn't it? Annette, I don't know. She always talks about how proud she is, but then, her girlfriend came looking for her, right? I know that Caitlyn bought birth control pills from Doreen, and... I'm not sure about the others. The thing is, if you say it out loud, it will get to one of the doctors, and they send you to counseling. The community...it's tight, and it's safe, but they want you to go in a certain direction."

"You have alternatives now," I reminded her. How I wished I could go home and take her with me. A black market for birth control pills. Mandatory counseling.

"That depends on what the judge says. In the eyes of the church, I'll never really be divorced though."

"They can't tell you how to live your life."

"Well, except they did for more than ten years. Where would I go?"

"You could come with me."

There it was, out in the open.

"I don't mean you have to be with me. I know this is all going very fast, for you, and the kids, and I don't want to add to that. All I'm saying is that you have a place with me...and it's safe."

"Tell me about the old me," she said, her eyes welling up. "Tell me what I wanted to do with my life...just so I know I'm not crazy."

So I did, and told her about her college plans, about New York, the evening we spent together, and the kiss. Today, we'd be honest about everything.

Tomorrow, a judge would determine the future—or was it really in our own hands?

❧

Paige

It was with a lighter heart that I went to bed that night. Dani was right—she was right about so many things, but I did need more time to figure out what my future would look like. I wanted to be with her so badly, but if I took her up on her offer, I needed to think about how to break this to Tom, Colin. and Mia. Maybe Tom wouldn't even be surprised. The more I thought about it, the more it made sense. It wasn't fair to stay with someone I didn't love, rob that person out of the chance to find happiness.

Could I really make Dani happy when she knew I had two children to take care of, when all I could offer her were vague fantasies? Maybe I could. Maybe I could undo all those detours and get back on the path that I was meant to be on all along.

If I had been all alone in this room, I would have slept naked. Even the idea made me flush with the sudden heat, making my face burn, igniting the hunger. It was almost scary—I'd never felt for Tom like that. It wasn't a woman's place, the reverend would say. I was sick and tired of being good and moral. I wanted more from my life.

The phone rang, and I jumped, the sound so unexpected in the stillness of the night.

The voice on the other end of the line was too.

"Peg...I just wanted to know how you're doing."

I blushed even harder, as if Tom could guess the thoughts I had just a minute ago. Maybe he would be able to, because my voice sounded strangely breathless.

"Okay," I said vaguely.

"This will all be over tomorrow. The police found nothing. They can't keep us apart any longer."

"Are you even supposed to talk to me? I don't want you to get into any kind of trouble."

"You're my wife," he said. "You belong with me. Whatever that judge says, right? Our family is the only authority. You remember that?"

Had he always been so patronizing?

"Did you know that I was a minor when you married me?"

"Does it matter now? You were almost eighteen, that's only a few months' difference. We have two beautiful children. They need us."

"I don't want to go to therapy anymore," I said, as if that was negotiable. I was well aware that he hadn't answered my question.

"Okay, sure, whatever you want. I miss you, Peggy."

"It's not Peggy."

"I'm sorry." He laughed self-consciously. "I guess I'll have to get used to that now...Paige. It's odd."

"What else do you know? About my parents?" The subject made me incredibly sad, and angry. "Did you know they never kicked me out? Did you know about New York?"

"Wait a minute, what are you saying? I only ever knew the story you told me, about everyone being so nasty to you, and that you had to pack your bags the day you turned eighteen."

"Don't lie to me, please."

"That is the truth. What crazy ideas are they putting in your head?"

Only they weren't crazy ideas, but my memories—and logic deduction. Either I had told him this story, or it never existed, and he'd known I was only seventeen. Both couldn't be true.

"Why, Tom? Why did you and Graham marry girls that were underage?"

"You are confused," he said. "We'll talk tomorrow after I bring you home."

I wanted to say that this wasn't a given, but I couldn't bring out the words, all of a sudden a lot more alarmed about the hearing. It could mean freedom or a life sentence. Meanwhile, my children were eager to be back with their father.

I couldn't win.

※

"We are talking about some undefined events that allegedly happened thirteen years ago, and very little can actually be verified. All we have achieved so far is to destabilize the environment for the children in question and endanger families. I am determined to put an end to this. Mrs. Bond, you may return home."

I turned to Dani first, seeing her shocked expression. Shocked, I assumed, because she knew no matter how much she had tried to encourage me, I wasn't that brave or rebellious. It's true what they say, that having children changes everything. I couldn't just run away. That didn't mean I wasn't disheartened by the outcome, not just the ruling, but the way the judge had phrased it. Tom would never let me have custody. I would never leave them behind.

So, I had to leave myself behind, once more.

❦

Tom came up to me right afterwards. Mia and Colin ran to him, hugging him tightly. The scene unnerved and frightened me. They hadn't enjoyed the unusual freedom of the past few days as much as I had. They just wanted to go home.

Home, where was that?

"Thank God," he said. "Now we can all go back to normal."

"I can drive you to the hotel," Dani said behind me. I expected Tom to object, but to my surprise he agreed.

"If that's okay with you? I'll get Colin and Mia home in the meantime, and we can have dinner together. I missed you so much."

It was Dani who frowned at his words. I felt torn in every direction—it was impossible to misinterpret the longing gazes of my children. Tom. Dani. I couldn't make a scene when so many people I knew were still around. Ashley and Graham were still there with the twins. Margaret. Tammy. It freaked me out to realize how many of the women were pregnant. Some of them, because they had always wanted big families. Some of them, because they simply had no choice. Had anyone talked to the police about the birth control pills? Would they find out?

We finally left the crowd behind and made it to the parking lot where I sat in the car with Dani, wishing time would stop.

She fastened her seatbelt and started the car, waiting silently for me to say something, maybe hoping.

"I would love to..." I started, then stopped, unsure how I could really express the turmoil inside of me. "I want to be with you. I want that so much, but it's impossible, at least right now. I can't leave."

"Bring the kids with you," she said. "It will be all right. It might be a little tight, but we can always find another place. Come back with me."

"I have to talk to Tom first. We are married. I have to go back and explain myself."

"That's not even legal. He married a minor with false documents."

"The judge said—"

"I don't care what the judge said!" Dani snapped, making me flinch. She apologized right away. "I'm sorry, that was uncalled for. But he can't make you go back if you don't want to."

"I'm a married woman. I can't run away from that." Maybe I was too much of a coward to run. Maybe the years had slowed me down too much. "I don't think you understand. I have no idea what I'm doing. Everything I thought was true is turning out to be a lie. I would like it all to stop for a while, so I'd have time to figure out what's going to happen, but what choice do I have? A decade of my life is gone. Much as I wish, I can't get that back. I don't know what's next, but I need to talk to him. I owe him that much."

"You don't owe him anything."

"You don't understand."

She sighed. "I guess you're right about that. I don't."

Dani was silent while I packed Mia's, Colin's, and my clothes. When I was done, she picked up the suitcase, then put it down again. She kissed me very softly. I could hardly enjoy it, one of those stress headaches building. It was like a tug of war inside my head. The new reality was starting to impose itself over the one I had believed to be true for over a decade. I shivered at the feel of her lips on mine, memory, dream, reality—sometimes I still found it hard to tell. I would have to come to terms with the fact that I'd been lied to, manipulated.

"You do what you have to do but know that you and the kids always have a place with me. You don't have to be with him if you don't want to. You don't have to have sex with him."

I laughed uneasily.

"Sex is the least of my problems right now. Don't worry. I'll be okay. You'll let me know if you find out anything new about...New York and what happened?"

"Of course."

When we reached the house, I told her she didn't have to come in with me, mostly for my benefit. I already felt saddened to my soul—but this wasn't just about me. If it had been, I would have asked her to take me far away. The temptation was great.

Instead, I said, "I always remembered that first kiss...and now I have more to remember."

Dani insisted on accompanying me to the door.

❦

Dani

"What do you want?" Tom asked with barely unveiled anger. That was meant for me. Paige disappeared into the house, and a moment later, I heard a happy squeal from Mia. "Haven't you done enough?"

I couldn't help it.

"Whatever that judge said today, he's letting you off the hook easily."

"Oh, right. And what do you understand about marriage?"

"I understand that Paige was underage when you married her with those false papers."

"Well, that was cleared up today. I didn't know. No one was harmed. I'll take that back. You harmed my family with those ridiculous accusations. Thank God that is over now."

Could he really be this ignorant? Innocent?

"We'll be in touch," I said.

"I'd rather you weren't. Jarrod assured me today that there is no more reason to bother our family. Have a good day, Detective."

Knowing there was nothing I could do at the moment, I left, but I wouldn't go far. I didn't care what Jarrod had to say, the judge, the FBI even. There was something wrong about these marriages, and I would find out. If it cost me my job, then so be it. It wasn't worse than spending all those years not knowing if Paige was still alive, wondering if I had made it easier for someone to prey on her that day.

Someone—who?

I started organizing and packing up my own files. I wasn't going anywhere, but I had to make up my mind where to go from here. The husbands. None of them had a record as we knew, but there had to be some connection.

The school.

The hospital.

Janet Tyler and Brittany Dawson.

I sat down between piles of papers and folders, distracted from my musings. Paige, kissing me in the restroom. The moment in the hotel room that almost led to more, leaving both of us wanting. I could understand that this was going too fast for her, that she needed more time, but there was still some odd sense of obligation that held her back, not just for the children. She was aware of it, but she couldn't fight it. Or maybe she didn't want to, and bringing back the past had done nothing but create a momentary confusion?

What if I had read the signs all wrong, and something happened, but then it had been Tom who helped her pick up the pieces? No. She said she wanted to be with me. And they were in counseling...in any case, she felt indebted to him, and there seemed nothing I could do about it, like there was still an invisible wall separating us.

More than ten years of my life were gone too. With that realization sinking in, I wanted to cry, punch something, or raid the closest liquor store. The minibar wouldn't do, not at all. Maybe it was true that one reason why I had never given up hope was the fantasy that somehow, we'd be together in the end, that those tentative feelings could translate into an adult relationship after so much time no matter what.

She was married, but that marriage wasn't legal.

My work here wasn't done.

⁂

I made a detour by Paige's house where all was quiet. I knew I had to be careful, but damn it, even so I nearly went to knock on the door. Paige had said to keep her up to date in case I found out something new. I'd have to deliver something new.

I stopped at a diner to have a bite, aware of the curious looks from some patrons. I didn't have time to follow the press much, but most residents had to be aware of the investigation—I imagined it didn't happen all that often around here that the

FBI came to town. I wanted to find out more about Janet Tyler, how much she knew about Brittany, and maybe why Jarrod had marked her as "sister."

I parked a few blocks away from her house and waited until it was dark. There was never any shortage of files to study or patterns to look for. Someone had orchestrated this, chosen the women and the men who married them. The more I thought about it, the more it made sense. At least three of the women were previously either in relationships with other women, or had planned to be—so was this an anti-gay hate group with extraordinary means, attempting to slap us in the face, because we had won the right to marry? There I'd thought these people had moved on to creating bathroom hysteria, finding just another cruel and unnecessary way to turn people's lives upside down.

Could you do that, mess with a person to the extent they completely changed their life's design? They had tried, with their fraudulent version of "therapy," and even if some still held on, we knew that it was a hoax, something that didn't work and had only served to harm people. Paige's parents would have never stood for any of this crap, so why target her?

I had a dead neurosurgeon who could have answered some of those questions for me, if she were still alive—and a missing woman who probably had even more answers for me.

I hadn't seen Annette in a while, but she'd firmly believed she'd wanted to break up with Rose Kerry on that camping trip.

Paige was in an accident that required brain surgery.

You couldn't change a person's sexual orientation through surgery—or even try, could you? This was all over, sins of the past—right?

Brittany had worked with trauma victims. She wouldn't have let herself be drawn into something illegal...or if she had, there would be the reason for her to commit suicide.

I called Viola whom I caught on her way out.

"I thought you weren't on the task force anymore."

News travels fast.

"I need you to check something for me. Please."

"If it has to do with Paige MacGregor or Dr. Dawson, I'm not sure I should. The lieutenant made it very clear that as far as this department is concerned, this case is closed."

"Go see if you can find Hawkins and ask about the encrypted files."

"Danielle. Please, for the love of God."

"I think there's a hate group behind this. They have money, influence, and skilled people on their side. I think they're trying to change sexual orientation through brain surgery."

"Wait..." At least she didn't right out say I was crazy. "Didn't someone try that already?"

"Yeah, and it wasn't that long ago when you think about it, but this is different. If what I think is true, they are a whole lot more sophisticated and sinister than anything we've ever heard about before."

"Dani...I think you're tired."

"I sure am, but that's not why I came up with this. Think about it. It makes sense."

"In what universe? Those crazy people are the fringe these days."

"They still get laws written and passed."

"That's an outright conspiracy theory. Are you really sure you want to go there?"

"I am sure that there are patient files on that key all right, but they are not of celebrities. Maybe Dawson killed herself because she couldn't live with what she had done, or maybe she wanted to go public, and she knew they would come after her and Elaina. And if all of that is true, it would explain why some of the locals are hesitant to dig deeper."

"Wow." I could tell that she was, at the very least, intrigued. "That's horrible to think about. If that's true, Rose Kerry wasn't wrong about brainwashing. How do you explain Caitlyn Hoyt? She wasn't gay but traded one ass of a husband for another."

"Maybe there's something we don't know yet. Please, just check on the key and let me know what happens, okay?"

"I'll see what I can do," she said, and I remembered Chief Larkin had used the same words.

At least, I had some friends left. I hoped.

I decided to talk to Janet again, find out more about Brittany's work at the hospital. Something had to give.

It was a quiet residential area she lived in, though the architecture was more individual than in Paige's neighborhood, different-sized front yards, the occasional wrap-around porch. Janet's house was at the end of the street.

The next moment, reality was altered in a disturbing way as hands pushed me hard enough for me to lose my balance and stumble. A booted foot kicked me in the stomach, and in the split second before the pain registered, I recognized the man's furious face.

Jason Geller.

"You...get the hell out of here, bitch!" He came up with a couple of other, even less original names to call me, but at least I had time to get to my feet, training kicking in. Somehow, I didn't think I could count on much help from anyone in this town anymore. He had caught me off guard, and the asshole was strong, but he hadn't counted on my growing frustration ever since I'd come here and kept banging my head against walls. He went down, but not before getting a punch in. I felt the blood spurt from my nose, but finally, I managed to get my gun and point it at him.

"Stay down!" I hissed, getting my cell phone with the other hand and calling 911.

He did, but that didn't keep him from talking.

"We don't want your kind around here."

What did he mean? Cops who did their jobs—or lesbians?

"Yeah, whatever. It looks pretty bad for you right now, but you can still help yourself. Tell me who arranged your marriage with Caitlyn."

"Are you fucking crazy? I married Katie because I wanted to. You jealous, bitch? Not like anybody wants your crazy ass."

I tuned him out as the sirens sounded in the distance, thinking that whoever had started this, must have overlooked something—Paige still wanted to be with me, so whatever they'd done to her, the old life, the original, was strong enough to override some of the damage done.

❧

At the police station, I cleaned up a bit in the bathroom, realizing with grim satisfaction that I had bled more on him than on me. I gave my statement, but I was careful not to mention what I had done in that area of town, or my latest theory. I wanted to get back out there as soon as possible.

The officer who took my statement regarded me with a mix of curiosity and sympathy. I couldn't blame him.

"Are you sure you don't want to go to a hospital?"

Not in this town, I almost said.

"No, thanks, I'm fine. Just make sure you keep him this time. That should be more than enough to revoke bail."

He didn't argue, and a few minutes later I was on my way back to visit Janet Tyler. I needed answers more than ever, from whoever could give them to me.

When she opened the door to me, she stared at me in shock for almost a full minute.

"Now, come on, it's not that bad, is it?"

"What happened to you?"

"Mr. Geller, if you must know, but that's not important right now."

"Jason? Oh God. Come in, Detective. Does that mean he's finally off the streets for good?"

"For a while, at least."

"That's good. He deserves to be locked up for a long time after what he did to Caitlyn...and you, obviously."

She led me into the living room where she took a bottle and two glasses out of a cabinet. "I don't know about you, but I need a drink, and you look like you could use one too."

"Oh my God."

We both turned around at the sound of a voice. Tyler shook her head.

Caitlyn Hoyt was standing in the doorway.

❦

Detective Michael Jarrod stood in front of the two-way mirror, talking on the phone as he watched Jason Geller who was waiting for his lawyer. The man was in for a bad surprise. The high-priced law firm who had made sure his bail was set ridiculously low the first time, was out. They didn't mind defending a guy who beat up his wife, but they did have a problem with this particular one.

It seemed sudden, but Jason Geller with his violent ten-dencies had always looked good as the fall guy. One of them, anyway.

Chapter Thirteen

Paige

Now I had a bedroom separate from the kids again—that didn't mean I had more privacy. I had hoped that after everything, making it an early night meant just that. I was exhausted, and at the same time too wired to sleep, anxious about what might happen, grieving for things that were never going to happen now.

When Tom tried to kiss me, it was the worst possible moment, and of course, he had no idea what was going on in my head.

"Paige," he said. "Don't you think it's time? It's been too long. When we have another baby, it will take your mind off all the bad things."

"No." I realized with dread that I hadn't taken the pill this morning. How could I have forgotten? I never forgot.

"You know what the therapist said."

"Who is he, God?"

"Could you just try to pretend you're enjoying yourself?" Tom asked. There was a hint of impatience to his voice that I hardly ever heard, certainly not in the bedroom.

"And why would I do that?"

"Because you vowed to!"

I made as much room between us as I could in the double bed.

"Yes, I did, and maybe I was in no condition to do so. I'm sorry, Tom. I can't do this anymore."

"What the hell are you talking about? I'll make an appointment with the counselor first thing in the morning."

"I won't go. I told you I won't go back, and I will not have another baby!"

His expression was truly shocked.

"They got into your head," he whispered. "I should have never let you go to that hotel. They got to you. What did they do to you?"

"No one did anything to me, but maybe I finally woke up for real." I pushed back the covers and got out of bed, starting to pace. "I know what you did for me, how you were there for me after the accident, when I was all alone, and I'm grateful. But I stayed with you for all those years, and I think it's time to be honest. We're not happy."

If anything, the dread in his expression intensified. Tom kept trying. I didn't think he understood that there was nothing he could say to change the way things were.

"I am happy! I've always been happy with you, and our children's home is here with us. You can learn to be happy again. They can help you."

I couldn't deal with the entitlement and ignorance any longer.

"There's nothing wrong with me." That was probably debatable, but still. "I don't need help. This is the way I am."

"So, it's true? She seduced you when you were young?"

"What? No. No one seduced me. All I want is a freaking moment to myself!"

"You're a mother. You don't get to do that."

"Watch me."

I couldn't leave the house, true, but I didn't want to sleep in the same room with him tonight. I went down to the living room where I sat on the couch, feeling trapped and furious.

What did that mean? Who had told him about me and Dani?

Dani

We still stood in Janet Tyler's living room, unmoving. Even with my head hurting, I realized this could be a big break.

"Caitlyn, why?" Tyler chided softly, not happy that Caitlyn had come out of hiding.

"This is becoming crazy," Caitlyn said. "I swear, I didn't know he was going to do this. We can't hide out here any longer."

"How come you found a place to hide out here in the first place?"

The two women shared a look.

"Janet is my sister-in law. She and Jason haven't been on speaking terms for a long time. I knew I could trust her."

I waited.

Caitlyn sighed. "Part of me hoped this would all just go away, and that Jason would stop looking, but of course nothing is ever that easy. Now that they know you're on to them, they will try even harder. If I want my children to be safe, I need to speak up."

"Who are they?" I asked, oddly thrilled even though I hurt all over. It didn't matter. If there was anything to my theory, I would finally be able to save Paige.

"You'll be disappointed to hear that I can't tell you any names. You must understand that back then, I was desperate. I couldn't see a way out, and then this woman came to see me at work and asked me if she gave me a ticket to freedom, would I use it?"

She laughed bitterly. "That was my ticket, marry Jason. Ironic, wouldn't you say?"

"You never got a name?" I asked incredulously.

"I didn't ask for one. They told me that the less I knew, the safer it was for everyone. They'd make sure Christopher wouldn't find me. They set up something for the anniversary trip, and at a restaurant, they got me out. In return, I'd agree to a new therapy trial run. It was about helping victims of trauma to forget their memories completely, something that had never been done before—by therapy and surgery. Especially the last part was in the early stages of development, but I assumed they knew what they were doing." She shook her head. "I've been like in a cloud for some time, and after my first marriage, believe me, that was a blessing. I didn't forget everything—and I still ended up with Jason."

"How did you meet him?"

"We were introduced at a party. I remember Ashley and Paige were there, but I didn't know them then."

"What about their husbands, were they there too?"

"Graham was... I think Tom might have been too. It was a faculty event. Come to think of it, the therapist pushed really hard after that, said I was still young and could turn my life around, have a family. At some point I believed it. I really thought they meant well, why else would they have gotten me out of a horrible situation? And here I am, hiding from my second husband with my three children. It didn't work out so well."

"You think Jason knew about all this? That he was in on it?"

Caitlyn shrugged. "I can't really tell. He had many secrets from me."

"That is helpful though. I talked to my partner at home, and she's trying to obtain some patient files. This is not right. Someone exploited your situation for their sick experiment."

"It sounded good in theory, but at some point...The doctors were always pushing for us to have more children, and if you try to buy any form of birth control around here, they make you go to counseling. You wonder why Paige had only two? There's a black market, and we both got lucky."

That was it. I couldn't let her stay in that house for a minute longer.

"I want to find the people who did this to you, and I want them to pay. Are you going to help me?"

Caitlyn shared another look with Janet, and after a long moment, she nodded.

I had hope again, even when Caitlyn told me that I shouldn't put much hope in the local police. I had my suspicions after the way Jarrod and the FBI agents approached the case, but I still had one ace up my sleeve. They didn't count on my association with Chief Larkin. I hoped he would have news for me soon, especially when Caitlyn could prove that my theories weren't exaggerated.

Not only would I save Paige from the mockery of a marriage, we'd get to all of them who had created this bizarre situation. No wonder Brittany Dawson was grappling with guilt. They had to have something on her to get her to work for them in the first place.

We had to investigate the hospital and the school. We had to figure out what exactly had been done to these women.

"You have no idea what you're up against," Caitlyn said. "They kidnapped people and performed brain surgeries on them."

"Not all of them though."

"No. I guess they thought I was malleable enough because I wanted out. With the others...I don't know. Someone had to have watched them."

Who? What we once thought of as random incidents had clearly turned out to be a concerted effort. I kept coming back to Paige's hospital stay, the accident, and the unclear story of her and Tom. Did that accident even take place, or was it something they told her?

He had to know.

Likewise, Annette's husband Maxwell, for whom she had allegedly left Rose Kerry without a warning.

"I'll be back," I promised as I got to my feet. "For now, I think it's best not to tell anyone that I found you."

Both Janet and Caitlyn looked relieved at that.

"Jason will go down for everything he did, but I want to make sure that there's no danger for either of you. I'll be in touch."

The situation was disconcerting—I had no idea how far the reach of those shadowy people was, and they had gotten pretty far already, covering this up for over a decade. Still, I felt calm and serene with my decision. There wasn't much Tom could do. The judge had said they could live together, but that didn't mean the marriage was legal.

He opened the door to me, the annoyance in his expression quickly vanishing when he saw my face.

"What the hell happened to you?"

I didn't answer but walked straight into the living room where I found Paige on the couch, a comforter wrapped around her. I realized quickly what had happened. She had come back, but not spent the night in the marital bed.

"This ends now," I said. "You're coming with me."

Her eyes widened.

"Dani, oh my God, what happened to you?"

"I'll tell you later. I need you to get ready now."

"I thought we'd talked about this. Mia and Colin..."

"They will come with us. We'll stay in the hotel for a few more days, then we'll go home."

"Have you lost your mind?" Tom asked angrily. "What are you even still doing here? Everyone tells you to go home, and you're still trying to sell your conspiracy theories? Based on those bruises, I guess someone finally had enough."

"Tom!"

"Don't, Paige, it's okay. We'll leave in a bit. There's nothing he can do."

"I wouldn't bet on it. You have no idea. Our community doesn't work like that. We don't leave, we don't separate families."

"You'll be able to work out custody, as I assume you are Mia and Colin's father."

At this point, he might have punched me if I wasn't already looking this pitiful. I continued, "But Paige is free to go wherever she wants to. Your community can't keep her from leaving."

Something struck me as odd, this term, the community. The people were talking about it like it was some sort of club, yet there was still no visible leader I could identify.

"Do you want to come with me, Paige?"

"No, she doesn't want to. I'm calling the police if you don't—"

"I do," Paige said, her voice quiet and firm. "I want to come with you."

"Okay. You pack some things for you and the kids, you all get dressed, and we'll go."

"This is ridiculous," Tom complained.

"You and I will talk meanwhile. I need you to tell me all about the community."

He cast an incredulous look after Paige who was going up the stairs, then Tom turned back to me.

"You'll regret this. Everyone is talking about how you were obsessed, how you started this personal crusade once you found out Paige was happy here. What do you think you have to offer her? Rumor has it you were fired already."

"Well, those rumors were wrong," I said, even though the implications of his words were unsettling. I had to go home soon, talk to the lieutenant in person, and make him understand the progress we'd made. "I'm giving you a chance here. I believe you actually care about Paige. Caitlyn Hoyt wasn't so lucky when she met Jason Geller. I know you were at that party, and so were Paige, Ashley Bennett and her future husband."

"So? What does that prove? We often have these events in town."

"You didn't know Paige before the accident. There was no accident."

He cast a nervous look to the upper floor. No sign of Paige yet.

"You need to leave it alone. They might even let you get away with taking Paige, but then you have to stop."

"What did they offer you—or should I say, what did they have on you?"

"I didn't need to be bribed," he said indignantly. "I fell in love with Paige pretty much right away."

"When did you first see her?"

Tom sank into a chair, raking a hand through his hair.

"You can't tell anyone about this, ever. If my mother found out...Hell, if they did, I'd be in for more than marriage counseling."

"Who are they?"

"I don't know. They gave names like Smith, Jones...The therapist is with them, and so are some doctors at the hospital, but

I don't know for sure. Hell, I never cared, because this life was all I ever wanted. I have a good job, a home, a family. You're destroying it."

"There's nothing wrong with having those dreams. There's everything wrong with rape."

"Rape? You have no idea what you're talking about! Paige believed me. She thought there was an accident, and that I'd known her shortly before. What difference does it make now? We have two children!"

"It makes all the difference in the world." Paige stood on top of the stairs. "I only slept with you because everyone kept telling me how lucky I was to have you, and that I had no choice. Why did I ever believe them?" The tears were streaming down her face. "How could I believe them that my parents didn't want me? That I wasn't in love with a woman?"

"Because this felt right," he said. "It's natural."

"How about illegal? Paige, I'm really sorry about all this, but you see why it's not a good idea for you and the kids to stay. Other women have been tricked into marriages like this."

"No." For the first time since I had come here, I felt like Tom was actually scared. "They told me it would all work out after the surgery, and it did. I love her, and I love our children! Why do you want to destroy this?"

It turned out he had been tricked as well.

"There's nothing to destroy. Paige never had a choice in this, but she does have one now, and I believe she made it."

He shook his head.

"This will never work. They're going to come after you."

"Jason Geller already did and look where he is now. You can't scare us."

"I'm getting Mia and Colin," Paige said, turning to go back up.

Tom let us go. Fortunately, the kids were tired enough to be almost asleep on their feet.

Tomorrow, we'd have to explain to the school why we were going to take them out. I booked Paige a room like she'd had before, with two double beds. There wasn't much conversation before we retreated to our respective rooms—we were both exhausted. Tomorrow was another day.

In the morning, I laid out my strategy to Paige while Mia and Colin were busy with their breakfast.

"I'm not at all sure that Jarrod told me the truth about the medical files. I don't want you to worry either, but once we're home, I'd like you to see a doctor that's not in the pocket of these people. I swear, getting you into a safe place, finding the kids a new school, is priority now, but I need to go see a few people first. I know this is tough on you—I'm sorry. Caitlyn told me some things that sounded a lot like what Tom said, and I believe that Geller has something to add."

"So, you found her after all." Paige was surprisingly calm even after the barrage of revelations. "She was also married off to some guy they chose for her?"

"It appears so. I think the same is true for all the women we've found so far, though Caitlyn remembers more. Annette seems to have a completely false recollection of the events."

Paige shook her head. "It's like we've been living in some-body's sick fantasy. Why would they do this? Why me, or any of the women, for that matter?"

"I want to find out, but frankly, you are most important right now." That earned me a faint smile. "I mean it. I've been hitting walls from the moment I found Caitlyn's number, and it's no coincidence. Someone's trying to stall me, and I keep wondering if it even could be someone in my own department. Whatever. I'll ask a few more questions, that's all I can do. I want you to be comfortable."

"Comfortable." Paige laughed a little at that. "Do you still want *me*?"

"If you're okay with that. When you're ready," I said without hesitation.

"What if there are other women, some that we don't know about yet? I mean...I didn't have it so bad, but Caitlyn..."

It was on my mind all of the time, but for the first time, I had to admit to myself I might not be able to take it much further. I might not be able to keep my promise to Rose Kerry.

"I know. I'll do what I can, I promise."

"If I can help in any way, tell me."

I nodded. I had to give it one more try...but then I had to focus on her, just like I always had. Not for me, but to make her see that we could find a way to make up for that lost time.

"What do you think the doctor might say?" she asked.

"I'm not sure," I said honestly. "But they wanted to keep all of you healthy."

It wasn't much, but it had to be enough of a comfort until we could figure out the whole truth.

❦

To my utter surprise, Jason Geller had accepted a deal and had already been transferred. The officer at the front desk wouldn't tell me where he was, and Jarrod or the FBI agents were nowhere to be seen. Frankly, I was looking forward to going home, escaping this bizarre place where time had stopped.

Next on my list of people to see was Annette Montgomery. She opened the door, shrugged when she saw me, and went back to the living room. I saw that she was in the middle of folding an enormous pile of laundry.

"I guess you came to say goodbye," she said. "I'm sorry you had some bad experiences here."

"Oh, it wasn't all bad. I could close a couple of my own cases and help colleagues. Most of all, I was able to bring closure to a few loved ones."

She sighed. "Rose still doesn't believe that I chose this, does she? I wish she could give it a rest."

"Some of the women were tricked into marriages, possibly drugged." If there was never a car accident, why else would they keep Paige at the hospital? How had she gotten hurt after disappearing in New York? "The same could be true for you. The timeline doesn't add up. I don't know how they did it, but they gave them false memories." All of the women should undergo some tests to determine the extent of the manipulation. As long as I didn't know who was behind this bizarre project, controlling the community, I couldn't do much. "They gave the men a pile of lies as well."

"No one had to be tricked into marrying me." She sounded indignant.

"When we came by your house, you knew that your name was Annette, not Annie. You don't remember that you and Rose talked about marriage?"

To my surprise, her eyes welled up with tears.

"But it's not the right way to live. This...it's natural."

"Who told you?"

"I don't know!" she snapped. "The doctors, the reverend, people in school—everywhere. I've lived like this for years, and these are the things I remember. If you want me to turn it all upside down again, you're asking too much."

Again?

"Someone turned it all upside down before, and they were wrong to do that to you, and the others. Annette, have you been sent to therapy as well?"

She shook her head. "No, Maxwell and I never had that kind of problem. I saw a therapist a few years ago because I had lots of stress headaches. I think she still works at the hospital."

The hospital...Paige had mentioned that she'd seen a therapist as well while she was still there. If I could find another connection with Brittany, someone who could tell me more about what her role had been...It was no secret any longer why she had so much money her new employer didn't know about. This sick little experiment spanning over many years, involving brain surgery and likely, kidnapping, didn't come cheap.

"Annette, I don't think you decided to break up with Rose. I think you might have been abducted."

"But I love him! I love my children!"

"I'm not denying that. I'm saying that somebody probably intervened."

"You don't know what you're saying."

Neither of us had heard Maxwell come in. Between my experiences with Jason Geller and Tom, I braced myself for some more unpleasant communication.

"There's talk, sure, and they praise us for being a traditional family, but we never listened much to that stuff," he said. Annette didn't seem too surprised. I was.

"I have no idea about a kidnapping, but Annie was hospitalized for severe headaches several times. They were trying to find the reason for them, and we were so happy when they did."

"How do you explain Rose Kerry? Or the fact that Annette was an activist before she wound up here?"

He shrugged. "Annette didn't talk much about her life before she came here. I knew she broke up with her girlfriend. That's all, I swear." He shared an anxious look with Annette. "Sweetheart, maybe we should have talked about this before."

"How could we know?" she asked, a desperate tone to her voice. "We don't even know now. They could still take me away."

"That is entirely up to you..." I started.

"I don't mean you," Annette said. "The people who started this...If I don't fulfill my God-given potential, they could take me away."

Maxwell shook his head. "I'm not going to let that happen. Besides, with the investigation, they're cautious now. It's already out in the open."

I listened with growing dread. It was time to get Paige and her children out of here, and make a big splash, before anyone got the idea they could still contain all that information.

Had "they" made women disappear who didn't comply with their dystopian fantasy?

"Who told you about Annette?"

"I don't know, his name was Jones or something. I didn't pay attention to it much, but when we moved here, we realized that all the families in the neighborhood had a similar lifestyle. Like I said—we played along. I never thought of anyone different as unnatural."

"Then why did you stay?"

"You don't understand. We got promotions, better mortgages, a great school for our children...Many parents would make a deal with the devil to have that. I'm afraid we did."

"I can help you," I said. "I need to go back home for a bit, but I'll be back soon. In the meantime, if you have any communication, emails, paperwork...Anything that might refer to favors you have gotten, and Annette, your hospital stays."

"What does that have to do with anything?" she asked.

"They might have operated on you without your consent," I said, seeing Maxwell's eyes widen in shock.

"What?"

"I'll get back to you when I know more. In the meantime, don't tell anyone."

One more trip, and I could get Paige, Mia and Colin and take them home.

The therapist Annette had mentioned wasn't at work, but I caught the hospital's head psychiatrist between patients. He wasn't amused.

"I've talked to the police many times since this chaos started. Why do you think there's anything to add now?"

"Some things have changed. You were aware of the treatment Paige MacGregor received here."

"I read the files. I'm not a surgeon, so don't expect me to go into detail. She suffered some memory loss after the accident, was confused about what to do next, so we worked on that."

"And Annette Montgomery? Headaches? Was there a mention of surgery in her files too?"

I saw the flash of alarm before he caught himself.

"Not as far as I know. Look, I have patients waiting. I don't know what you expected to find."

The problem was, I was finding more than I could handle. After I got Paige home, it would be time to contact Chief Larkin again.

❦

Paige

Once again, I was exhausted, but too wired to sleep, too anxious about the days to come. Truth be told, I was relieved to leave Tom and the house behind, more than I could have ever thought. I'd been okay hiding out as long as the truth remained in the shadows, when I couldn't trust my own memories. Now that the pieces were coming together, I knew it was time to go.

I couldn't care less about the condescending looks the school's principal gave us when Dani and I went to pick up Colin and Mia, telling her that they weren't coming back. I was more worried about them, how they would adjust in a new environment. I wasn't going to try and keep them away from Tom. Still, all of us would have to deal with the changes. I'd have to find a job. I might find a way to go back to school, but that would be difficult, starting from scratch. I tried not to think about the fact that I'd have to see another doctor for tests, and what the results might be.

Then there was Dani, irresistible and troubling, on the other side of that door. It was kind of her to give me time until I had figured things out...When would that be? And what would happen once I came to some conclusions?

I was afraid.

Back when I was a teenager, and only recently, I had built up our relationship in my mind so much, and I worried she had done the same. What if the reality wasn't all that, what if it was no different from the boredom and resignation I'd come to feel at Tom's side?

It couldn't be.

I'd never felt with him what I felt when Dani and I kissed, that moment on the edge of something different, new, amazing. Could I do it? What if Mia and Colin were never going to be okay with this?

Tomorrow, we'd all go with Dani to where she lived, still close to the town where we had all grown up. The thought made me cry again, because I couldn't envision a happy future with Dani without acknowledging that I bought into the lies of strangers, that my parents had died not knowing whether or not I was okay.

Didn't I deserve to be happy? Or Caitlyn, and the other women?

Someone else had decided for us. Never again.

⁂

Ken Jansing stared at the photograph of his niece, a picture taken before the "incident," as he talked to the psychiatrist.

"I don't care how difficult this is. Some of us invested a lot of money in this project, and we'd hate to see all of this money go down the drain." Especially since he had been promised lots more if she was out of the picture. It looked like one person had caused a lot of trouble. He couldn't understand it. "Just one cop, and you can't handle her?"

"Her transfer is a go. I can't speak for the other families though, if they will keep quiet..."

"The other families are none of my concern. I have to be sure that none of this ever gets out. I'll take care of the rest."

"I can't promise..."

"You better," Jansing said and tapped the button to end the call. He missed the good old days when you could slam a phone. Damn those amateurs. It had been too good to be true, his niece hidden away in a community where the husband was still the head of the family, and she was busy with housekeeping and looking after her children. Living with a false name and ID, and jumbled memories. He had been slightly intrigued by the possibilities of the project, but the true reason why he'd suggested her was a lot more pragmatic.

If she ever found out that her biological grandfather had included her in his will, she could also uncover that there was a fortune waiting for her—not if Ken had any say in it though.

She had enough visits to psychiatrists and therapists under her belt by now that he might be able to bribe another one. Still, he was furious, after giving so generously to the people who wanted to create a community where women knew their place.

He wouldn't let them drag him down with them, if push came to shove, but they weren't there yet.

There was still the cop to take care of.

Chapter Fourteen

Dani

During the drive home, Colin was staring out of the window miserably while Mia was occupied with a coloring book. She was the easier one, and it came as no surprise. None of the couples in the community had openly rebelled against the rules, even though some might have believed in them more than others.

Paige was pensive as well, and for now, I decided not to disturb any of them in their musings. I had a lot on my mind, too.

When I left home, I did it for the faint chance of a clue. Now I knew where those women were, if not who had taken them and placed them into a very particular situation. Maybe I'd never have all the answers, but I knew I needed to get whatever I knew out in the open, tell the story loudly, so Caitlyn could come out of hiding, and Annette and Maxwell could decide what to do next without fear. I had to talk to Rose too, try to explain what I didn't yet fully understand.

I wished I could have some quiet uninterrupted time with Paige, but of course that was near impossible right now. I had to keep my promise, give her time.

We also had to eat, and to keep things simple, I had invited all of us to my parents tonight. I had warned them about my run-in with a criminal and asked them not to say anything in front of Paige.

The moment of our arrival was much more emotional than I imagined. I never knew how aware they were of the impact Paige's disappearance had on me and my subsequent life. They hugged me, then her, and greeted the children in a way that was a lot less awkward than I had ever been able to.

"It's good to see you, Paige," Dad said. "We're happy you're all right."

Mom nodded.

"This is incredible. I'm glad you're all here. There's a bathroom to the left, and one upstairs if you'd like to freshen up a bit. I've got some appetizers and a glass of wine ready for you. Well, I guess you two don't like wine." She crouched in front of Mia and Colin who both looked intrigued. "Apple juice? Coke?"

I breathed a sigh of relief. After juggling so many obligations in the past few days, it was good to leave some minor decisions up to Mom and Dad.

"We can't stay too long."

"Oh, but you're not going to drive out to your apartment tonight? We prepared the guestrooms for you."

So that was settled too. Finally, something was going right.

⁂

I excused myself later to call Viola, the call going to voicemail, and a reporter I had worked with on numerous occasions. She'd be thrilled to hear about the story—of course she already knew about the women, but I could give her more, information and theory. We scheduled a meeting, and I was about to end the call when Mom walked into the kitchen.

"Are you okay?" she asked softly. "I know we're not supposed to mention it, but..."

"I am. Sorry, I didn't mean to scare you. One of the women there was in a domestic violence situation, and the guy didn't appreciate me intervening. He's in jail now. And Paige, she's okay."

"What a miracle," she said, and I didn't think she meant it in a religious sense. You didn't have to be religious to call it that. Then again, good old-fashioned detective work had led us there as well.

"Yeah."

"I heard a little bit about it in the news. I was surprised they didn't talk about it more, but...I'm even more surprised about those well-behaved children in my living room. I remember Paige was quite adamant about having a career before even considering kids."

"People change," I said vaguely, wondering how much she had really guessed. Alice had been over many times, even when we were already in college. She might have mentioned something about Paige, I didn't know.

"They do. How is Alice doing?"

Truth be told, I didn't have much time to think about her after she accused me of past indecent conduct. "Better, I guess. We all are."

"And Lois?" she asked softly.

"Lois and I aren't together anymore. I always knew...Most people couldn't handle this, me." I poured myself another glass of wine. "I don't know what would have happened if I hadn't found her." I shrugged. "I guess I would have kept looking."

"But you did find her. Are you..." She let her words trail off, obviously unsure how to ask the question.

"I don't know," I said honestly. "Paige has been through a lot. I...I haven't talked about it a lot, but people have been interfering with the investigation at every turn. There's still so much to figure out, but I'm running out of vacation time, and frankly, I'm tired."

"You found her. That's the most important thing right now. I'm sure everyone agrees you deserve a break."

My vision blurred a bit at that. It was true. I found her. Now I had to make sure that no one could take her away.

The next day, we conferred over breakfast what to do next. I called my GP to make an appointment, to get started. I would go with Paige and explain the situation, and we'd take it from there.

Paige would have to do some research to get the kids back into school. We had a couple of more weeks until the summer vacation. Certainly, everyone would understand the special circumstances we were dealing with, but she needed to get them in somewhere.

I had to go back to work. I was going to meet with Charlie Scott, the reporter who was hoping to break the biggest story of her life.

There was a lot to consider.

Mom offered to come with us and help Paige with the school issue. I saw Mia's eyes lighten up. At least there was no complaint from Colin, so we left later that morning.

Paige held me back at the door. I was almost expecting her to tell me to cancel on Charlie.

"Tell her everything we know," she said. "Everything."

"Thank you. It's important for all of you to be safe. Once the truth is out there, they can't hurt any of you."

She nodded. "I will help you in any way I can. If you need me to talk to her, I will."

So that was settled. She stepped forward and kissed me. "I'm so grateful for your parents welcoming us like that. They barely know me."

"They know I care about you," I said, brushing my fingers over her cheek. Would we ever have that moment to ourselves? And when would that be?

Scott was ecstatic about the material I brought her, if flabbergasted—and outraged.

"It's incredible that this was even possible, right under our noses. What were they trying to build, the good old days?" I thought of Annette who wanted to stay with her husband and children, regardless of the fact that Rose was still waiting for her. Caitlyn, going from one bad situation to the next. And Paige. *My* Paige.

"It looks that way, and it seems like some people pumped a lot of money into it. It's some crass and brazen way of conversion therapy as well, so it might be worth looking into the usual suspects."

"Why aren't you?" Charlie asked.

"I exhausted all my resources." And myself. "I don't know who exactly the culprit is, but someone has been throwing obstacles in my way. The local police may be involved. I don't know, at this point I'm even wary of my lieutenant's various attempts to call me home. The latter, I don't want to see in print."

"All right, all right. I'll send you the article for your approval anyway. Jones or Smith, huh? They weren't very original."

"They were clever, though. I am certain that they were somehow involved in Dawson's death, and that they sent Geller after me. I want this out in the open. There's not much more I can do unless we find what's in the encrypted files."

She looked a bit doubtful. "It's a lot, I'll give you that, but much of it is still speculation. I'll do what I can with it."

"It will stir up something, I promise you."

⁓

I had brief conversations with Rose Kerry and Caitlyn. Rose was disappointed, as I'd expected, Caitlyn cautious.

"This will work out," I said. "Once it's public, you'll be safe to be out in the open. You won't have to worry about Jason."

Next on my list was finding Viola whom I still couldn't reach. First, I went to the department, intent on telling the lieutenant I was going to come back to work.

"Frankly, that's earlier than I expected. I'm glad. What changed your mind?"

"I didn't, really. I'm shifting my priorities. Paige MacGregor chose to come with me, and after we go public, the other women will be safe too. By the way, did Viola take time off? I can't reach her."

"Detective Marsh isn't working for this department any longer," he said. "She asked for a transfer. Don't look so shocked, Ryder. Since you started your crusade, we are under constant scrutiny. This needs to stop. You call that reporter and tell him he can't print the article."

"Charlie Scott is a woman. And that's not possible!"

What was Viola thinking? Had somebody pressured her?

"Oh, it certainly is. If you refuse to stand down and do your job for once, I won't have a choice. If I see any bizarre conspiracy theories in the paper tomorrow, you'll be fired."

I didn't need any more proof.

"Why, is it because you have something to lose yourself, lieutenant?"

"Be careful," he warned. "You still have options at this point. You could lose them very soon."

"Why did Detective Marsh leave?"

"You'll have to ask her. She put in the request, and I approved it."

"This isn't over yet. I have friends in the department as well."

I didn't wait any longer. I left his office and returned to my desk from where I called Chief Larkin. His secretary put me on hold, and I did some impatient doodles on a piece of paper.

"I can put you through to Chief Larkin now," the secretary said.

"Yes, thank you."

"Danielle, what can I do for you?"

I didn't waste any time.

"Have you found out anything about the task force?"

"I would have called you. I asked my guys to look into it, but they seem legit. Look, is it possible that you were taking this too personally?"

"What? No! They practically denied every clue we found, and I bet you there is no news on the fake IDs."

"Those weren't high school kids, from what I understand." His tone was soft and gentle.

"That's my point. Professionals did this, and someone should try to find them, hold them accountable. That's our job."

"I understand. I promise, I will let you know if I hear anything. For now, I'm sorry, but I have to let you go."

I hadn't even told him about the article, or that I might not have a job anymore come tomorrow—but at least I still had a friend I could count on.

Charlie sent me the article later that day, and I approved it, knowing well that the lieutenant might make good on his promise. I came home, deciding that I wouldn't tell Paige or Mom about the threats. They might try to change my mind.

Mom and Paige had made progress and found a couple of schools that were willing to take in Mia and Colin after the summer vacation. Everything would be okay. I tried to tell myself that, but I still felt antsy, the numerous warnings ringing in my head.

⁂

Paige

I was incredibly grateful that Dani's mother had helped me with the school applications. I hadn't been to their house often when I was younger, because Alice was more Dani's friend than I had been. They were still as friendly and welcoming as I remembered, and especially now, that did a lot of good for me.

Only a couple of days until I'd see the doctor. She would make recommendations to further assess my situation.

We finally made it to Dani's apartment, calling it a night soon after take-out dinner. Mia and Colin were asleep in the guestroom, and I was wide awake on the couch in the living room. Dani had offered me her bed numerous times, but I felt too bad about chasing her from her bedroom. She had already risked so much because of me—I thought it wasn't fair to rob her of a good night's sleep on top of it.

My thoughts kept circling around her though, drawn to her in a way I couldn't and didn't want to stop.

I was in love with her, had been for a long time. What was it really worth, that feeling, or my fake marriage to a man I had mostly tolerated?

What the hell was I waiting for?

I doubted that the article would change so much—our names had been out there since the press got wind of Caitlyn's case. I had no more excuses, just my own fears.

Tom and I had had sex before with the kids in the house—and it was nothing I wanted to think about right now.

I wasn't even sure if sex was what I needed at the moment. I needed her, to be close to her.

I got up, tiptoed across the room and the hall to her bedroom, opened the door carefully. The room was dark, only a sliver of moonlight coming through the half-closed blinds. Dani was asleep, her back to me. I went closer, lifting the sheet and slipped underneath, thrilled, worried. There was no reason for the latter. She had made it pretty clear that she was interested, and given the fact that I was no longer underage, she had no reason to step back once more—or did she? I snuggled closer, delighted by the warmth of her body against mine. I reached out with a trembling hand to trace my fingers down her arm, and, emboldened by hope and attraction, leaned forward to kiss the back of her neck.

"Paige." Her tone was warm, inviting, hopeful too. That was better than *What the hell are you doing?* Not that I had much of an idea, or experience. I just knew that this was what I wanted, what I had wanted for a long time—and I knew she felt the same. I slipped my hand underneath her tank top, reveling in the feel of soft, warm skin. It all came rushing back to me, dreams I'd had, fantasies about being with a woman. In some way, I still felt like the teenager I'd been, unsure but pretending the opposite—but this was different. I was a grown woman. I could make my own decisions, even if for years, they'd been taken out of my hands.

Dani drew a sharp breath when I brushed my fingers over her nipples, cupping her breasts gently.

"Are you sure?"

"Please, don't ask me that another time." I didn't want to think about what would happen tomorrow, or in the next week. The time when all my days had been the same, cleaning up after the kids or Tom, trying to be what was expected of me, was over. No one could tell me what to do anymore.

"Okay," she said, a smile in her voice. I could feel her relax against me, and so I resumed my explorations, my heart hammering, knowing that my earlier fears were unfounded. Nothing had ever felt like this. I'd never felt this urgency being with Tom. This wasn't just something to pass the time—I couldn't turn back from this, ever.

I brushed my fingers over the fabric of her slip, causing a delightful shiver. I wasn't quite sure how it happened, but the next moment I found myself on my back, with her on top of me. I couldn't stop the sounds even before she touched me, before we lost our clothes in quick impatient movements, the feel of warm skin a relief and a tease.

"You'll always be safe with me," she whispered. "I love you."

Of all the promises that people had made to me over the years, this was the one I believed. I knew it to be true.

I might have been confused for a long time, but my body wasn't. The pleasure was almost overwhelming, until it was...I had always known that this was where I belonged, with her.

Everything else would be coming together easily, right?

Chapter Fifteen

Dani

I had fallen asleep with Paige in my arms, naked, a smile on her face. I woke up alone. Since we still had a lot of work to do in order to wrap up the loose ends of the decade long mystery, I didn't make too much of it, not when every fiber of my body was still alive with the memory of last night.

I had expected her to be shy or hesitant maybe, ready to let her dictate the pace—it turned out Paige was passionate, and eager to make up for what we had lost, no hesitation. She'd been spelling each of her fantasies, with lips and fingertips, on my body. I couldn't wait until we had the chance to do it again, but first, we needed to get to work. I had to see what the fallout from Charlie's article would be, and if I still had a job. After putting on my PJ shorts and tank top, I checked my phone, startled at almost a hundred messages. I'd have to get to them later. Some things were more important.

Paige was in the kitchen, fully dressed. She was wearing an apron, standing over a pan of eggs, and another with bacon. There was a fresh pot of coffee. Not the worst way to start the day.

I remembered being in awe of New York City as a younger woman, as if all the colors and sensations were intensified. All of that was gone the moment Paige went missing, and the world turned bland and gray.

Now, the colors were back.

I stepped behind her to kiss the back of her neck. "Good morning."

"Hey."

She didn't move away until we heard the sound of footsteps, giving me an apologetic smile when Mia walked in, rubbing her eyes.

"Sit down, Mia. Where's your brother?"

"He wanted to sleep longer," Mia said. "Are we going to stay here? Colin says he wants to go home."

"We're going to stay here for a little while," Paige told her. "You and Colin are going to another school next fall, remember?" She fixed a plate for the girl.

"It's going to be fun," I said. "It's an adventure." Even Mia had noticed the awkwardness, and her answering smile was much too adult for my taste. These were Paige's children, and I'd find a way to be okay with them. I knew I needed to. I just couldn't get over the fact, not yet, that she never had a choice when it came to having them.

"Will you be okay on your own for a bit?" I asked. "You don't have to clean up, I can do that later. Maybe you'd like to take the kids to the park, or for an ice cream…" I realized I had never even asked her about her financial situation, too eager to take care of everything. We would have to figure out something. If we could get to the people who started this sick experiment, we might be able to get some restoration for the women and their children, and she could go back to school if she wanted to. There was still so much to talk about, to figure out—but she was here, and she wanted to be here. That was all that mattered at the moment.

"I'll be fine. Don't worry. I just might have to think of something creative to get Colin out of bed."

"Good luck with that. I'll check in with you as soon as I can."

I hugged her, and to my relief, she hugged me back tightly. Mia was focused on her breakfast—she didn't seem to mind. I had the feeling Colin would be harder to convince, but I had other things to think about first.

On my way to meet Charlie, I drove past Viola's house, startled that there were no more drapes in the windows. The front porch was empty, and there was a For Sale sign in the front yard. That was quick, and more than odd. I still couldn't reach her on her cell phone. What happened?

I found Charlie in the small café, looking depressed as she was nursing her latte. She was wearing tinted glasses, and a baseball cap. I didn't make the connection until she shook her head and said, "I'd rather have a shot of rum in it, but I can't be seen in public drinking for breakfast. Wow. I didn't see that one coming."

"What do you mean?" I asked, bracing myself for something bad...Viola's sudden transfer couldn't be a coincidence.

"We broke the story last night. This morning, we were called into a meeting. Turns out, the paper was sold recently—none of us knew anything about it. The paper's new owners who said they had no use for us any longer—me, the editor, the photographer, we are all unemployed as to a few hours ago."

"What?"

"My reaction exactly. You stirred up some powerful shit, and there are people who aren't happy about it. It's obvious that they want to kill the story."

"What are you going to do?"

"Well, I'm not going to lie down and take it," she said.

"I'm with you, of course, whatever you need. I'll let you know if I find out anything else, and Paige will talk to you."

She nodded. "That won't give me my job back, but maybe I can still clear my name. This is just so odd. It never happened before, with any story. Someone decided to take control overnight."

"Do you know who's behind this?"

"If I did, would I still be sitting here? I'd like to talk to Paige. What's your next step?"

"I'll talk to my lieutenant. I want some answers."

"Be careful," she said somberly. "There are some people who didn't want this story to get out."

"It's too late though."

"Sure, but they always can call us hysterical and over-zealous."

"Many women went missing, six of them turning up in this dystopian fantasy—and we know there was a little over a dozen more that we haven't been able to find in the neighborhood, from Brittany's files."

Charlie leaned back in her chair. "Too bad we can't ask her."

"They won't be able to put the genie back into the bottle. My partner was transferred after I asked her to check something for me. The lieutenant must know where I can find her."

"Maybe you should stop asking people for a favor for a while," she suggested. "I'm sorry. This story is bigger than we thought. We have to find out who's behind this."

"We will, don't worry."

The lieutenant was furious, even more so than when I had taken time off to follow the lead on Caitlyn Hoyt. He was a cop, for Christ's sake. Had he been bought? How could he think it was okay to leave a woman in a bad situation like this—and the others?

"Frankly, I don't get it. Aren't we supposed to catch the bad guys? You'd be okay with abandoning Caitlyn and the other women?"

"I thought I made myself clear."

"Unfortunately, yes. You don't want me to do my job."

"That's enough, Ryder. It's over. You no longer work for this department."

"You're firing me? I can't say I'm surprised. I wonder who *you* are working for. The city, the people…That's clearly not it."

"Be careful," he warned. "You have no idea what you're doing. You can't follow simple orders. You're a liability for your colleagues."

"You mean Viola?" A horrifying thought sprang to mind. What if they had done more than just mess with her career? It all started with Brittany's case. She had taken her own life, and we still could only guess why.

"Where is she?"

"It would be better for both of you if you didn't contact her right now."

"Why? Is she even still alive, or did someone make another convenient suicide happen?" I didn't miss the flash of alarm in his expression. "You know about all this, don't you? I figured as much. You tried to keep me on a tight leash, and when that didn't work, you fired me. You're going to try and discredit me the way the paper's new owners are doing with their employees?"

"I don't know anything about that," he said, impatient. "Detective Marsh made a decision that benefitted her career, and frankly, it's not good for anybody's career to be associated with your name right now."

"So, you're more worried about your career than you are about the women who were kidnapped and practically sold into illegal marriages?"

He shook his head. "It wasn't like that. They were doing okay."

"What happened to you? You know I could go to IA over that, and I'll probably have to. I'm not going to accept this."

"You better. Otherwise, I cannot guarantee what's going to happen next."

"Is that a threat?" I asked incredulously. "I can't believe this." I spun around to leave. I was almost at the door when he said, "Detective Ryder, you have to understand. I have a family."

"Well," I said, turning to him, "I have one now, too. Excuse me."

"Is that so, Detective?"

His tone sounded surprisingly bitter. Or maybe I shouldn't have been surprised. I had met enough criminals who felt entitled, offended by the fact a woman had exposed them…This should have been different though. I had worked for this man almost seven years. I couldn't believe he was dirty, but it was becoming harder to deny that.

"Is Mrs. Bond your family now, or couldn't you live with the choices she made for herself?"

Oh God. Talk about bad surprises. Was I about to learn that my supervisor was a homophobe too?

"Talk to me," I said. "Maybe I can help you."

He actually laughed at that.

"Clear out your desk, Ryder. If you want to enjoy life with that new family of yours, I advise you to let it go."

"Or what?"

"Go!" he snapped, so I did, walking to my desk in a haze of disbelief. This was where it was all going to end? I had always known I was ready to make sacrifices, if only Paige turned out to be okay. This wasn't a necessary one. I could still do my job. His decision wasn't a legitimate one by any means—there was too much evidence.

I opened the top drawer of my desk with a key. There were still the results from the face recognition software, the women who had matched Brittany's photo folder. I frowned at the bent edge of the folder—this was certainly not how I'd left it. The photos were still inside, along with a sim card. Where did it come from? I always locked that drawer. Something told me I needed to know what was on the card, and I didn't want to use my computer for it. I'd have to go home and find out.

I tried to call Chief Larkin on my cell again. This time, the secretary told me he wasn't in, and he hadn't told her when he'd be back.

Later. I wanted to know what was on this card.

❦

Paige

When I took Dani's advice and went to the park two blocks away with Colin and Mia, I had no idea there would be reporters already, sticking microphones in my face. I had a story to tell all right, but I wasn't sure what Dani had agreed on with her friend. I held on tightly to my kids' hands and repeated "no comment" over and over again.

Finally, I made it to a café not far from Dani's apartment where I sat them down in a corner booth and counted the cash I had left. I wouldn't make it far on that, but it was enough for ice cream and a coffee.

I was shaken by my encounter with the journalists who had so many questions. Would they think of me as a fraud or a coward, because I didn't have all the answers? Because I had left the community to be with Dani?

I was in love with her, more than ever before, but I was also aware that this could be the biggest challenge of my life. It hadn't been all that hard to be an obedient housewife, because there was nothing I needed to decide. At the same time, it had been slowly driving me crazy, especially lately. I needed to find my way out of this. For my children. For myself.

I needed to tell that story.

I hoped the reporter, Scott, would still be interested in meeting me. This could be the catharsis I'd been hoping for...and then I could maybe start to explain to Mia and Colin why I couldn't stay with their father any longer.

I could stop feeling guilty, and angry, and take charge of my life.

❦

Dani

I'd ask Charlie to come by later, but first I needed to have a moment with Paige. It became even more important when I noticed the small group of reporters huddled near the entrance of my apartment building. I hoped they hadn't harassed her—I was well aware that even with everything that had happened between us, she was still vulnerable, her connection to her new reality perhaps not as firm yet...I had to be careful with every step. I had to do my best to protect her, and at the same time, she was right: We couldn't let go yet. Annette Montgomery might choose to stay with her husband freely, but the others might not. I was also curious as to what happened to Jason Geller, if someone had used him as a diversion. He wasn't on my priority list though.

When I opened the door, Paige walked into my embrace, leaning into me even though Mia and Colin were sitting at the dining table. The boy regarded us curiously, though in the past days, he had become less hostile.

"We're going to draw lots of attention," Paige said.

So she'd had a run-in with the reporters after all.

"I'm sorry. I didn't know they'd jump on it right away."

"Well, it's been a story for a while now. I'd much rather tell it on my own terms. What if we ask Charlie here? And take a trip to the community?"

"I don't know. Charlie will be happy to talk to you, but most people in the community weren't so open..."

She cast a look at her children a few feet away. "Let me speak with them first. They will have something to say. Hell, we didn't know we spent over a decade in a prison, trapped in our own minds."

I knew she was talking about the surgery and intense manipulation before and after, their psychological impact—but there were even more tangible crimes that had been committed.

"You were trapped in more than one way," I said. "You were kidnapped and held hostage. They're going to pay for it, and they know it, so they will try whatever they can." I went to sit down with her in the living area. "Viola and Charlie already lost their jobs over it." Well...technically I had too. "Lieutenant Thorne fired me today."

"What? Can he do that?"

"I will fight it, don't worry. I believe he's involved too. I think I found new evidence, but I'm wondering if it wouldn't be better if you and the kids stayed at my parents' for a bit. Just until we can put some of those people away."

"And when will that be?" Paige shook her head. "You looked for me all those years. You never gave up on me. I'm with you now. I want to know the truth as much as you—if not more. It's my brain they messed with."

"Okay. I understand. Come join me in my office for a moment?"

She followed me, and after I'd closed the door behind us, we kissed hungrily, a tad desperately.

"Still sure?" I asked, unable to keep the smile out of my voice. I didn't have a lot of time for them, but I'd had some lingering doubts.

Paige smiled too. "Don't get me wrong, life is still pretty confusing these days. But I remember you. I remember I wanted you. Now I know why...Did that sound bad? Of course, that's not the only reason, but last night was wonderful."

"I think so too."

I finally produced the card I had found clearing out my desk and put it into my computer. I had seen the files before, in their encrypted state, but now the gibberish of numbers and letters had been transformed into words, sentences and graphics. I couldn't help staring. Brittany Dawson's secrets, unraveled one by one.

Viola had to have left them with me. Where was she? Somewhere safe, I hoped. She could take care of herself, but we'd never been up against anything like this.

I opened one of the files, realizing it was indeed a patient file, containing their development from intake to release. Some of it had obviously been written by Brittany, judging from the surgical jargon, other parts were from the psychiatrists and attending physicians. I recognized names of people I had spoken to at the hospital.

I was pretty sure Brittany wasn't supposed to have that in her private possession.

It was everything. Now the letters and numbers I had found on lists earlier made sense—this was how the files were grouped.

The term "guided confabulation" caught my eye. I took a deep breath, angry, frustrated. Who was responsible for this madness?

Next to me, Paige was quiet when I opened her file after a moment of hesitation. There it was, her story, the real one—point of contact: New York City, July 31st, 2003. Diagnosis: Undesirable sexual orientation. Guided confabulation: Negligent parents, conflict with friends, boyfriend. Recommendation via: Ken Jansing.

"What the hell is this?" Paige asked, angry tears in her voice. "Who the hell is Ken Jansing, and why is my sexual orientation any of his concern?"

The name rang a bell, somehow, but I couldn't put my finger on it.

"Let's find out," I said, and typed him into the internet search engine. It only took a few seconds to turn up several pictures of the businessman, smiling and shaking hands with celebrities, politicians and...damn. I hadn't expected this. Jansing with Chief Larkin at a fundraiser. It didn't have to mean anything. He met with lots of high-profile folks—but at least I might be able to carefully ask about Jansing, if Larkin's secretary ever put me through.

"What are we going to do with all of this?" Paige asked. She sounded overwhelmed. I was too.

"One step at a time. Let's call Charlie and see what she thinks about visiting the community."

⁂

After hanging up with Charlie, we continued reading. It appeared that we'd been right about Caitlyn's story—she had tried to get away from Christopher Hoyt, accepted an offer that seemed too good to be true, and ended up with Geller.

Paige's file didn't detail how she had broken her leg, but it did prove that there had never been a car accident. They grabbed her in New York and drove her away to the hospital where she had been "treated" subsequently. I felt furious, and helpless at the same time. What was it with those people playing God? They had drugged her, kept her under for long periods at a time. What else?

"I woke up with my leg in a cast," she said. "They did that."

Not to mention a completely unnecessary brain surgery. Up until now, I had reserved some sympathy for Brittany, but she was a criminal like the rest of them. Once this information got out, heads would roll for real. The husbands might be able to cut deals if they came forward.

What a nightmare.

I'd be able to prove to Annette that she had indeed been kidnapped, taken from that hiking trip, her mind manipulated into thinking the life in that cookie cutter neighborhood was all she'd ever dreamed of. Her situation was only more complicated by the fact that she still claimed to love her husband...Who could really tell if it was true, or the result of someone creating an alternative story, and stimulating her brain so she would believe it?

Her father's name was mentioned in the "recommended" section. He had thought of her sexual orientation as "undesirable" as well. Margaret's story was similar, only a former colleague had recommended her. After her disappearance, he had bought her now thriving business, go figure.

There were more files, of women from the picture folder that we had not yet found. They were either offered a way out of a bad situation, or "recommended" by somebody—all of them were expected to live the lifestyle, docile women, obedient to their husbands, having a number of children. No contraceptives were allowed. If a couple hadn't had children in a while, mandatory counseling was their only option. The therapists had only one job—bring them back on track. I'd been right to assume they wanted to keep the women healthy, though they didn't mind causing confusion. The files didn't say anything about surgeries gone wrong. I felt sick at the thought of what could have been, and what we still might uncover.

The Amnesia Project, as this dystopia was titled, aimed to bring back simpler times, where everyone knew their place, and life hadn't been complicated by the liberal agenda and the PC police. At this point, I wanted to throw something, or punch someone.

I didn't have the time. We still had to figure out why Ken Jansing had unleashed this nightmare on Paige and her family, on all of us.

The doorbell rang. Charlie had arrived. Before I went to answer her, I pulled Paige close to me.

"We'll get through this," I promised her. Of course, we would. We had survived worse.

Charlie was excited about the development. "This is gold," she said. "Together with Paige's statement, and if I can get some of the others, we'll nail them."

"I like that idea. The sooner we get our jobs back, the better."

"Yeah, even though this won't be easy. Have you heard the Chief's statement today?"

"What do you mean?" I asked, feeling uneasy. He had encouraged me over almost a decade. He was going to look into the task force for me...

"Wait, I'll find it for you." She searched for the video on her phone, then held the device out to me. I could hardly believe what I was hearing.

"Detective Ryder has been under enormous stress during the last years. The disappearance of her friend was a traumatic experience, and finding her was too, in a way. She did not approve

of the lifestyle choices the women made, and because of that, she went too far. I am sorry to hear that her supervisor had to let her go, and I hope she'll be able to move on." A reporter asked him about the false IDs.

"You have to understand the cases vary, but the FBI is making good progress on finding out who is behind these IDs. At this point, the women are safe and living a life of their choice. We should respect that. Thank you."

I was dumbstruck. How could I have trusted in this man?

"You were focused on one thing," Charlie said softly. "Plus, he delivered the lieutenant to you as a likely suspect."

"Thorne knows something, too."

"Yeah, all those people know something to some degree...if Jansing and Larkin knew each other, maybe we should go right there."

"This could cost us more than a job," I warned her.

"The truth needs to come out."

"I agree," Paige said. "I lost thirteen years of my life. Someday, I'll have to explain all of this to my children, that we, that our family, were part of an experiment I never consented to. I want those people held accountable, all of them."

"Let's do it, then," Charlie said. "We'll go back to the community, get a statement from each of the women, confront them with this new evidence and get their consent to put it out on the internet. There is no turning back."

"You can have mine right now."

I felt slightly more optimistic, and a tad wistful. Alice, Joy, and I had been close friends like this once, certain that no one and nothing could tear us apart. We all had lost something, but now, we had the ultimate chance to make it right.

Everyone responsible in this would pay.

Chapter Sixteen

Paige

I was oddly excited to go back to the old neighborhood, as a visitor. Charlie had slept on the couch and never questioned the fact that I went to share Dani's bed. Nothing happened that night, except that in her arms, I had the best night's sleep in forever. Mia and Colin would be excited too. I hoped Tom would make time to see them—as much as I blamed him for his part in this misery, he was still their father, which meant he had some responsibility for their well-being. We would explain things to them when the time was right.

For now, all I wanted was for the people involved to tell the truth—that they had kidnapped and assaulted women from all over the country in order to create their sick, twisted idea of the ideal society, *Stepford Wives* and *The Handmaid's Tale* wrapped into one deluded fantasy.

I had never been in a condition to consent to any of it, marrying Tom at the age of seventeen, having two children, not more only by the grace of Doreen and her black market birth control pills. Charlie would likely be interested in talking to her as well. We would get to the bottom of this, all of it, and Ken Jansing, whoever the rich entitled asshole was, would apologize to me and the others.

Maybe I was still dreaming.

In any case, we woke up early, and I got the kids ready for the road trip.

"Are we going to see Dad?" Colin asked.

"It's possible."

In the old days, I was told never to show up at his work unless there was an emergency, but I didn't feel bound by the rules of the community any longer. Hell, we weren't even legally married. He had married Peggy, a person who didn't exist, a character in a play written by some mad scientists.

I had left the stage. My life was my own now.

We were almost ready to leave when Dani's phone rang.

I could tell from the way her expression changed instantly that it was serious. No surprise there. Charlie had put up a video including my records from the encrypted files last night, and it had gotten thousands of hits in those few hours. Somebody was bound to react.

"It's Viola," she said. "I have to meet her right away. You go without me—I'll meet up with you later today."

I didn't like this, and she sensed my hesitation.

"You can trust Charlie. The sooner you get started, the better. I'll join you as soon as I can."

"Is it going to be dangerous?"

Dani kissed me softly. "I don't know."

I wished she hadn't been so honest with me at that moment.

"Okay," I said, clapping my hands, forcing a smile. "Who's ready for a road trip?"

Dani

Viola's call came at the worst possible time, but of course, I couldn't ignore her. I needed to hear the whole story, and together we had to figure out how to protect her too. I felt guilty for involving her in this in the first place—then again, the constant resistance of other colleagues might be messing with my mind. We were police officers. What else should we have done?

This was our job. Once all was said and done, I was going to have a long talk with IA so they could find out who else had been complicit in the kidnapping of these women.

Recommended. Tammy Grey's husband was still MIA with the daughter—gaining sole custody had been his goal. Maybe she was actually better off with the new husband, though did they really think she could forget about her first child?

I was still stunned by the blatant disregard for those women's lives and their choices. They made them lab rats, experimenting on humans without their consent to create a community, and then, society, of their choice.

People involved in the school board, the hospital, clergy and the police. Maybe, FBI even. It was outrageous how they had abused their power, but all of this would come to light bit by bit.

The address Viola had given me was on the outskirts of town. She had said to hurry, and that she wouldn't be able to stay long. I doubted Lieutenant Thorne's explanation of a transfer—she sounded more like she was on the run. So many lives ruined. No more.

I was determined.

I drove through a suburban neighborhood, stores and restaurants sparse though it wasn't by far as bad as the almost identical houses in the "community." I wondered if the architects and contractors who had built those houses knew what they would be used for. At this point, I didn't consider anything impossible. I had to drive around the block a couple of times to find 7 Columbus Street. When I checked my watch, it was barely after seven. I could still join Paige and Charlie before noon—maybe I should ask Viola to come with me. As long as we were all together, we were probably safer. I got out of the car and walked up to the front door of the small bungalow. No one had followed me. I hoped we could make this quick.

She opened the door before I could ring the bell.

"Viola! I'm so glad we can finally talk." We didn't hug often, but I assumed the circumstances warranted a gesture of affection. I was so glad she was okay.

"I am so sorry," she whispered.

I didn't realize what she meant until Chief Larkin stepped out of the room to the left. He was holding a gun on us.

"I'm sorry," Viola said again. "They found me."

Chapter Seventeen

Paige

Everything would be fine. I kept repeating that mantra in my mind as we neared the community, though it didn't take. I had no reason to be so antsy. Mia and Colin were behaving, Charlie was easy to talk to, and even if the other women didn't want to get involved, I could give her plenty of material.

Dani would join us in a few hours. Of course she would—right? That phone call worried me. Maybe I was paranoid, and for sure, I couldn't be suspicious of the woman who had been her friend and partner for years...At this point, anyone could be involved. We didn't know. Wasn't it better to be safe than sorry?

Then again, Viola's career was on the line, like Charlie's and Dani's—because of me. Not just me, but my story certainly played a part in that. I should trust them to know what steps to take next, as I was in no condition to do that planning myself.

I leaned back in my seat, wondering what I could do with my life after all of this.

Dani was certain that once the responsible parties were arrested, we could get a settlement out of them. After all, there had to be some serious money in this "experiment." But how long would that take? Did I really want to go back to school and be one of the oldest students? Once upon a time I had been certain. I had made plans, thinking that an education would save me, would help me save the world. I hadn't been able to save one single person.

Instead, I had accepted all the lies they had told me for over a decade, let my family and my friends down.

Would Dani come to the same conclusion at some point?

I couldn't worry about that now.

I had to find a way to convince Ashley and the others to join me. Piece of cake.

***

Ashley offered us a piece of cake and coffee. Since it had been a few hours since breakfast, we gladly accepted. The conversation went a lot easier than we had expected.

"I will tell you my story all right," she said darkly. "They gave us so much trouble because we couldn't have children, me, mostly, as if I wasn't blaming myself already. I'm glad we could adopt the twins, and they finally backed off, harassed the other women instead. That sounds bad. Of course, the others didn't deserve it either. I just needed a break so much."

"What do you want to do?" I asked, already jealous at the thought that someone else could have specific plans.

She shrugged. "I'm going back to work, I guess. Graham and I decided to separate."

I didn't know if that was good or bad news to her, so I waited.

"He didn't know that I was a minor when we got married. I'm not sure how much that counts anymore, but it hit him hard. He says it's not right, and so we should take our time to figure out what we want. They took away my choices and destroyed the only good thing that came out of it."

"I'm sorry about that," Charlie said. "Thank you for talking to us. We'll lure them all out, and someone is going to pay."

Ashley looked doubtful. "They've done this for at least a decade. They must have had time to prepare, have their people infiltrate institutions. What makes you think they won't continue to get away with it now?"

Because they couldn't. Because they had taken away too much from all of us already...and because Dani had promised. I believed her.

We went to Annette Montgomery's house where we found her over a couple of open suitcases.

"Detective Ryder isn't here with you? I believe she would be happy to see this," she said matter-of-factly.

"Why is that?" I asked.

"I'm leaving my husband, all right? It was all too much in the end. And no, I don't think there's going to be a romantic happy ending with Rose. What were you all thinking? I'm pregnant. Even if she was still interested, I can't put that on her. That's not the life she chose."

I could relate to that, uncomfortably so. But Dani had spent thirteen years of her life looking for me. We could be a family.

"She knows what happened, that you didn't have a choice in the matter either. Your children will understand when they are old enough. What matters to them is that you stand by them." I looked over to Colin and Mia who were sitting quietly in the corner with Annette's youngest who wasn't in school yet. Would they understand? So far, they hadn't asked too many questions. I assumed they would come at some point. I was nowhere near ready. "All I know is that we have to speak out. We have to be on the record so that nothing like this ever happens again."

"You can print what I say, but...never again?" She laughed bitterly. "Worse things happen every day. Look at Caitlyn. I guess we were lucky, considering."

That was one way to look at it.

⁂

Dani

"I didn't want to believe it," I said. "I guess I was just really naïve to think you were too smart to be involved in something like this."

Larkin laughed.

"I'm sorry, but you got it all wrong. It's the smart thing to do, at least it was before you went a little overboard with all your conspiracy theories. Involving the press? That was not a good move, but at least we have the chance to contain it now."

"By killing me?" At this point, I was still more irritated than afraid. I might have been in denial. He seemed amused at the suggestion.

"I don't plan on killing you, Danielle, at least not if I can avoid it. Come on in. I assume you have many questions. Detective Marsh here and I will do our best to answer them."

I shot her an incredulous look, and she shook her head.

"I swear I didn't know about any of this until the results from the encrypted files came back. The chief himself made sure that I was let go, but I managed to plant the sim card in your desk."

"All the information is now available to the press, some of it is already online. A reporter and Ms. MacGregor are talking to the other women as we speak. There is no turning back."

"Oh, you would be surprised," he said. "Sit."

With his gun still trained on me, I had no choice. I was beginning to worry. Paige might realize something was wrong if I didn't join them soon, but what could she do? There was no one left we could trust.

"All right, humor me. Why would a man I considered to be fairly intelligent be involved in an experiment evoking the good old times?"

"Fairly intelligent? Oh, that hurts. You said it though—those actually were good times. Women claimed their place in the house, as mothers and wives. They had time to take care of the children and didn't take jobs from hard-working men. I remember such a time, you know."

I was going to throw up.

"And you got together with a bunch of other nostalgic Neanderthals," I mused.

"Oh Danielle, can we stop it already with the name-calling? This is one of the most important experiments in human history. People have tried many different things in gay conversion therapy, but they didn't have the funding or the guts to go all the way."

"You did," I said, angry at myself because I never saw this coming. All those years, Larkin encouraging me to forge a career instead of a crusade, had been the sexist homophobic jackass sitting across from me—and an excellent actor. Something else came to mind—all of the women we knew to have been kidnapped or bribed into the experiment, were white. No surprise there. The unholy trinity, sexism, racism, homophobia...you rarely found one without the others.

"We did all right. We got them all, the best and the brightest, surgeons, psychiatrists, and a few actors as well. Not all of them were easily convinced, but most of the time, we found something to get them there. Everyone has a price."

"Brittany Dawson wanted to adopt a child with her wife," I said.

"Oh yes, bleeding heart Brittany. If she didn't kill herself, I might have shot her for being so careless with sensitive information. You shouldn't have ever gotten to Caitlyn Hoyt."

"But when I did, Jason Geller became your scapegoat."

"Didn't he make a great one? Keeping the focus on Caitlyn for a while, one unlucky woman, trading one asshole husband for the next. It happens. Nothing shady there."

"Except we had a bunch of asshole husbands marrying underage girls."

He shrugged. "It's not like they were children. It's good for women to have children earlier, and you saw all the beautiful children in the community. Too bad you did whatever you could to ruin their lives."

I didn't bother to argue. I cast a quick sideways look to Viola, but she was looking away.

"What are you planning for me if you don't want to kill me? I'm not going to keep quiet about this. The public has a right to know. I'm sure quite a bit of taxpayer money went into this as well."

"You would be surprised," Larkin said. "We had parents, husbands and relatives who were quite eager to get their wayward women into the program."

"Ken Jansing. What was his problem with the MacGregors?"

"Don't get me started on Ken, he's become a real nuisance. He couldn't wait to have his niece out of the picture so he could claim the family heritage."

"What? Paige's parents weren't rich."

"Oh, they were. She didn't exactly luck out with her adoptive parents, or her biological uncle."

I sat, absorbing all of this for a moment. Jensing was Paige's uncle, related to her biological parents. He'd wanted her gone.

"I don't understand. Where were her parents in all of this, and why didn't it ever come up in the original investigation?"

His smile made me shudder. "You never stop asking questions, do you? Here's a story for you: Paige's mother got pregnant very young, the father was out of the picture right after he learned about the pregnancy. Paige's grandfather, who had amassed a fortune, made his daughter put the baby up for adoption. Later, he had regrets and wrote Paige into the will. Tragically, both of Paige's biological parents died young, and so Paige was the only one standing between Ken and this incredible wealth. He really couldn't care less about the belief system we built this on, but he was a generous donor, so we couldn't say no, could we?"

"This is disgusting."

Viola finally held my gaze for a split-second. Larkin was just a few feet away, his hand around the revolver relaxing. Between the two of us, we might be able to overpower him. He hadn't searched me yet.

"You might think so, but for other people, you are part of the problem and always have been. At least these women found the righteous, natural path."

"They were forced to undergo brain surgery! And no matter what Dawson and other doctors did to them, the memories still came back. Interesting, isn't it? There was something stronger than all the manipulation you exposed them to."

"You mean like true love? Now you're just silly. Some responded better than others. MacGregor is confused. She might see you as an easy way out right now, but what do you think is going to happen to the children? You think they're going to accept you as their dad?"

"That's just ridiculous—and none of your concern."

"Well, in any case, it was nice chatting with you, but I'm afraid we have to move now."

He turned towards the door.

Viola and I both moved at the same time. I pointed my gun at him, as he spun around and shot her. She'd been close enough for her blood to spill on my shirt.

"Don't even think about it," he warned. The act was gone, and all I could see was a ruthless psychopath. "She might make it, but not if you cause any more trouble."

The front door opened, and the next moment four men trained their rifles on me.

"You have to help her!"

"Yeah, sure, you do that," Larkin said with a shrug. "We might still have use for her. As for Detective Ryder here...everything as planned."

Within seconds, I found myself face down on the floor. Somebody wrenched my arms behind my back and cuffed my wrists. Larkin crouched next to me, a smile on his face as he produced the syringe. "We've indulged you for a long time, but that's over now. It's about time that we introduce you to the merits of our extraordinary project."

❧

Paige

"Why isn't Dani coming?" Mia asked.

"Maybe she's never coming back," Colin mused out loud. If they hadn't been children, I might have shaken them, as their words reinforced the nagging worry.

We had retreated to a diner with Caitlyn, Terri, and Margaret.

Charlie kept collecting their stories. I was grateful that this was happening, but at the same time, I found it hard to concentrate, finding dubious comfort in sugar and caffeine. The only reason why I thought I could do this, go public and let everyone dissect what had been my life of the past thirteen years, a life that seemed to vanish like reality had before, was that I counted on her to be by my side. Just like she'd always been, even if I hadn't known when I was despairing over my dull and yet challenging days—when I was thinking of things to tell the counselor, embarrassed about the questions I knew he would ask. I hoped they would arrest him too, the creepy voyeur.

It was late in the afternoon.

I was going crazy with the growing fear...no, really, maybe I was going crazy.

"She'll be here soon," Charlie said, but she didn't sound or look too convinced.

Chapter Eighteen

Dani

I didn't know how much time had passed when I woke up, dizzy and disoriented, in a hospital bed. My instinct was to jolt upwards, but I was held down by wide leather restraints. Even the small movement they allowed caused a blinding headache to flare. The room blurred before my eyes. After an endless moment, my vision sharpened again.

This time, body and mind didn't waste any time reminding me that I was in a pretty desperate situation.

"Danielle. Good to have you with us," Larkin said. "I'd like to explain a bit more of your future to you."

"Viola?" I rasped. I thought I might actually be sick, remembering the scene, her blood on my hands. Some kind soul had washed them...wait. I was wearing a hospital gown. Someone had put that on me.

"She'll pull through. I told you, we only employ the best and the brightest."

"You're not going to get away with this."

"You think? I believe we've come pretty far, and whatever you were trying to do, the experiment will continue. Did you really think those six you turned up were our only subjects? Wouldn't be worth the cost for the counterfeiter who made the passports."

I wasn't much surprised, though the thought was depressing. Even more so, knowing he was telling me all these things because he didn't expect me to get out of this alive.

"What's...the plan?"

"For now, I believe you're just fine in this bed. Like your colleague, you asked for a transfer far away, too embarrassed about all the crazy shit you stirred up. Paige will surely find comfort in her husband's arms. You were so curious about this, you should experience it first-hand. And don't worry, after you've healed, we'll find you a good husband too."

"You are crazy!"

"You'll never be able to understand the genius behind this. It's a good thing you don't have to worry about it any longer, isn't it?"

He patted my cheek and then turned to leave the room.

It took me a moment to realize it wasn't the bed that was shaking. It was me.

~

Paige

At nine-thirty, Colin and Mia were both sleeping in the backseat. Charlie had all her interviews, and she had uploaded parts of them already. An hour later, someone had flagged them, and they were taken down, only to reappear within a short time. We were going viral. People were astonished and disgusted by the extent of the project.

At the moment, I couldn't care less about any of this.

"I don't want to stay in the hotel. We have to go back."

"And do what?" Charlie asked. "Dani said she'd come here. She got held up. Maybe Detective Marsh knows more than she imagined, or Dani had to take measures to keep her safe. She will be here soon."

"What if she isn't coming? We need to—" Report her missing. I nearly slapped my hand against my mouth. Was that how everyone had felt when I disappeared without a trace in New York City?

"Let's go to the hotel and regroup, okay?"

I wanted to shake her. How could she be so calm?

"We can make a video. They can't be so bold to take her, but if they did, we'll send them a message."

I thought about this for a moment.

"I think I have a better idea."

When I told her the address, her eyes widened. "Are you sure? It's kinda late."

"Yeah, so? He owes me. I'm going to collect."

"All right. Let's go."

At five to ten, we were ringing the doorbell, two scared adults and two exhausted children.

My pretend husband looked at us with an expression somewhere between astonishment and exasperation.

"Really?"

Colin was completely awake now, jumping with joy. "Daddy!"

Mia sleepily followed into the hug.

"I need to talk to you."

"I'm surprised," he said, but stepped back so we could come inside the house. "I thought everything was already on the internet."

"Don't," I warned. "Can the kids go to their rooms for a bit, maybe take a few books or toys?"

"At this point, does it matter if you take any more? Go," he addressed them. "Your mom and I have some things to talk about. When we're done, we'll call you and there might be some ice cream."

I bit my tongue. I wasn't happy with scolding him nor loading Mia and Colin up with sugar, but I needed them out of the room for a bit.

I needed to act, or the fear would overwhelm me.

"Have you been contacted lately? By the people who came up with this crazy idea in the first place?"

"Peg...Paige," he said, impatient. "You know it wasn't all bad. If you don't have anything else to say, please leave. And who's this? Your cop friend didn't stick around?"

"She's the only one who never gave up on me in thirteen years and you know it. I need your help. You owe it to me."

Charlie looked on with interest.

Tom shook his head. "I can't imagine how or why you came up with all this. What is this about? I thought you were enjoying the spotlight."

"This is not just about me, and you know it. The truth has to come out either way. Dani is gone, and we have reason to believe—"

He turned away as he spoke. "If that's the case, I'm very sorry, but I don't know how I could help you. I don't know how to contact these people. The last time, they came to me."

"What about Ken Jansing?"

Tom faced us, surprise in his expression. "You met him?"

"No, I haven't, but I know he's involved, just like Dani's boss. What can you tell me about him?"

"He came by once, a few months ago, to see how you were doing. Before you start, I didn't know he was funding a huge part of the project."

"How can we find him? Can you call him?"

"At this time of night? You must be—"

"Call him and tell him we'll come over. Then call Millicent and ask her to watch the kids. Charlie will stay here, and I'll come with you. Do it already!" I yelled at him, and for a moment, it felt really good. Tom didn't have a temper, but I knew I had a right to my anger nonetheless. He had manipulated me into a life I hadn't chosen. It was about time he paid his dues.

"He's a donor. I doubt he can tell you much about...All right. I'll call him."

Charlie and I waited as he made the call.

"Good evening, Ken. It's Thomas. What I—yes, I know it's late. It's kind of an emergency. What about Danielle Ryder? Is she going to be a problem?" He looked puzzled for a moment. "Yes, I understand. Can you meet me there? Thank you."

Ending the call, he said, "I don't think it's a good idea for you to come."

"He 'recommended' me, and he seems to know where Dani is. So, yes, this man has a lot to answer for, and no, I'm not afraid of him."

"You should be. He's loaded. He can make all of us disappear if he wants to. I...I don't want you to get hurt."

"It's a little late for that, don't you think?"

He had the good grace to look self-conscious at that.

"Okay, you can come, but I want you to be careful. Those people are unpredictable."

I almost laughed, but then I might have cried, so I aborted the impulse.

<hr />

All those years I had wondered what might be happening to Paige. Chief Larkin hadn't lied to me this time: I was experiencing it, with the exception that now, I knew who they were. I knew I couldn't let fear cloud my mind, but it was hard not to give in to the lure of it. The drugs in my system didn't help.

I sure was scared of what they could do, and what they had callously done to many women before. They wouldn't succeed, right?

Because I'd always remember Paige, and that I loved her.

Except that for years, she had tried to live as Peggy Bond, wife of Thomas Bond, because they had manipulated her into thinking that had been her plan all along. This was different. They couldn't possibly think that they could do the same with me, now that I knew...

A shudder wracked my body as realization sank in. They could do a lot more. Playing with a person's brain had consequences, and I might wake up unable to speak or walk...or remember anything.

No.

They couldn't win.

I refused to believe in a world where these rich men could behave like spoilt brats all through their lives, a world where Paige and I would only have this small window, just a moment of our own.

Not fair.

Not possible.

Paige

"We know that the initiators of The Amnesia Project bribed and threatened high-ranking officials to get their way. We know

some of you thought it was wrong, and if you are among those, now is the time to come forward."

While sitting next to Tom in the car, I was watching Charlie's latest video. She was clear and precise, calm, convincing. Her voice broke through the haze of panic that threatened to engulf me every time I imagined what they might want Dani for—or if they had already killed her.

I couldn't allow myself to think that way. I didn't make it out of my dull, not to mention illegal, marriage only to have the person I loved taken away from me so soon.

"We're here," Tom said, resignation in his tone. "Remember, this is the guy who made them aware of you in the first place. You walk over that threshold, I'm not sure I can protect you."

"You said that before," I said, even though my heart was hammering. "I'm ready."

"Good. Let's go."

A woman, probably the housekeeper, opened the door to us. I hated this man already before I'd even first seen him in person. Why me? Why had he decided I should be a subject in this sick experiment?

When he finally came to greet us, I recognized him from the pictures Dani and I had looked up—otherwise he was a complete stranger to me.

"My dear niece," he said and stepped forward to embrace me. For a few seconds I froze, unable to react or process what he'd said. Then I disengaged myself from the unwelcome hug and slapped him.

"You son of a bitch!"

Niece? What did he mean? Did it matter anymore?

"I'm not responsible for her manners any longer," Tom said, and I wanted to slap him too. I nearly did, but I had bigger fish to fry at the moment.

Ken Jansing laughed, amused by my reaction.

"That's how you greet me after all these years? I'm hurt."

"You had me kidnapped and sold into a marriage I never wanted," I said sharply. Tom flinched. I was grateful he'd brought me here, but I couldn't muster much sympathy for him otherwise.

"Yeah, that. You could have done worse, don't you think? You were young. I thought you could be convinced to get on the right path. Seeing how all of this is ending, I guess I was wrong. If it makes you feel any better, they screwed me over too."

"About that," Tom said. "How about you help us, and we help you get back at them?"

I couldn't care less. He was behind all this, had given them money to make me disappear, and played a cruel game with my parents—but I had to hold back my questions until we had found Dani.

"That's why you come here in the middle of the night? Oh come on, Tom, you know my lawyers will take care of that. They will crush them if they must."

"I don't know, they have been pretty clever too. You've been playing that game with them long enough to know, so...You might want an ace up your sleeve."

He studied me curiously. "Did you tell him to say that? Last time I checked, Tommy here doesn't do much unless he's told. What ace are you talking about?"

"Danielle Ryder," Tom said. "Look, we both got something to lose in this, and we've both been betrayed by those people who promised a 100% perfect result."

I cringed. They were talking about me. Stubborn, resistant, if for a long time only in my mind, I hadn't turned out like they expected.

"Let's get her and let her finish her crusade. The thing is, she cares about Paige a great deal. We'll be the ones helping, taking down the monster. We walk away, but all the doctors, cops, clergy and whoever else was involved, take the fall."

It was a deal too good to refuse, right? I wasn't at all sure if Dani and I agreed to letting him go, but we could always come back to that. For now, I needed her to be safe.

"You're quite clever," Jansing said. "Your mom and your grandfather would have been proud of you."

I had many more questions, as this obviously related to my adoption as a baby. Now wasn't the time. Ken Jansing was not a decent man, but for the moment, he was our best bet to free Dani.

Talk about a deal with the devil.

"I'll see what I can do," he said.

❦

Dani

The chief came back with a doctor who put something into my IV line that turned my arms and legs into jelly within minutes.

"Can't risk you running away," Larkin mused as he undid the leather restraints. "We think that you really deserve this, after trying so hard to solve the mystery. We'll show you around and explain everything before your surgery, because after that...you never know."

He helped me into the wheelchair the doctor had brought, the touch making my skin crawl.

"You're going to do...surgery on Viola as well?"

"She had hers already, but not what you think. The bullet only did some minor damage. She's recovering. Let's give you a tour now."

Out of the room, he wheeled me along a hallway and into a spacious elevator. "Let's take it from the top, shall we?"

I wanted to run all right, scream, but I could neither move nor get enough air into my lungs for the latter. In any case, I'd get an idea of the layout of the place—if it wasn't too late already.

No. Paige would return the favor. She'd be looking for me, and she wouldn't give up, even with fewer resources available to her. When the elevator doors opened, I was introduced to a spectacular view from the conference room, a huge glass wall allowing me to see into the room and beyond. The lights of the city were amazing.

"This is where we hold meetings," the doctor explained unnecessarily. He was mid-forties, a pretty type who could have played a doctor on TV. He seemed unimpressed by my predicament or the role he played in it. "The project manager only comes to the important ones, most of the time it's the assistant project managers and their staff to update the local community leaders. As you've noticed, Ms. Ryder, we have successfully inserted loyal members of our group in schools, the health department and law enforcement. This is important to keep things running. On the floor below, people do the vetting work—find doctors and psychiatrists, surgeons, specialists, and find out how we can convince them to work for us."

"You threaten them," I finally said. "I assume Brittany Dawson's death put a lot of pressure on many?"

"Oh yes, that was a terrible loss for us. She was a genius with the scalpel."

I couldn't help but shudder.

"Well, we still have good staff, and you don't have to worry. All of them are brilliant neurosurgeons. You're in good hands. I understand that in most cases, it's just about stimulating certain areas. Sensations combined with the guided confabulation manifests the new memory."

That was frightening and insane enough. Fortunately, it hadn't always worked in the way those evil genii had predicted. I had another question though.

"Why?"

"Here's someone who can explain it better than any of us," Larkin said, turning to the man in the white coat who had just exited one of the offices.

"Dr. Carlson, if you have a moment. Ms. Ryder—"

"Detective."

"Detective Ryder, then," the chief acknowledged, as if it was optional, "has some questions for you. In fact, she asked the ultimate one. Why try to implement such a brilliant idea in a time that has long been hijacked by the liberal agenda?"

"Well, miss, it's true what the chief is saying. Too much has been taken from us. And we're taking it back."

"Taking what back from whom?"

I wasn't stupid. I had always known men like that existed, feeling deserving of more than their share—I was interested in how he would justify himself. This was way beyond a misogynist joke made in a bar, or even a right-wing politician ramming through his policies.

"I know you think of this as an affront on your free will."

"Well, for one, I'm not here of my own free will," I reminded him.

"We don't harm women. We give them a chance to develop their full potential," Dr. Carlson insisted. "Those women were happy before you ripped them from their families. See, you might enjoy sex with other women and even fool yourself into thinking that you were somehow born that way, but you're trying to go against nature."

"They were so happy that most of them needed counseling."

I had always thought of sexists on a scale from irritating to dangerous, but this individual was certifiable.

241

"Danielle, deep down inside you want to be normal. We will help you, so you no longer need to fight the impulse."

"What I really want is a cold beer and a burger with fries. And all of you in a straitjacket."

I wouldn't go down easily. That, I promised myself, and Paige.

Chapter Nineteen

Paige

We were back at the hotel—not that sleep was any option for me. Ken Jansing had insisted that we couldn't visit the facility now without raising suspicion.

We had a plan: I would ask to talk to the project manager about my case, on how to reverse some of the "damage" to the program my life on the outside had caused—pretending I wanted to go back to Tom. Hopefully, it would be enough of a distraction to get to Dani.

It was a bad plan. They could try to capture me again and do only God knew what to me. I didn't trust Ken. I didn't know if I could trust Tom, but I had to do something.

Together with Charlie and Caitlyn, we regrouped at my old home. I had briefly snuck into Colin and Mia's rooms and kissed them goodnight, then thanked Millicent who had spent the night in the guest room. Given the situation, she was going to stay a little while longer—and she had gone through a surprising evolution as well.

Unable to sleep, I got up around 4:30 to make coffee, and she joined me in the kitchen.

"It's early. You could sleep a little while longer."

She laughed wryly. "I don't know, I don't think anyone's sleeping in this house. Your reporter friend is preparing a new video...For a long time, I didn't want to believe any of this could be true. I thought you were just stubborn, not knowing how much of a good thing you had."

"It could have been worse. Caitlyn was mistreated. Tom never did that, and he's helping me now."

Grudgingly, but yes, he did. He'd be playing along with the getting back together lie.

Caitlyn and Charlie would be our backup. We didn't even have a location yet.

"Did you ever love him?" she asked wistfully.

That was a hard question because I had no easy answer for her.

"I care enough for him to know we can't be together. He'll find someone new, who actually chooses him."

"I'll be here to take care of the kids as long as you need me," she said. "God, I was so angry at you, at times, and then at him when it all came out. How could he let those people talk him into something he knew wasn't right? I'm all for big families, but you can't force that on women anymore."

"No, you can't," I agreed. "That's why we must bring this to an end."

"I hope you can."

Me too.

Dani

The tour continued, and at the end of it, I was privy to almost all of The Amnesia Project's secrets—I assumed there might be a few left, but that wasn't really important any more. A bunch of mostly old men, some younger, had banded together to make sure their vision of the world would continue to exist. They were scared to death of the prospect of complete equality for women.

They created a time machine through bribery, extortion, and threats, and put together a team of genii to guide the women they chose through the process. All of the women were young and white, some of them had previously come out, much to the chagrin of a family member.

Ken Jansing, Paige's uncle, didn't give a damn about Paige's sexual orientation. He simply wanted her out of the way, and TAP was as good as any solution for that.

"Your surgery will be tomorrow," Chief Larkin said once we were back in my room. "Don't worry about anything. We'll give you a new life, and you'll have a lot more to show for than in your old one.

I had to think, and fast, which wasn't easy with the drugs muddling my mind. At least, the feeling in my arms and legs seemed to be back to almost normal. Seeing what this beast had been able to do over decades—not just the chief, but the collective band of well-funded criminals—was terrifying. It was also motivating. I probably had one last chance.

"Chief, can I talk to you for a second?"

"I don't see why not." He certainly didn't feel threatened by a woman tied to a hospital bed. He was a trained officer of the law after all, carrying a gun.

"Thank you," I said after the doctor and psychiatrist had left. "I just hoped to clear everything between us. Tomorrow, everything will change." How I was able to talk to him without showing my hate for him, I didn't know. They had done this to Paige, lied and lied, falsified documents—all in their self-righteous quest for a society that celebrated patriarchy instead of exposing and overcoming its hypocrisy and the harm it did.

"That is true. What else do we need to clear?"

"I learned a lot from you." That wasn't a lie. For the rest of my life, I'd be wary about trusting male authority. All those years he had seemed like a benevolent uncle, offering pep talks that brought me back from the verge of obsession...reining in the leash, was more like it.

"You are welcome, Danielle. Given where we are now, I wish I had done better."

"Oh, you did a great job pulling the wool over my eyes for a long time. That's over now. The doctor might think this is part of the program, but let's be honest. If anything goes wrong tomorrow, no one will care. I might still end up dead, or trapped, because that would be the easier solution for all of you."

He didn't confirm nor deny.

"I'd like to go to the chapel. There is a chapel in here, right? I think you owe me that."

My suggestion put an awkward embarrassed smile on his face. I knew the chief came from a family where it was mandatory to be visible in church.

"I didn't know you prayed," he said eventually.

"Yeah, about that. I didn't use to, but I started when a bunch of maniacs kidnapped my best friend's sister."

Larkin pondered this for a long, nail-biting moment.

"All right, why not. Let's pray for the best possible outcome, that all goes well tomorrow."

"Thank you," I said again.

"You're welcome, Danielle. I'm glad you're making your peace with the inevitable."

"I don't see much of a choice."

Paige

Jansing had kept his promise and managed to get us into the facility. We were all sitting in Dr. Carlson's office, the psychiatrist I remembered from my early days in the clinic. I had to stay calm and friendly with the people who had stolen a big part of my life in order to save Dani—and make a deal with the devil. I still didn't understand what Jansing had to gain from forcing me into the program, but I assumed those questions could still be answered later.

I was terrified to be in a place where people had so callously ignored my basic human rights, but there was no alternative. We weren't able to see the project manager, but Dr. Carlson had agreed to see us.

"So, we've come to the conclusion it would be best for our family to get back together," I said, ending my pitch. "I was hoping you could help us to find our path again."

The bastard didn't even look surprised. He was counting on all of us being so confused by our real authentic lives that we would come crawling back. I could have told him that the women waiting for us outside, and I, had no such intention. We were angry.

"We will certainly do everything we can to help you. I see you've had counseling sessions already, but maybe that won't be enough. Over the past five, six years, we have built several retreats for couples and individuals. I'll have to clear it with the project manager, but I believe you'd be eligible."

I shared a look with Tom who seemed to be just as surprised about this. It was just getting worse. If those wasted hours with the counselor were any indication, I could just imagine what a retreat like that would look like. I knew that some women in the community drank when they could get their hands on alcohol, or used pills other than birth control, to fight the ever-present guilt. How come you aren't pregnant? Aren't you having relations with your husband? It was worse when women took part in the scheme. I had instinctively known that there was something wrong with these people, but still, for a too long time, they managed to trick me into believing that something might be wrong with me.

This wasn't about me. I wouldn't leave here without Dani.

"Tell me more about the retreats."

Chapter Twenty

Dani

Just as I had imagined, the chief helped me back into the wheelchair and brought me to the chapel where I struggled to my knees in the pew. I might have exaggerated the struggle a bit. He stood next to the pew, waiting. I wouldn't go as far as asking him to join in—I didn't think he had a prayer for me. I was determined not to let him touch my mind or my brain, him or any of his rich bored cronies.

I folded my hands and leaned forward, centering my thoughts, focusing.

Please, Paige, forgive me if this doesn't work out. I hoped she would find her way, that she would find solace in the companionship of other women who had been through the same. That all those doctors, cops, clergy and whoever else had been involved, would have their asses thrown into jail, and that they'd pay to those women for the rest of their sorry lives. Amen.

"What the—"

When I slid down to the floor, Larkin reached out to help me up. My fate was decided within seconds. I reached for his gun and pulled the trigger once. His grip vanished, and I got to my feet and ran, his angry scream following me.

My next steps were crucial. I had to get out of here, but I wasn't likely to achieve that goal in a hospital gown. Earlier, during my tour, I had seen a couple of supply closets. I had to get to one of them, get some scrubs and find my way out.

Piece of cake.

I heard voices and footsteps on the other end of the corridor and ducked into a doorway. Fortunately, they weren't coming my way. I made it to the closet unseen, and quickly donned scrubs and hid my hair under a cap. I didn't have shoes, obviously, but I put disposable shoe covers over my feet. There was no saying how much time I had, a few minutes maybe, more if Larkin was seriously injured. No one knew that he had taken me to the chapel.

I had to get to a phone and get the police in here, call Charlie too in case the whole police department of this town was corrupt and in the hands of the community.

I almost made it, but when I walked past the office door left ajar and heard the agitated voices inside, I couldn't leave.

Paige

"You can't do this. You can't—"

I could tell Tom was uneasy with the turn of events, but I wasn't sure he was brave enough to intervene.

"Please, calm down, Mrs. Bond," Carlson said. "It's better we start calling you that again, right? Don't you worry. We'll undo all the damage easily, and you won't even remember."

"The public already knows. You won't get away with it this time."

"Gentlemen," Carlson said, getting to his feet, "I thank you for your cooperation."

"Don't screw it up this time," Jansing muttered, getting up as well. Tom hesitated.

"Please, Mr. Bond, I have to ask you to leave too. The reorientation is not easy for our test subjects, and your wife has had lots of exposure to damaging influences. I might have to call in some help..."

"No." I wouldn't let them do this to me all over again, not a chance.

"I agree with Ms. MacGregor. Your sick little experiment is over. You let her go. You—Carlson, get away from that desk. I assume you have a gun in there."

I just stared at the apparition in front of me, Dani, wearing scrubs, including the cap and shoe covers.

It was probably too early for knee-buckling relief, but I couldn't help it.

"Miss Ryder," Carlson said, his voice dripping with condescendence. "I believe it would be a good idea to move up your surgery to tonight. You can't think you'll get away with this."

"No." Tom stood finally up. "No more of this. It's not working. You gave us all that bullshit about how this is supposed to be good and natural? You made us marry women who tolerated us at best."

I wasn't sure what that meant exactly, but I couldn't feel sorry for him either.

"What do we do?" he asked Dani who kept the gun trained on Jansing and Carlson.

"Do you have your cell phone with you? Call 911. Paige, call Charlie."

251

I was just beginning to relate the story to her in a breathless, rapid pace when the alarm sounded.

"What is this?" Dani asked sharply.

Carlson laughed. "Whatever you did to get out of that bed, someone has noticed. The building is under lockdown. Neither of you is going to get out of here anytime soon. Mr. Jansing, I'm sorry for the inconvenience."

───

Dani

I had made the right decision. In my mind, there were no doubts. The police were on their way here, and I hoped that there would be strength in numbers, and the statements of Charlie, Paige and Viola, who was hopefully near and recovering, would help my case. Thomas Bond had finally made up his mind about which side he wanted to be on. Fortunately, for the sake of his children, he had made the right decision too, and most likely, he would get away unscathed. I still resented him for even thinking for a minute that his decisions hadn't been harmful to Paige. As long as we had to make sure the story would be told correctly, I could work with him.

I caught Paige's gaze on me, and I wanted nothing more but to hold her close. Of course, we couldn't do this in front of the two men who were still gloating, because they couldn't think of a world where they would ever have to concede—regardless of the fact that I was the one with the gun.

I realized that my hand was trembling, just barely, but I noticed. I could tell from Paige's worried look that she had noticed it too. Had she ever fired a gun before? Had Tom?

I supposed with the lockdown, we were at least safe from Larkin.

I was so tired, but this close to the finish line, I couldn't give up, could I?

"Please, Danielle, give up. When security comes in here, it will be best for all of us if they don't see you with a gun, right? If the worst possible happens, how do you think she will ever get over it—the woman you claim you love?"

I knew he was going to try and get the gun, but he never had the chance as the next moment, the door opened, and several armed officers streamed inside—one of them was familiar. I held my breath as I recognized the female FBI agent from the task force, one of many people who had told me to let it go.

It seemed like Carlson recognized her too.

"Agent, finally."

She shook her head, her expression disgusted. "It's the end of the road, Doctor. Detective Ryder, I believe we will have some important matters to discuss."

"Larkin?" I asked.

"He's in custody. He'll need some patching up, but he'll be behind bars soon. We'll move Detective Marsh to a hospital that is not run by these clowns."

"I'm not sure I understand..."

"Frankly, I wasn't sure what was going on at first," she said. "But too many people tried to block this investigation, and I realized why. We'll talk later."

"Of course."

Paige gave me a small smile. Jansing and Carlson all but spat at us when they were led out of the room.

"Thanks for your help," I said to Tom, and turned to Paige. Her face was the last thing I saw before the world turned grey, and then pitch black.

Paige

I'm not proud to admit that for a moment, I panicked.

"Dani!"

I was by her side and on my knees within seconds, and fortunately, she came to even before the paramedics made it into the room.

"It's okay. Don't be scared."

I was scared, if a little less than a few minutes ago. I didn't have the words to even begin to express what I was feeling. All I could do was hold her hand while the tears kept streaming down my face. I felt so much regret for what we'd lost, and at the same time, gratitude that we were getting this second—or third—chance.

Tom left with one of the cops. I stayed while the paramedics tended to Dani.

"Ms. MacGregor?"

It took me a moment to realize one of them had addressed me.

"I'm fine," I said quickly. "They drugged her. Please, just make sure she's okay."

"Another hospital? Damn." Dani was quickly getting back to her old self. "I was hoping I could avoid that."

"I'll come with you. And I'll find out about Viola."

"The police will want to talk to you."

"Indeed, but we know where to find you."

I realized the FBI agent both Dani and Jansing had recognized was still in the room. "We will talk to your ex-husband,

and we'll see you at the hospital later. It's important we get the details from everyone before we find them online."

If there was some mild scolding in her words, I didn't care or mind. As long as they didn't try to separate me from Dani any longer, I'd be okay. We'd be okay. I wiped my face while Dani, back on her feet, argued with the paramedics.

"Come on guys, not a stretcher. I can walk just fine."

We finally made it outside and into the ambulance. I took her hand again, and this time, I didn't let go until we arrived.

⁓

I waited for Dani to get settled and then left the room while they ran some tests on her. I checked in with Millicent who assured me everything was fine with Colin and Mia. Tom had called her too.

With everything else out of our hands for the moment, I waited until I was allowed back into Dani's room. There would be no results in the immediate future, but given the plans the doctors had with her, I was hopeful that they hadn't changed their MO much. The first phase had been to keep us under for long periods of time to confuse us. Then, surgery. I shuddered at the thought that this might have happened to Dani.

I was likely to cry some more before the night was over.

For the moment, I was happy to have some privacy with her. I wasted no time, slipped out of my shoes and lay down beside her.

"The agent, and I assume, Charlie, are going to bother us soon," she said with a sigh. "How are you?"

"I'm not the one who fainted."

"I didn't faint." There was some heartfelt indignation in her tone, making me laugh. I was so grateful this little episode was most likely harmless. It was hard to trust anymore. I was likely to struggle with this for years to come, and that was not a pretty thought. She tightened her fingers around mine as if reading my mind.

"All right then. Viola is doing okay. Yes, the agent said she'd come back, but I think they'll be busy arresting people all through the night. This, they won't get out of."

"Good."

We were both silent for a moment, grappling with the magnitude of what had happened in the past few weeks.

"All of them owe you a lot. It might be some time though, before any of it is decided in court."

"Yeah, I know. I have to get up off my ass and get myself a job."

"Not tonight. Maybe never. Hey." She leaned in to kiss me before I could ask what she'd meant, and continued. "You'll stay with me, right? For Colin and Mia, we figured it all out for next semester. We just might need a bigger apartment."

I was very much okay with not making any more major decisions over night.

"I love you," I said. "I want to be with you. It's what I always wanted."

"I love you too. Once we're—"

The knock on the door interrupted her, and Charlie, in the company of the FBI agent, walked in, reminding us that there was a lot of work to do before we could ride off into the sunset—or something like that.

Chapter
Twenty-One

Dani

Over the next few hours, we learned even more astonishing truths. The agent shared with us that she'd become increasingly suspicious when every member of the task force was told to push a certain line, keep me out of the loop as much as possible.

"I'm sorry for testing you too, but I had to know whom I could trust," she said.

"I understand. It wasn't easy to figure out."

For sure, it wasn't. Lieutenant Thorne had been blackmailed, Larkin was one of the founders of the project together with Carlson and the yet to be identified project manager. I thought of something.

"Please, make sure Geller doesn't get to cut a deal. He doesn't know anything, at least not more than the other husbands who are willing to talk. They just wanted him to go away to make it look like Caitlyn's was an isolated case of domestic abuse."

Paige had sat up when Charlie and the agent came in, but she still sat close enough that I could feel her shudder. Her story was terrible enough. We both knew it could have been so much worse.

"Will do. There's one more thing..." Her apologetic tone made me wonder if she had bad news to share. "We found Gloria, the nurse that was part of the problem."

"That's good, right? She can corroborate a big part of the story?"

"I'm afraid that won't be possible," the agent said. "She died three years ago, from complications related to an alcohol addiction."

I held back a curse. Paige looked even more apprehensive. It wasn't hard to imagine what had driven Gloria to excessive drinking.

"We're still looking into that, though. It's possible she confided in someone—we'll keep you updated. By the way, when you come back to work, you'll likely see some changes. Lieutenant Thorne is cooperating—as you can imagine, Chief Larkin is not. There could be an opening soon," she hinted. "Thorne implied he might retire."

I couldn't think about this now. I was becoming too tired to even process much more of this. At least, the bottom line remained: The good ones had won this time. The Amnesia Project would be dismantled, hopefully forever a warning to future generations.

Not that I was holding my breath—people were never that good at learning from the past, otherwise this could have never taken hold the way it did.

No matter what they had done to us—we had the rest of our lives to be together.

Fortunately, the visit to my GP and subsequent tests confirmed Paige's good health. Once more, a team of scientists and investigators was put together to determine the scope of the Amnesia Project, after more arrests turned up more files and cases.

I had taken a few days off beyond sick leave so we could start looking for an apartment, and preferably, move within that time frame as well. I had some difficult conversations with Elaina and Rose Kerry as well. They reminded me uncomfortably how I could have been one of them, left behind.

Mom and Dad helped us out a great deal, and one evening, we all had dinner at their house, me and Paige, Mia, Colin, Alice and her husband and kids, and Joy.

It was the first time we could all celebrate the happy outcome, and in my mind, I was flirting with even bigger ideas. Mia and Colin were adjusting to the new situation. They were excited about each having a room of their own in the new apartment.

I was, frankly, excited about being a family, too.

Alice caught me out on the deck, and for a moment, the silence was awkward.

"Thanks for inviting us," she said eventually.

"Of course. Look, I know you had doubts about—"

"Yeah, I did," she interrupted me. "I am sorry. I really am. I shouldn't have made assumptions, especially when you never gave up on her. I was...in a bad place for a long time. I'm in therapy now."

"That's good, but some of your assumptions weren't too far off," I said, bracing myself. I wasn't sure bringing up all of it was such a good idea, but I needed all of it out in the open, no more secrets. "That night, when you and Joy were out clubbing, she kissed me. I told her nothing could happen, and that's why she was pissed at me the next day."

She turned to me, her expression surprised.

"That's all?"

"Well, that's a lot. If she hadn't been angry with me..."

"Dani, stop. They had been planning this. They were going to take her during the trip no matter what. You did the adult thing. It didn't matter to their plan...Wait. You didn't spend all these years thinking...?" She didn't wait for an answer, just stepped forward and hugged me.

It didn't hit me until that moment that I had waited this long for someone to say it out loud. It wasn't my fault. It never had been. It finally sank in.

The next moment, Paige and Joy joined in on the hug.

The past had finally released us from its clutches.

꧁꧂

There was still a lot to find out about what exactly Paige's inheritance was, and how much of it Ken Jansing had spent. We hired a lawyer and a PI to deal with the details, and I asked Paige the question. Not The Question, but one that, in my mind, needed to come before: "Will you come with me to New York for a few days?"

Paige seemed surprised, but she simply asked, "Why?"

"It was such a dream for all of us, and it became a nightmare. I went back a couple of times, thinking I could find something there, a hint, anything. There have been so many changes, and I think you'd like to see them. I think it would be good for both of us."

"Yes, sure why not?" It was settled. Mia and Colin would spend the four days with my parents who had formed a great rapport with them.

Paige and I would be able to close this last chapter before the new life began.

She wasn't sleeping in the guest room any longer, but so much had happened in such a short time that we hadn't done much other than fall asleep in each other's arms. When Paige turned off the lights and slid under the covers with me, she was all naked, the feel of her warm skin assuring me that tonight would be more than a fantasy. We hadn't even been able to talk much about what happened that other night, or that it should be a subject given our plans.

It was all priority now with her hands all over my body, her lips on mine.

"I can't believe I had to spend all those years apart from you," she whispered. "I want to make up for every single one of them."

I was starting to believe she meant it literally when the play of her fingers became urgent, then turned into a whisper-soft tease only to increase in its intensity again, leaving me breathless. I had to bite my lip, reminding myself that we couldn't wake the kids.

My hips rose as I pressed myself against her hand, unable to hold back the gasp. Paige kissed me deeply, her fingers slowing down. She didn't wait long before starting all over again, kissing her way down my body.

I'd never experienced intimacy like this, being able to let go completely. Finding her, I had finally found myself.

❦

Paige

We were on the way to New York when the PI called us with solid numbers. Together with what Uncle Ken hadn't spent, it would be enough to get Mia and Colin through college and beyond. It was something reassuring in this sad and bizarre story. I couldn't think too much of my biological parents or grandfather at this point—I had enough to deal with, the grief over the parents who raised and loved me, and getting my life back together. Getting the life I always wanted.

I could get my degree if I wanted to, and why the hell not? We might not be able to turn back time, but all of a sudden, there were a lot of options open to us.

I felt giddy on this road trip, alone with Dani, the trials of the past behind us. At the same time, going back made me more apprehensive than I had shared with her. This was the place where it all happened, the crossroads. I didn't remember the exact moment. I wasn't even sure I'd recognize the street. In any case I was looking forward to seeing New York City again after my last visit had unexpectedly been cut short by a gang of misogynist criminals.

In retrospect, it was still hard to believe their entitlement, a bunch of men who had plotted my fate and that of others behind closed doors. I imagined them sitting in leather chairs, puffing cigars and whining about the good old times when women knew their place. There might be always people like that, but we had gotten out, and we were telling the stories. We were here to warn people. In my opinion, that was a good thing.

Once we were home and Dani went back to work, possibly in for a promotion, I would meet with the other women to start a foundation. Our goal would be to reach out to women who had been in the same situation, provide support for them and their children, and eventually go beyond that and help others, women in desperate situations who had no one that would come looking for them.

"Are you okay?" Dani asked softly, catching on to my sudden shift in mood.

"Oh yes. Just making plans."

"That's good."

"Yeah."

We found our hotel in downtown Manhattan in the late afternoon. Dani parked her car in the garage, and we went up to our room to freshen up before going out for dinner...The shower unexpectedly took longer than planned when she joined me.

Later, we took a walk, and I finally realized the crowded street where I had been kidnapped wasn't by far all that Dani wanted to show me. I thought about her coming here, all alone, wondering what had happened to me, carrying the irrational guilt with her, always.

In a somber mood, we took a moment to visit the completed 9/11 memorial. The One World Trade Center was finished and open to the public. Tomorrow, we would visit the High Line.

Eventually, we found an Italian restaurant where we got a corner table, a bit of privacy in the always hectic and busy city.

"Thank you," I said.

Dani didn't need a lot of explanations.

"I made a couple of trips," she said. "I thought it could heal me...but there was always something missing. Not anymore."

The waiter brought our wine, and we clinked our glasses together, taking a first sip.

I thought of my existence as a Stepford wife, so unreal and far away now. I remembered thinking that when I first came out, I told my parents I wasn't sure whether I wanted children. Maybe, maybe not. I never ruled it out—and I was happy to have Mia and Colin. All the pieces were falling into place.

"I understand what you mean. I really do."

"You don't regret anything? About...us?"

"No, of course not. Where are you going with this?"

"You were always so much more confident. I admired you. I learned from you, even in those days when I had no idea...I love you, Paige. A lot has changed in those years, but that hasn't.

This is why I needed some time alone with you, here, to ask you."

"Yes. Oh my God, yes," I blurted out when she set the small velvet covered box in front of me. "There better be a ring in this box?"

She laughed, though her eyes were welling up at the same time. "Of course there is. So, you're going to marry me?"

"Yes," I confirmed. "And it will be my first marriage...and my last."

"We don't have to go back to that street. Not tomorrow, not ever."

"It's okay," I said and opened the box to uncover the beautiful white gold diamond ring. "I want to. I know I can do this. I know now."

We had our meal, and then a glass of champagne with dessert, and took a cab to the hotel after.

No more fear. In the end, love had conquered all. Lucky for us that even the smartest researchers don't know everything about the human brain.

❧

Dani

We went back to that street after all, on our way to the High Line. It wasn't as spooky and scary as I remembered even from my later trips, just a busy street with people going into every direction. This time, I held on to her hand, knowing one thing for sure:

We had won.

Epilogue

Dani

2019

"Lieutenant? There's someone who wants to see you. She doesn't have an appointment. A Rose Kerry?"

I didn't really have time, but this impromptu visit had me curious. I hadn't heard from Rose in years, ever since our last conversation on the phone. Annette lived on her own with her children now, and as far as I knew, they hadn't gotten back together.

"I have ten minutes," I said. Mariah nodded and went to bring her in.

When I'd first met Rose Kerry, she had been as desperate as I had been at the time, hoping to find out what happened to the woman she loved. I had been lucky, given my happy ending and new beginning—she hadn't been so lucky.

Rose walked inside, and I got up to greet her.

"It's been a while," I said as I shook her hand. "How are you doing? I hope you don't mind I'm having my lunch. Otherwise, I won't get a bite all day."

"No problem, go ahead. As for the other question..." She sat in the visitor's chair, crossing her legs. "I'm good. I got my PI's license a couple of years ago."

"Good for you. Congratulations."

The experience of nearly losing someone we loved, then being reunited under complicated circumstances, had left its mark in both of us. We didn't have any more illusions of what humans were capable of doing to each other, because they were assholes, or because they thought of themselves as better, default persons. Her clothes and her demeanor were a tad edgier than I remembered.

"Thanks."

"What brings you here?"

"See, I couldn't convince Annette. This whole time, she has been torn between what we had, and the family she had with her husband. She can't stay here or there."

"I'm sorry about that." I was, genuinely. I was reminded every day of how different my life could be, if Paige hadn't remembered as much as she did, if her circumstances had been slightly different.

"I know." Rose made a dismissive gesture. "That's not why I'm here though. I've been working on this case for almost three months now...and I think someone's at it again."

Her words felt like a gut punch. This wasn't possible. Together with other women who had left or were rescued from The Amnesia Project, Paige had started a foundation. She had written a book and been in TV interviews. People were more cautious now that the truth was out—were they really?

"How? That can't be."

"This is already bigger than what I can do. I want you to take a look at this." She laid a folder, about two inches thick, on my desk. "I really hope you can help me. I'm not sure they have the same sophistication as those other guys, but there's definitely something in motion, and it's the same ideology. Get them married young, as many kids as possible, if there's anything 'undesirable' about them, try to change it with all means possible."

I wanted to scream. Or cry. Punch somebody. "I'll read this and get back to you as soon as possible," I said in a calm tone."

"Thank you, Dani." She handed me a business card and got up. "I'll see you soon."

"They never give up, do they?" I said, resigning to the fact that life in the comfortable bubble Paige and I had been living in, was over.

"No. But neither do we."

That was at least one thing we knew with certainty.

And we'd win again, over and over until they'd stop.

About the Author

Barbara Winkes writes sapphic crime drama and Christmas romance. She loves writing characters who get the job done, whether it's stopping a predator or saving cherished traditions—while still making time for love. She lives with her wife in Quebec City.

barbarawinkes.com

www.ingramcontent.com/pod-product-compliance
Lightning Source LLC
Chambersburg PA
CBHW050720180626
46814CB00002B/523